PEANUT BUTTER PANIC

Also in the Amish Candy Shop Mystery series
by Amanda Flower

Assaulted Caramel

Lethal Licorice

Premeditated Peppermint

Criminally Cocoa (ebook novella)

Toxic Toffee

Botched Butterscotch (ebook novella)

Marshmallow Malice

Candy Cane Crime (ebook novella)

Lemon Drop Dead

And in the Amish Matchmaker Mystery series

Matchmaking Can Be Murder

Courting Can Be Killer

Marriage Can Be Mischief

PEANUT BUTTER PANIC

USA Today **Bestselling Author**

Amanda Flower

Kensington Publishing Corp.
www.kensingtonbooks.com

KENSINGTON BOOKS are published by

Kensington Publishing Corp.
119 West 40th Street
New York, NY 10018

All Kensington titles, imprints, and distributed lines are available at special quantity discounts for bulk purchases for sales promotion, premiums, fund-raising, educational, or institutional use.

Special book excerpts or customized printings can also be created to fit specific needs. For details, write or phone the office of the Kensington Sales Manager: Attn.: Sales Department. Kensington Publishing Corp., 119 West 40th Street, New York, NY 10018. Phone: 1-800-221-2647.

The K and Teapot logo is a trademark of Kensington Publishing Corp.

First Printing: September 2022
ISBN: 978-1-4967-3461-7

ISBN: 978-1-4967-3462-4 (ebook)

10 9 8 7 6 5 4 3 2

Printed in the United States of America

In memory of Sheryl Hendrix

ACKNOWLEDGMENTS

The Amish Candy Shop Mysteries is my longest-running series to date, and that's all thanks to you, my Dear Readers. If you didn't care about these books and about Bailey, Aiden, Jethro, and the entire community in fictional Harvest, this series would have ended years ago. Thank you for reading, buying my books, checking out my books from the library, telling your friends, and reviewing my books. It truly makes a difference.

Always thanks to the wonderful team at Kensington, especially my editor Alicia Condon. I'm blessed to have been able to work with all of you for so long. I don't take it for granted. Thanks too for my agent of over ten years, Nicole Resciniti. She has guided my career in the right direction for over a decade and I could never thank her enough.

Thanks too to reader Kimra Bell.

Very special thanks to my dear friend Delia Haidautu. I still laugh whenever I think of our adventure of making thousands of buckeyes for a fundraiser in high school and the hundred or so we lost in that massive vat of chocolate. That experience definitely inspired the recipe and the use of buckeyes in this book.

Love and thanks to my husband, David Seymour, for his love, support, and emergency food deliveries while I wrote this and every book.

Finally, I thank God for letting me write for a living. I still pinch myself from time to time over it.

CHAPTER ONE

"Careful! Don't drop the turkeys! We will be ruined if we don't have turkeys on Thanksgiving! Why do you have them here anyway?" Margot Rawlings cried as she buzzed around the Harvest village square like a spinning top. Her short curls bounced as she pointed at the young volunteers and barked orders. "Chairs over there. No, no, no. Don't put the kids' table facing the playground. All they'll want to do is run off and play instead of eating their dinners."

A young Amish man who was carrying a crate of thawing turkeys looked as frozen as the poultry in his hands. After Margot yelled at him, it seemed he didn't know what to do.

I smiled at him as I approached, carrying a box of display dishes for the dessert table. "You okay, Leon?"

Leon Hersh was an Amish teen who volunteered often

for Margot's many events on the village square. Since Margot had taken over the Harvest social calendar a few years ago, it seemed scarcely a week went by that there wasn't something happening in the small Amish village in Holmes County, Ohio. From concerts to weddings to Christmas pageants, the square had seen it all. Thanksgiving week was no exception.

In fact, Thanksgiving was going to be bigger and grander than any event Margot had ever thrown before. There would be a community-wide Thanksgiving meal for the village. It would include both Amish and English residents and be followed with a lighting-of-the-square ceremony to usher in the holiday season.

Margot had been working on the event for months, which meant that everyone else in the village had been too. She was great at drafting help. I always thought if the U.S. military brought back the draft, Margot should be at the helm of the effort.

Leon blinked his bright blue eyes at me. "She's scarier than the bishop's wife."

I hid my smile. I knew the bishop's wife, Ruth Yoder, as well as I knew Margot. I also knew Ruth would have wanted to be seen as more formidable than Margot. I certainly wasn't going to tell her what this young man had said. "Why don't you take those turkeys to the church? They'll be cooked later today by the church volunteers. Just leave them on the counter and the kitchen staff will know what to do."

He nodded. "*Danki*. I should have thought of that in the first place. But when Margot shouted at me to get the turkeys from Levi Wittmer's poultry farm, I brought them here where I knew she would be. I wasn't thinking." He nodded at the horse and wagon that was parked along

Main Street. "My wagon is right there. I'll take them over now."

The back of the wagon was laden with crates just like the one in Leon's hands. My brow went up. How many turkeys had Margot ordered from the Wittmer farm for this event? Then again, as many as eight hundred people had said they would come for the celebration tomorrow afternoon. It was possible she would need every last turkey.

"That's a good plan, Leon, and can I give you a tip?" I asked.

He nodded.

"Give yourself a break. You're doing a fine job. Just remember Margot is, well, let's just say she is very exacting. For better or worse, she treats everyone the same. It's not you."

He licked his lips and nodded. "*Danki*, Bailey. The Esh family is right; you are very kind for an *Englischer.*"

I smiled, taking no offense at the "for an *Englischer*" comment. It was one I had heard before, and many times since I'd moved from NYC to Harvest.

With the crate in his arms, he hurried back to his wagon, loaded the turkeys into the back with the others, and drove around to the church, which was just on the opposite side of the square on Church Street.

It was a gray and cloudy day, as was typical at the end of November, but there was a bright blue patch of sky above the church's tall white steeple. The forecast for tomorrow, Thanksgiving morning, was clear skies and warmer temperatures. The weather was something that could never be guaranteed in Ohio, but I hoped for the sake of the festivities that the prediction was accurate.

I could only imagine the flurry of activity that must be

happening in the church kitchen at the moment. When Margot and Juliet Brook, the pastor's wife, had put their heads together to sponsor a village-wide Thanksgiving dinner, I don't believe they realized how much work it would take.

Then again, maybe Margot, who was one of the hardest-working people I had ever met, knew. However, I bet all the activity had taken Juliet by surprise.

"Bailey King!" Margot pointed at me. "Just the person I wanted to see."

I sighed. Maybe I agreed with Leon just a little. Margot could be scary, and nothing was scarier than being caught in her crosshairs when she had an assignment for you, which in my case was all the time. It seemed to me that whenever Margot spotted me, she had something she wanted me to do. At least I knew I wouldn't have to drive to Wittmer Poultry Farm to collect the turkeys. I didn't think I could stand seeing a bunch of turkeys walking around flapping their wings right before Thanksgiving.

She marched over to me. As usual she wore jeans, running shoes, and a sweatshirt. However due to the chilly temperatures, she'd added a quilted barn coat over her sweatshirt and fingerless gloves on her hands. "I stopped by Swissmen Sweets well over an hour ago looking for you. Charlotte said you were away on an errand in Canton." She put her hands on her hips. "What are you doing traveling all that way this close to Thanksgiving? Don't you have enough to do right here at home? I hope you don't plan to go to New York this weekend. The village needs you."

I rubbed my head because I was already getting a headache as I tried to remember the sage advice that I had given Leon about Margot. The advice had flown right out of my head. All I could think was that he was right—she *was* scary.

"I'm not going to New York this weekend," I said as calmly as possible. "I only went to Canton to run an errand."

It was none of her business, but I had gone shopping for a housewarming gift for my boyfriend, Aiden Brody. I knew with Thanksgiving, Black Friday, and Small Business Saturday coming up, I would be so busy in the shop that I would not get another chance before I saw him.

He'd just moved into a new apartment in Columbus, and I felt I had to give him a gift to show my support of the move when in fact I wasn't feeling the least bit supportive. The last time we'd discussed where he would live after he completed his months of training with BCI, Ohio's Bureau of Investigations, he'd promised he would come back to Holmes County, so a new apartment nearly two hours away was not great news.

For over a decade, Aiden had been a sheriff's deputy in Holmes County. That was how I'd met him, but earlier this year, he had been given the chance of a lifetime to work with BCI. He had made a good impression on the department when he collaborated with them on a case last summer. From what I had been told before, after his training, he would be returning to Holmes County to work as a remote agent who specialized in Amish cases. Instead, he'd been moved to one of the largest cities in Ohio. I didn't know what this would mean for our relationship. Part of me thought when Aiden returned to Holmes County we would seriously begin talking about marriage and having a family—all those things that I knew we both wanted but were afraid to say aloud to each other.

I didn't tell Margot any of that. Instead, I said, "I came as soon as I could."

She folded her arms as if she had doubts. Margot was typically a tightly wound woman, but I don't think I had ever seen her this worked up.

"Is something wrong, Margot?"

She threw up her hands. "Something always goes wrong when it comes to these events, but it's never been anything I couldn't handle until today."

My eyes went wide. For Margot to admit that she couldn't handle something was unheard of. "What is it?" I braced myself to hear something about Leon and the turkeys. My brain was already scrambling for ways to defend the quiet teenager.

"My mother is coming!" she wailed.

I stared at her. That was not what I had expected her to say. "Your mother?"

"I know, doesn't it sound horrible?" She moaned.

"Why is it so horrible?" I asked.

"She's never attended one of my events. Ever. My whole life long. And the first one that she comes to is the village Thanksgiving dinner. Why did she have to pick this one? Why couldn't she have tried a concert or a bake sale or the Christmas parade next month? I have a camel at the Christmas parade. Everyone loves the camel. Would it have killed her to wait one more month?"

I knew Melchior the camel who makes a regular appearance at the village Christmas parade. He was nice as far as camels went but a bit of an escape artist. I wasn't sure a camel running loose was the best way for Margot to impress her mother, but what did I know?

Margot began to gasp for air.

I placed a hand on her shoulder. "Are you okay?" I

glanced around and noticed the volunteers who were setting up for the big meal tomorrow were watching us. If Margot noticed their stares, she gave no indication of it. "Do you want to sit down?"

She brushed my hand away and took a few deep breaths. "I'm fine. I don't want to sit. I don't have time to sit. I have to leave for the airport in an hour to pick up my mother. Everything has to be perfect here." She grabbed my arm. "Bailey, I need you!"

"Me?" I squeaked.

"Yes, I need you to oversee the preparations for Thanksgiving. Everything has to be perfect for tomorrow. Perfect. I know I always want things to be perfect, but I'm not kidding this time. I can't fail in front of my mother again."

Again? I wanted to ask her what she meant by that, but before I could, she said, "You have to promise me." She thrust her clipboard at me. "This is the list of everything that has to be finished. Guard it with your life. There's a checkmark next to the items that have been completed."

After a cursory glance, I noted that there were very few checkmarks on the page.

I tried to hand the clipboard back to her. "Margot, I'm honored that you would trust me with such an important job, but there is so much to do at Swissmen Sweets today. We have been making many of the desserts for tomorrow's meal, and we're getting extra candy ready for Black Friday and Small Business Saturday. This is our biggest weekend of the year."

She would not take the clipboard. "You don't understand. You have to help me."

"What about Juliet? She's always willing to help."

"I can't ask Juliet," Margot said as if it was the most

ridiculous idea she'd ever heard. "She's in charge of the food preparation happening at the church. And to be perfectly frank, you're the only one who even has any remote chance of doing the job as well as I can."

I frowned. "Thank you?" I wasn't sure this was an honor I wanted.

"You don't know my mother. She expects perfection. Always and in all things."

I guessed Margot was in her sixties, so her mother had to be over eighty years old, and yet Margot still feared her?

She took a breath. "Mother, the honorable Zara Bevan, was a powerhouse attorney and the first female judge in Holmes County. She excels at everything she does." She paused. "Until she had me."

I had known Margot for a while now, and I had never known her to undervalue herself. Even when something went terribly wrong at one of her events—like a dead body—she handled it with the efficiency and confidence of someone who always believed that they were in the right. However, at the moment, Margot looked anything but confident. She looked terrified. The honorable Zara Bevan must be a force to be reckoned with indeed.

"Where does your mother live now?" I asked. "Where is she coming from?"

"Fort Meyers, Florida. She moved there about fifteen years ago. She can play outdoor tennis all year round down there. She says indoor tennis is not the same. She's eighty-six years old and still plays tennis every day. She was even in the senior Olympics! How many people can say that their mother is a senior Olympian?"

"I can't think of any others," I admitted. "It seems your mother has achieved a lot."

"You have no idea. All she does is achieve, and she expects the same level of achievement out of everyone around her. Out of me!"

"Has it been a long while since she visited you in Harvest?" I asked.

"You can say that. She hasn't been back since she left. I try to get down to Florida for at least a few days every winter to see her. But between you and me, I'm always ready to come home at the end of the visit. Actually, I'm ready to come home before the visit even starts. I don't know how I'm going to survive this weekend." She grabbed my shoulders and shook me slightly. "Bailey, I need your help. I'm desperate."

I glanced down at the clipboard again and thought about the mile-long list that I had left on the kitchen island back in Swissmen Sweets just a few minutes ago. How was I ever going to get all of this done?

But I said, "All right, I'll help you."

Really, there was nothing else I could do.

CHAPTER TWO

Margot was a smart woman, and she didn't wait around to see if I would change my mind. To be honest, I regretted my promise to help as soon as the words were out of my mouth. I didn't have time to take on this massive project, but even if I could work up the nerve to say so, I never got the chance because Margot ran across the green to the church as if the heels of her sneakers were on fire.

I could only assume her getaway car was parked in the church lot. I looked up from Margot's list, which seemed to grow longer by the second. What on earth did "Dancing Pilgrims" mean? As far as I knew, there was no dancing at the first Thanksgiving, and pious pilgrims would not be the first group of people that I thought of cutting a rug. Also, did she want to offend the many Amish in attendance? Amish folks didn't dance at all.

"Everything okay?" a kind yet gravelly voice asked.

Lois Henry stood a few feet from me. In her arms, she held a half dozen woven cornucopias.

I consulted the list. Sure enough, number 158 read that Lois Henry would be supplying the cornucopia center-pieces for the tables stuffed with fresh fruit and flowers.

"I'm all right," I said. "Just trying to take it all in."

Lois cocked her head and her bright, spikey purple-red hair caught the sunlight. "You don't look all right to me. Is that Margot's clipboard in your hands? Does she know that you have it? I would put it down on the ground and walk away slowly if I were you. She guards that thing like a hawk." She swiveled her head back and forth as if waiting for Margot to jump out of the bushes that circled the large white gazebo in the middle of the village square. One chunky plastic green earring hit the side of her face as her head turned. Lois never met a piece of costume jewelry that she didn't love.

"She gave it to me," I said. "She had to go to the air-port to pick up her mother. She asked me to take over checking things off the list for tomorrow. It's quite a list." I flipped to the last page. "There are three hundred and eleven items on it." I let out a breath.

"Oh wow!" Lois gasped. "Zara is coming back to the village. We had better batten down the hatches. There are going to be fireworks!"

I stared at her. "You know Margot's mother?"

"Sure do." She whistled. "The woman is a powerhouse to be admired *and* feared."

I held the clipboard to my chest. "That was the impression I got from Margot too."

She held up the cornucopias. "Let me set these down and we can tackle that list together."

"I'd really appreciate that, Lois. To say that I'm stretched to my limit would not be an exaggeration."

"This is a big weekend for retail, and your business is booming." She dropped the cornucopias onto the same table where I'd left my display dishes when I went to rescue Leon.

"How do you know Zara?"

"Margot and I grew up together. She was behind me a few years in school, but the school was small. Everyone knew everyone else. Her mother was something. Back when we were kids, there weren't as many single moms as you have today. I think a lot of women stayed married because they felt like they didn't have any choices. Not Zara though. She was divorced and put herself through college and law school. All the while she was raising Margot too." Lois placed a jeweled hand to her chest. "As a strong woman who has been a single mom and married four times myself, I can appreciate that."

"Do you know why Margot wouldn't want to see her?" I asked, and then I held up my hand. "You don't have to tell me. I'm prying into their relationship, and that's personal business."

"Maybe you are just a little bit," she said with a wink. "But I'm not going to tell you anything that people over fifty in the village don't already know. Margot's mother can be harsh. Zara is not a person you want to mess with. I've seen her make grown men cry. My first ex-husband was one of the men she made cry at least twice when he came in front of her bench. He wasn't the greatest guy in the world, and in hindsight, I think both times he deserved it."

"I have never seen Margot so unhinged. Not even when a herd of sheep got loose in the center of town and ate all the flowers in her manicured pots or when there was a murder in the village. She took all of that in stride, but picking her mother up from the airport has her in a complete tizzy."

Lois nodded. "If I were Margot, I would be unhinged too. Zara is a perfectionist through and through, and she only really has respect for other perfectionists like her. As hard as Margot tried, she never measured up to her mother's standards of greatness. She wasn't pretty enough, athletic enough, or smart enough. She was a good student, but never had the highest grades."

Hearing this made me sad. "But I would say that Margot *is* very successful. With everything she's done for the village, she should be proud to show her mother her accomplishments."

Lois twirled one of her large rings around her finger. "Maybe. But . . ." Lois hesitated and twirled the ring again. "Zara was such a perfectionist, she was, well, rather obsessive. I don't think Margot had an easy go of it."

"Maybe things will be different now," I offered.

"Maybe." Lois shrugged. "Times were different then. Zara was a successful attorney in the nineteen sixties and seventies when being a woman in that field was a hindrance. She never let anyone judge her by her gender. I believe because Zara had to fight so hard for her place, she was even stricter in her courtroom—and in her expectations of her daughter. Unfortunately, it was a time when a woman had to come off as tough to be taken seriously in a man's world."

"I guess I can see why Margot would be nervous about her coming here, especially for such a major holiday."

Lois nodded. "I didn't have a great relationship with my parents either. They have long since passed, but I can understand how Margot feels. I certainly wouldn't want my parents as surprise guests."

I looked down at the clipboard. "In that case, I want to do right by Margot. She does so much for the village. I think we should try to put our best foot forward to show her mother how she's helped the village grow." I frowned. "But there is so much to do at Swissmen Sweets. I at least have to run to the shop and tell them what's going on."

"Millie and I can handle this list for a little while."

Millie was Millie Fisher, the village's Amish matchmaker and Lois's best friend. The two women were ideologically and fashionably miles apart but were kindred spirits in the best possible ways. They reminded me of myself and my best friend, Cass Calbera, who was a chocolatier in New York.

"Are you sure?" I asked.

She held out her hand. "Give it to me."

I put Margot's precious clipboard in her hand. "I won't be gone too long. I just want to run over to the shop and update them. I'll be back as quick as I can."

"Don't rush, honey. The lunch rush at the Sunbeam Café doesn't start for over an hour from now."

The Sunbeam Café was the café owned by Lois's granddaughter, Darcy Woodin. Lois worked as a waitress and hostess in the café during the busy hours of the day.

"I can't thank you enough for doing this."

"Go." She shooed me away. "Nothing will go wrong."

I nodded and jogged across the green toward Main Street. Lois's comment that nothing could possibly go wrong rang in my ears. In my experience, phrases like that were spoken just before disaster struck.

I waited for a buggy to roll down the street before I crossed to Swissmen Sweets. The newly washed windows sparkled in the sunshine. There was a fresh coat of paint on the window frames and the front door too. The words "Swissmen Sweets" were etched into the large picture window. Since I began working at the shop with my grandmother, I'd slowly made improvements, some small, like the fresh coat of paint, others more momentous, like launching the online store. A lot at Swissmen Sweets had changed over the last few years. However, the heart of the shop was the same. We still made candies and sweets using traditional Amish recipes and methods. We were still closed on Sundays and began the workday at four a.m. every morning to make the candies fresh for every customer who ambled through the door or placed an order in cyberspace.

As I stepped into Swissmen Sweets, Puff, the large white rabbit, and Nutmeg, the orange tabby, greeted me at the door. By their expectant faces I believed they thought it was lunchtime already, but it wasn't even ten in the morning yet.

I shook my finger at both of them. "You just had breakfast not too long ago."

My cousin Charlotte stood behind the glass-domed display counter, still surprising me with her English appearance. Charlotte grew up Amish, but just recently decided to leave the faith to live in English society. Her straight red hair, which I was so used to seeing tied back from her face in an Amish bun, was tethered in a long braid. Amish women didn't cut their hair. Ever. As of yet, Charlotte had not taken the plunge to cut her hair, but she was wearing it down and braided more often. It seemed to me that cutting her hair was the final step in her choice to leave the Amish community for good. Whether she realized it or not, she just wasn't there yet.

"I don't think Nutmeg or Puff believe you. They always feel they lack treats. Nutmeg has been watching the commotion out at the square through the window all day. It's like his personal movie theater." She looked at Puff on the floor. "I think Puff is jealous since she can't get up on the windowsill to look out."

I scratched Puff's head between her two downy white ears. "You will get extra carrots tonight. I promise."

She twitched her nose. I was certain that she was making a mental note about the treat. If I forgot, she'd remind me. Puff loved carrots.

"Why were you over there so long? You said you were just going to drop off the display dishes. . . ." She frowned. "I peeked out the window with Nutmeg when you didn't come back right away. You were talking to Margot. What does she want you to do this time?"

I made a face. It was a fair question. It seemed that every time I ran into Margot, she asked me to do something. This time had been no exception.

Maami came out of the kitchen carrying a fresh tray of buckeye candies. I could smell the heavenly scent of peanut butter and chocolate. Was there ever a better candy combination?

Maami was a petite woman with white hair that was styled back in an Amish bun at the nape of her neck. She wore a plain blue dress with a black apron over it and a white prayer cap on her head. There were remnants of powdered sugar on the front of her apron.

It was clear that she was in the middle of making more candies to sell this weekend, which was good. We needed to be making candies around the clock to be ready for the busy days ahead, which we hoped would bring the biggest sales in the shop's history. Ever since my cable television show on Gourmet Television went on the air, business had boomed.

When a television producer approached me two years ago to host a cooking show about Amish candy making, I had never imagined that it would do so well. Soon I would be headed to New York to film the third season. The show's success meant success for Swissmen Sweets. In the last two years our business had grown tenfold, and we were reaching the point that it could not grow any more and be sustainable unless we physically expanded the business. It was something that I had thought a lot about lately, but as of yet had not worked up the courage to discuss with *Maami*.

Charlotte reached for one of the buckeyes, and *Maami* pulled the tray away before she could steal one. "These are a special batch made just for Aiden. They are his favorite. Since he's recently moved, I thought it was only right to make him a batch of his very own. I'm going to give them to him tomorrow."

"I can take them when I see him Saturday night," I said.

Maami stared at me. "Won't Aiden be at the village for Thanksgiving?"

I shook my head. "He has to work. He texted this morning to tell me." I tried to keep my voice light so the disappointment I felt wouldn't show. Aiden was in law enforcement; his job was important. He was doing good work, but I'd be lying if I didn't admit that I was heartbroken at the idea that we'd spend yet another holiday apart.

Charlotte gave me a pitying look. I broke eye contact.

"I'll still be able to see him this weekend. I'm sure after he's more settled in Columbus, things will become easier."

"Of course they will," my grandmother said in her most soothing voice. "Now, back to what I overheard Charlotte saying. *Who* wants Bailey to do *what*?"

I said, "Margot stopped me on the square. She wants me to help her out at the square for a couple of hours. I hate to leave you all on such a busy day."

Maami waved away this concern. "Don't worry about it. We have production well in hand. I personally know that you have been working late at night at the shop over the last two weeks to prepare for this weekend." She eyed me. "You have even worked on Sundays, haven't you?"

My grandmother didn't approve of anyone working on the Sabbath, whether or not they were members of the Amish church. I knew better than to argue with her about that even though working on Sunday had made me feel better about the busy schedule of the coming week.

Her face softened. "You have been working very hard. Charlotte and I can manage for a few hours. Why does Margot need your help? I would have thought she'd have everything well in hand for tomorrow. She usually does."

"Margot is stressed. Her mother is coming to visit for Thanksgiving. She had to head to the airport and pick her up."

"Zara is coming home?" *Maami* asked.

"You know her too?" I asked.

"Too?" *Maami*'s eyes went wide.

"Lois knows her."

"Oh." Her face cleared. "*Ya*, of course she would."

"How well do you know her?"

"Not very well. She's a bit older than me, and I am

older than Margot. We didn't overlap much. However, I most certainly know who she is. She was a powerful woman in the county twenty years ago. I think there were many people who let out a sigh of relief when she left. I know people think that Margot can be forceful, but she is not nearly as . . ." She paused as if she were searching for the right word. "As self-important as her mother."

I wanted to ask my grandmother who exactly gave a sigh of relief when Zara left, but before I could, the front door of Swissmen Sweets opened.

It was still before ten in the morning when the shop officially opened, so I was about to turn around and let the customer know we weren't quite ready for sales yet. Only I found it wasn't a customer at all. It was Juliet Brook, and her miniature potbellied pig Jethro was in her arms. Jethro wriggled his black and white polka-dotted body to get out of his mistress's grasp as soon as he saw Puff and Nutmeg. The odd trio of animals were the very best of friends.

No one had told them rabbits should be afraid of cats and cats shouldn't be friends with pigs.

"Oh my, Jethro. Calm yourself," Juliet complained as she set the pig on the ground. His hooves skidded on the wide plank floor, and he bopped noses with first the cat and then the rabbit.

Juliet straightened and brushed off the sleeve of her brown and white polka-dotted coat. Juliet loved polka dots on everything. I never thought to ask her which came first, Jethro or the polka dots, but they certainly were a package deal as far as she was concerned.

Juliet placed the back of her hand to her forehead as if she might swoon. Knowing Juliet, it was entirely possible.

I stepped forward. "Juliet, are you all right? Do you need to sit down?" I pulled out a chair for her at one of the three café tables in the front of the shop.

"Oh, thank you, Bailey. I really don't know what I would do without you. You've just been a rock for me since Aiden moved away. I know he's a grown man, but I've missed him so much. And now he's not coming home for Thanksgiving. Can you imagine? BCI is working him too hard. He needs a break. What's a mother to do?" She placed a hand to her chest. "But I could never miss him as much as you have. I certainly hope this is not giving you cold feet about the wedding."

Behind me Charlotte's bark of a laugh was covered with a fake cough. I shot a look over my shoulder. For well over a year, Juliet had been hinting that she thought her son Aiden and I should get married sooner rather than later. If I was being completely honest, I had thought we might be at least engaged by the end of this year too, but that seemed unlikely to happen now.

"Is there something we can get for you, Juliet?" *Maami* asked.

"Oh, well I just came by to speak with Bailey." She looked down at her little pig, who was snuggled up with the rabbit in Nutmeg's cat bed. "You know tomorrow is a very important day for the village. This Thanksgiving meal will be a great event and will do so much to improve the relationship between the Amish and English in Harvest, but . . ." She looked down at the pig again and fell silent.

"But what?" I asked even though I knew very well what she was about to say. I wanted her to say it.

"Jethro is the best pig in the world. I think everyone is agreed on that point, but it's very tense at the church right now. . . ." Juliet went on as if she had to win her case. "Everyone at the church is working overtime to get all the cooking and baking done for tomorrow. I'm sorry to say that my little pig is underfoot. I took him upstairs to my husband's office, where the poor man is working diligently on Sunday's sermon. I will tell you, the reverend gets no rest at all, but Jethro broke out of the office. He just opened the door and waltzed back down to the kitchen. I told you he is a smart pig. I think you're the only one who can keep him away from the church kitchen."

I glanced down at Jethro, and he looked up at me. Within the last hour I had been asked to supervise the setup of the village's Thanksgiving and to watch a runaway pig. It was just like any other day for me in Harvest.

"I can watch Jethro," I said, because there really wasn't anything else I could say.

"Oh thank you, thank you," Juliet said. "The way you treat Jethro is just more proof that you will be an amazing mother. What a wonderful day that will be! I can't wait to hold my grandbaby in my arms." Her native Carolina accent grew thicker as it always did when she spoke with emotion.

After Juliet left, Charlotte chuckled, "I'm sorry, Bailey, I shouldn't laugh, but it seems to me that you always get stuck with that pig."

It seemed to me that was true too.

CHAPTER THREE

Before I left the shop and went back to the square to relieve Lois and Millie, I went over the very long to-do list that we had planned for the candy shop that day. Our other shop assistant, Emily Keim, a young Amish mother with the most gorgeous natural blond hair, arrived to help for the day. *Maami* and Emily would work in the back of the shop making candies for online orders and to sell in the shop over the holiday weekend while Charlotte would work up front. When she didn't have customers, she would package candy and fill display cases.

I looked up from the list. "I shouldn't be on the square for too long. Maybe Margot will only be gone for an hour or two longer."

Maami patted my hand. "Do not worry. We will do very well just the three of us until you return."

I squeezed her hand. "I know you will."

She smiled. "Maybe next year business will calm down a bit. We have been working nonstop for too long."

I noticed the tiredness on her face and the beads of sweat across her brow. I bit the inside of my lip. My grandmother's comment did not bode well for my plan to expand our candy business. I hadn't even told her that I had been looking for places to convert into a candy factory. I bit my lip a little harder.

My ambition to expand the business was for her too. With more space and more employees, she would be able to semi-retire. I knew that it would be impossible to convince her to retire completely, but it pained me to see how hard she pushed herself to keep the business going, especially when I was away filming in New York.

Even if I found the perfect location, she still had to agree to it. That wasn't going to be easy. I would do the research first and then talk to her about it. I promised myself I would.

I said goodbye, gathered up Jethro, and left the shop. The little pig wasn't too excited about being separated from his cat and rabbit friends, but I knew that if I left him behind, he would be just as much of a distraction to the workers in the candy shop as he had been to those at Juliet's church.

When I crossed Main Street to the square, I immediately noticed how much had been completed in the short time I had been gone. Lois stood on the steps leaning into the gazebo with Margot's clipboard in her hands; she appeared to be completely in control.

I looked down at Jethro, whom I had tucked under my arm. The little pig was about the size of a toaster, but weighed more than the giant frozen turkeys that were in the process of thawing in the church for the meal tomorrow. I set him on the ground. He looked up at me as if to ask whether it was all right to wander around the square.

"Don't leave the square," I said. "Or eat any food that you might find sitting around. Just remember, it's not there for you."

He wiggled his snout. I didn't take that for affirmation that he would do what I asked. Jethro was a sweet, funny, and adorable little pig, but no one would say that he was obedient, not even Juliet.

Lois waved to me and came down the steps. "I see you have been saddled again with the village pig."

I looked down at Jethro, who had his snout buried in the grass and was deeply inhaling all the wonderful scents. "Juliet said he was making things a little challenging in the church as the Thanksgiving meal was being prepared."

"I imagine that he was." Lois handed me the clipboard. "While you were away, we got six items checked off the list. There are maybe five more tasks that you can get done today, but the rest will have to be left for tomorrow."

Millie Fisher walked over to join us. She was an older Amish woman with white hair and friendly eyes. She wore a navy-blue dress under a brown barn coat and a white prayer cap on her head.

"Will Margot be here tomorrow to oversee final arrangements?" Millie asked.

I accepted the clipboard from Lois. "I assume she will, but now that I think about it, maybe I should have asked her. I don't honestly know when she plans to come back from the airport." I bit my lip. "Had you heard something different?"

She shrugged. "*Nee*. I was just so surprised when Lois

told me that Margot left in the middle of settling everything for Thanksgiving. That's not like her at all. Then again, I can't remember the last time Zara came to the village."

"Me either," Lois said. "I had just assumed she was dead."

"Lois!" Millie gasped. "That's a horrible thing to say."

"The woman is in her late eighties. It's not unlikely that she might have passed, and as far as I know, Margot never speaks of her."

Millie shook her head.

"I do want to thank you both for helping me out." I glanced at Main Street, hoping to see Margot's car even though I knew it was too early for that. The airport was almost an hour away. It would be at least two hours before she came back, and that assumed Zara's flight was on time.

Lois waved her hands. "No need. It was fun. Both Millie and I like to give orders."

"Speak for yourself, Lois," Millie said in return.

"I did." Her friend grinned. "I just happened to speak for you too."

Millie rolled her eyes.

I stifled a laugh at the image of an elderly Amish woman rolling her eyes.

After the pair left the square, I spoke with several of the young Amish volunteers and found that everyone knew what they should be doing. Lois and Millie had done a great job of assigning and confirming everyone's tasks. There wasn't much left for me to do. I wondered if I could sneak away to the candy shop, which had just opened for the day. There was already a line outside. People were dropping in to buy candies for their Thanksgiving get-togethers. It wasn't a long line, but I knew the ladies in the shop must have their hands full.

Jethro was under the long Thanksgiving table that stretched from one end of the square to the other. That table alone could seat forty people. Other tables of varying size peppered the square. In all, there was outdoor seating for four hundred people, and inside of the church there was an additional four hundred seats in the fellowship hall for those who preferred to eat indoors.

That was eight hundred at Thanksgiving. Harvest had a little over a thousand residents. Many of them were Amish and living outside of the village proper. Margot guessed that around two hundred residents would not come to the meal. People had been asked to sign up. Over six hundred did. Providing enough seating for eight hundred, Margot believed she'd covered all her bases, and knowing her, she had food for at least a thousand.

"Bailey King, I need to talk to you." A sharp voice broke into my thoughts.

Now, there were only two people in Harvest who shouted at me like that. One of them was Margot, and I knew she was at the airport picking up her mother. The other was Ruth Yoder.

Ruth Yoder was the bishop's wife in my grandmother's Amish district. It was the largest district in Harvest, and the majority of the Amish living in the village were members or related to a member. Ruth took pride in the district's status in the village, and she didn't stand for any threat to her community's reputation.

She and Margot were like oil and water.

Ruth was a stocky woman with broad shoulders and steel-gray hair that was pulled back into a severe Amish bun at the nape of her neck. She marched over to me with anger and determination in every step.

Quickly, I scanned my memory for what I might have done to offend her. The truth was it could have been anything. Ruth was one of the most easily offended people I had ever met. It was almost as if she sat at home thinking over what happened throughout her day and how upsetting it all was.

"Bailey King, I need to talk to you." Her tone was firm.

Jethro ran down the length of the table and hid under a bush next to the gazebo. To be honest, I wished I could join him. I didn't want to have this conversation with Ruth either.

It wasn't that I disliked Ruth. I knew she meant well, and no one cared more for her community, but the manner in which she went about showing that love could be off-putting to say the least.

She stood in front of me and put her hands on her hips. "Is it true? Tell me. Is it true?" She waited.

"Is what true?" I asked. I knew it was a dangerous question. Clearly, I should know exactly what had her so worked up, but I didn't have an inkling.

"Zara!" she practically shouted.

Leon, who was unloading folding chairs from a box truck a few feet away, jumped.

"Zara? You mean Margot's mother?" I asked.

"*Ya*, will she be here tomorrow for the Thanksgiving meal?"

It seemed to me that this was a loaded question. I knew the answer, of course, but I guessed by the way Ruth said "Zara" like a four-letter word that it wasn't the answer she wanted to hear.

"I will take your silence as a yes. We will not stand for it. We will not." Ruth stopped just short of stomping her feet. "When our district agreed to participate in this event, we didn't know that woman would be here. I can't sit at the same table with her. I can't even be in the same place with this woman. Do you have any idea of the heartache she brought upon the Amish community in Harvest?

I blinked. "No."

"That woman ruined countless lives with her harshness. You think Sheriff Marshall is hard on the Amish in Holmes County? He is nothing compared to her. I would take three Sheriff Marshalls over one of her."

I stared at Ruth, whose face was impossibly red by this point. That was a serious statement to throw around. Everyone in Holmes County knew of the sheriff's dislike for the Amish. Aiden had stayed on as a deputy in the county for so long for that very reason. He wanted to be on hand to help his Amish friends.

In the last election, no one ran against the sheriff. Even if someone had, he had been in the job for over fifteen years. It was unlikely that he would have lost. The people who would vote against him were Amish, but the Amish, with very few exceptions, didn't vote.

"What did Zara do?" I asked.

"I don't even have time to tell you everything she did. It would take a year to list it all, but in the time that she served as judge in this county, she unjustly sentenced dozens of Amish men and even a few women to prison." She took a breath. "One of those men was my younger *bruder*. He never recovered from it. To this day, even though he is out of prison and has been out for over a decade, he won't talk about what it was like for him during that terrible time. He never married because of it. He was the end of the male line for my family. How do you think that made my parents feel, to know that their name would end with my brother? She ruined lives, then retired to Florida as if the years she was a judge in our county meant nothing at all. It killed my *maam*. I know she died early of sadness at what happened to her son."

This was news. I had always gotten the impression that Ruth's family was perfect. What had her brother done to have gone to prison? Had he been framed? Was that what Ruth thought, that he had been sentenced unfairly? "Why was your brother arrested?"

Ruth narrowed her eyes at me and immediately I realized I'd stated my question incorrectly.

"You think it was his fault?" she asked.

I held up my hands. "I just wondered what he was charged with. I'm not making a judgment as to whether he was innocent or guilty."

"What he was arrested for is beside the point."

I didn't think it was, but I knew better than to say that.

"Now, will she be there or not?"

"I believe she will."

She shook head. "I was afraid you were going to say that. Then I have no choice but to advise my husband to forbid the members of the church from attending tomorrow. We cannot be at the same table with that woman, not after all the trouble she has caused our community."

"Ruth, Thanksgiving is tomorrow. You can't make that decision so close to the event. There are so many people who are looking forward to it." Margot came first and foremost to my mind. She was already hoping to impress her mother with everything she'd done in the village to build the community. If the Amish in the village didn't show up for Thanksgiving, her goal would be ruined.

Ruth pursed her lips.

"Ruth, please don't do that. So many of your church members have helped and been involved in the meal. They will be sorely disappointed not to be able to attend."

"I would have thought after all this time, Bailey King, you would finally realize how Holmes County works, but it is clear to me that you do not. I blame Clara for that. She should have taken a firmer hand with you."

"A firmer hand? I'm over thirty years old. I moved here as an adult with an established life and career. I'm not a child to be disciplined."

"Precisely. Sometimes I wish that you had just stayed away," Ruth spat. "Margot thinks she is the reason that Harvest has become such a 'travel darling' in the last several years, but we all know the truth. The *Englischers* aren't coming for the quaint life or the Amish culture. They're coming for you, the television celebrity."

"I don't think that's true. I know the show has made the village more visible, but Margot has worked tirelessly to bring in more tourists."

A car drove by, and a woman leaned out the passenger window. "That's Bailey King from *Bailey's Amish Sweets*! Oh! I can't believe I see her. Slow down, so I can take a picture." The woman hung out of her car with a cell phone and took photos of me.

"Now do you understand what I mean?" Ruth asked with a raised brow. "You need to take a moment in prayer and ask yourself what you are doing for this community. Does your fame make it better? Do you think that's what the people of Harvest want?" She smoothed the sleeve of her jacket. "Now, I must go talk to my husband about this matter with Zara. It's his job to protect the district from hurt, and Zara brings hurt with her. As the wife of the bishop, it is my responsibility to tell him what is going on this community. He's a busy man and can't know of everything that is going on without me. It's a wife's duty to be an asset to her husband." She narrowed her eyes at me. "You will want to ask yourself, Bailey, *if* you ever plan to get married, whether you will be an asset to your husband." She marched away, climbed into her buggy, and drove off.

I sighed. I hoped Bishop Yoder's common sense would prevail, and he would see that forbidding his district to attend the community Thanksgiving wasn't a good idea. However, it was hard to tell what he would decide. It was well known that Ruth Yoder had a great amount of influence over her husband.

Despite Ruth's pronouncement, everyone was still working, and after checking with a few of the event staff, I walked over to the dessert table and tried to plan my tablescape for the next day. I made a list of all the desserts that Swissmen Sweets was providing, plus the thirty-some pies that were being made by both Amish and *Englisch* women in the district. I asked one of the Amish men to help me set up a second dessert table. The candy table would be "serve yourself," but I thought it best if we had two or three people cutting and serving the pies. I was sure we'd be able to find some volunteers, but I added a note to the bottom of Margot's list so that it wouldn't be overlooked.

I had just finished planning my tablescape when Margot's small SUV pulled up next to the square. I gave a sigh of relief. Now I could leave and go back to the shop. It was close to noon and the line was no longer out the front door, but I knew the ladies could use my help.

When Margot got out of the car, the expression on her

face could only be described as defeated. In all the years I'd known her, I had never seen Margot with such a hopeless look about her, not even that one time when all those sheep broke loose.

A fortyish man climbed out of the back seat and opened the front passenger door. An elderly woman took his hand as she exited the car. She had short, silver hair, and wore an expensive trench coat over a gray pantsuit. The skin of her face was tight and smooth, but her hands were wrinkled. She carried a large, patent leather bag with her. I guessed that it must be Zara. Who the man was remained a mystery.

Margot's eyes were the size of dinner plates when she walked up to me. I smiled, but she didn't smile back.

"Hi Margot," I said. "We have everything well in hand for tomorrow. I made a couple of additions to the list." I held up my hand. "Not to worry. Nothing major at all. It's just for things we want to make sure we don't overlook. The tables are in place and the bushes have been trimmed. Most everything else will have to wait until tomorrow morning."

"That's very good news," Margot said in a clipped voice.

This surprised me. Usually there was nothing that Margot enjoyed more than going over a punch list. She got great pleasure in checking items off.

I smiled at Zara and the man as they approached, walking arm in arm. Her high-heeled boots weren't the most practical footwear for walking on grass.

"Bailey," Margot said. "I'd like to introduce you to my mother, Zara Bevan. Mother, this is Bailey King, she's the chocolatier I was telling you about with her own show on Gourmet Television. She has brought so much interest to our little village."

Zara held out her hand to me. Her nails were perfectly manicured and painted a deep shade of maroon. She wore gold rings, and I was pretty sure a real diamond tennis bracelet. Zara had money and wasn't afraid to subtly show it off.

She squeezed my hand briefly in the same way some-one would squeeze a piece of fruit in the supermarket to test its ripeness. "It's so strange to me that someone with so much promise would give up a life in the city to live here. If you were doing well in New York, what use do you have for Harvest?"

Wow, okay then. Straight to the punch. "It's a wonderful place to live. I love Harvest and the people here." I pointed across the street. "I run Swissmen Sweets with my grandmother."

She looked over her shoulder. "I thought that was an Amish business. Are you Amish?"

"No, I'm not. My grandmother is." I left it at that. In all honesty, it really wasn't any of this woman's business.

Zara nodded. She was a beautiful woman. Even though I had been told she was eighty-six, she didn't look a day over sixty. If it had not been for her hands, I would have said she was even younger. Between Zara and her daughter, she looked like the younger person. Margot's face was blotchy and her curls sprang out of her head as if she had been pulling on them all day. I took the deflation of her springy curls as a warning sign. Margot pulled on them when she was especially agitated.

A growling sound came from the older woman's purse. I stared at it.

Zara patted the bag. "Not now, Gator. Hush you."

The growling only intensified.

"It's my dog. I take him with me everywhere. He's tired from the flight and doesn't want to be confined any longer. I should let him out to have a runabout." She handed the bag to the man standing next to her. "Will you help, Blaze?"

Blaze—who had yet to be formally introduced—looked as if "helping Gator" was the last thing on earth he wanted to do. But he took the bag from Zara's hands and set it on the ground. He unzipped it, and a creature popped up.

I thought "creature" at first because the dog was so fluffy I couldn't tell his head from his tail. I found out quickly though because the little puff of a dog jumped at me with jaws out.

I hopped back.

"Gator, be nice!" Zara said.

The man grabbed Gator just before he could bite me. I didn't believe "nice" was something in Gator's vocabulary. He clipped a leash on Gator's collar and set him back on the grass. The little dog shuffled around our feet. I took care to keep at least one eye on him at all times.

"It seems odd to me that you would come back to work for the Amish after leaving," Zara said.

I bristled at her tone. "I don't work for the Amish. My grandmother and I are partners. I didn't leave the Amish either. I grew up in Connecticut."

She pressed her lips together as if she didn't believe me. Likely due to her years with a gavel in hand, she appeared to be looking for cracks in my story. I could see as a judge she would be a tough woman to convince of one's innocence. It was no wonder a lot of the Amish didn't care for her.

The man named Blaze stepped forward and held out his hand to me. "I'm Blaze Smith." He chuckled. "Sorry that Gator tried to take a piece of you. He's a little devil."

Zara frowned. "He's spirited, and we love him dearly. Don't we, my dear?" Her question sounded like a threat.

"We do," Blaze said with a dazzling smile. "I call him a devil out of pure affection."

I wrinkled my brow. Was Blaze another child of Zara's? A friend? I couldn't quite pinpoint what the relationship was.

As if she read my mind, Zara said, "Blaze is my boyfriend. We've been together for six months now and could not be happier."

Out of the corner of my eye, I peeked at Margot. She looked as if she might actually throw up. I guessed that her mother having a boyfriend who was young enough to be Margot's child was a surprise to her too.

Blaze beamed at Zara's words. He had straight white teeth that appeared even whiter against his tan skin. Laugh lines ran from his eyes and around his mouth as if he spent a lot of time in the sun. His eyes were bright blue and cheerful. He smiled down at Zara. "That is so true. I had been coaching Zara in tennis for a couple of years and finally worked up the nerve to ask her on a date. The rest is history."

Behind them, Margot bounced from foot to foot as if she could not stand still.

Clearly, this was an uncomfortable topic for Margot, so I changed it. "We are all very excited to have you here for Thanksgiving. This is our first village-wide feast, and Margot has worked tirelessly to bring it all together. She's done so much for the village. This is a real celebration of what a close community we have become in Harvest."

Zara sniffed. "To me it's wasted talent."

My eyes widened. "Wasted talent?" I asked.

Zara narrowed her eyes at her daughter. "Margot could have done anything in this world. She inherited such intelligence from me. She could have been a doctor or lawyer. She could have been something important. Instead, she decided to stay in Harvest and have a family. What a waste. It's not what I raised her to be."

I didn't know what to say to that. Margot wouldn't meet my eyes. I had always thought of Margot as a strong woman, but it seemed she was folding into herself at her mother's criticism. And now, I could completely understand why Margot hadn't wanted her mother here for Thanksgiving. To be frank, Zara Bevan wasn't that nice.

"When you get to be my age, you realize that you have no time for pleasantries. If I think something, I say it. I have earned the right to speak my mind."

Not knowing what else to say, I turned to Blaze, who appeared to be the calmest of the three. "You play tennis?"

Zara answered for him. "He's an accomplished tennis pro. He's trained with the very best. Several of his students have played at Wimbledon and the US Open. We plan to go next year, don't we, love?"

He flashed his white teeth again. "We do. And I have trained Zara Bevan. There is none better than you. I've looked far and wide and you are the very best."

Zara's smile was like that old expression, the cat who ate the canary. I had a feeling she was quite proud of herself to be dating a man half her age.

"Mother," Margot interrupted. "Perhaps you and Blaze would like to go to your hotel to freshen up and relax after your long trip. Tomorrow will be such a busy day."

Zara narrowed her eyes at her daughter. "I do not need to freshen up. I always look well. I spend enough money on my appearance to do so." She picked up her dog. "But Gator does need a nap. He's had such a long day. Blaze, you will have to brush him when we get back to the hotel. His coat is all in knots."

A grimace flashed across Blaze's face.

"I could use some freshening up," Blaze said. "Not everyone is as naturally gorgeous as you, my love. I could use a midday cocktail as well."

I bit my lip to stop myself from saying good luck finding that in Holmes County.

"I'll just take you to the hotel then," Margot said, and then turned back to me. "Bailey, can you stay on the square for a little while longer?"

I sighed as my candy shop to-do list flashed across my mind. "Sure."

CHAPTER FOUR

When the alarm on my cell phone went off at four on Thanksgiving morning, I quietly turned it off. I didn't need the alarm to wake up. I had been awake for over an hour staring at the ceiling. There was so much on my mind. I worried over everything I needed to do that weekend, the possible expansion of the shop, and my relationship with Aiden. Of the three, my relationship with Aiden was the most troublesome.

I might not have been so worried about it if I knew that he would be in Harvest that weekend as we'd originally planned. But, as I'd discovered, plans could change quickly, particularly with a boyfriend in law enforcement. Aiden was the newest BCI agent, so he would most likely have to work holidays. Crime didn't take Thanksgiving off, unfortunately. Even so, I had been unable to hide my disappointment on the phone the night before.

"You have to work most of this weekend, don't you?" he had said. "This way we can get together Saturday night when you're less stressed and the shop is closed for the day."

"I know you're right."

And he was right. It just didn't feel right, not even a little bit.

I threw off my blankets and got up. I wasn't going to spend any more time having a pity party for myself. There was far too much to do. I got ready for the important day and ran downstairs. Puff waited for me at the bottom of the steps.

I scooped her up. "Puff, today is a day to count our blessings." I squeezed the chunky rabbit to my chest. "You're one of mine. Let's put all of our worries aside until tomorrow. It's Thanksgiving. It's a day to be grateful."

The rabbit wriggled her nose and tried to wriggle out of my arms. She liked to sit on my feet and enjoyed a good scratch between the ears, but she did not like to be held. One thing she disliked even more than being held was being forced to wait for her breakfast.

She squeaked. It was a high-pitched sniffing sound and just about the only noise she made, but I knew it meant she had had enough.

I put her down. "All right. All right. How about some carrots for breakfast since it's a special day?"

She shook her little cotton ball tail in anticipation.

After I fed Puff, I corralled her in the kitchen for the day using a baby gate. Typically, I would take her to the shop, but there would be so much activity on the square, I knew she'd be much more at ease at home.

The Thanksgiving celebration wasn't until two in the

afternoon, but Margot expected Charlotte and me to be there at nine to finish set up. That gave me a few more hours to get some work done at Swissmen Sweets. Many of the candies we'd made the day before had to be packaged. *Maami* wouldn't be happy with me for working on a holiday like this, but it couldn't be helped. She really had no idea how many times I worked all day on Sundays, usually from home. That had gotten worse since Aiden joined BCI. Before we spent almost every Sunday together.

Again, I shook thoughts of Aiden from my head. Be grateful. Worry about that tomorrow, I chanted in my head.

I knew myself well enough to know that chant wasn't going to hold me all day.

It was still pitch black when I went out my front door. I pulled the hood of my coat up over my ears. Knowing that parking would be at a premium around the square, I opted to walk.

The air was cold, but not in a biting way. The forecast promised sunny weather and temperatures in the fifties that afternoon. That was about the best we could hope for in November. Margot was wise enough to have outdoor space heaters peppered around the square for the event.

I wished I had thought to bring a scarf as I ducked my head and walked toward Apple Street. I turned on Apple, which ran perpendicular to Main Street, where Swissmen Sweets was located, without seeing a single soul.

I hadn't expected to. It wasn't unusual for me to see no one when I walked to work at this time of day. Besides, it was a holiday, though I supposed a good number of people were up thawing turkey for the day.

I reached the corner of Apple Street and Main. The gas

lampposts that lined Main Street were brightly lit as well as the lampposts on the square. I could see the shapes of the tables and chairs for that afternoon's meal.

I was about to look away and head into my shop when the figure of a man walking across the green caught my eye. I stopped in the middle of the sidewalk and watched him. There was nothing illegal about walking around the square so early in the morning. It was essentially what I was doing, but there was something about his movements that struck me as odd. He was quite tall, and I wondered if it might be Abel Esh. I frowned. Abel would be just the one to be creeping around the square in the dark. Could he have already been released from prison?

Abel had been arrested last spring for gambling schemes and causing accidents at a racetrack in Wayne County, which was the next county to the north of Holmes. He pled guilty and was sentenced to thirty-six months in prison. However, due to the prison overcrowding crisis in Ohio, he was only to serve a few months, or so his sister Emily Keim told me.

Emily, who was estranged from her brother, had heard it from her sister Esther.

Abel and his sister Esther owned Esh Family Pretzels, which was right next door to Swissmen Sweets. When I first moved to Harvest, my relationship with the Esh family was tenuous at best. Esther didn't care for me, mostly because she thought that I'd stolen Emily from the family business. After she married, Emily came to work part-time for me. She couldn't stand working for her overly critical sister any longer.

Last spring, Emily and Esther made amends. Emily still worked for me but the two sisters were speaking again. My relationship with Esther was much better too.

Although I wouldn't say that we were friends, she did wave to me when she saw me in the street. Sometimes. It was a slow process to win over Esther Esh.

Abel, on the other hand, was a completely different story. He drank, gambled, and sulked around the village with the world's largest chip on his shoulder. I continued to wonder why he even claimed to be Amish any longer. It seemed the only thing Amish about him was his clothing. He certainly didn't follow the other edicts of the religion. My only thought was that if he left the church, his farm would go to Esther and he would have to work. Working wasn't something Abel did.

Even before he went to prison, Esther did all the work on their small farm and at the pretzel shop. He did nothing at all from what I could tell. However, as long as he was Amish, he was the head of the family. There were so many things about Amish culture that I admired, but there were parts that made me uncomfortable too, such as Abel having authority over his unmarried sister just because he was a man.

I wished that Esther could kick her brother out of the house. But if she did that, she would be the one in trouble with the district, not Abel.

If he was released from prison, did that mean he had been welcomed back into the district and was living with his sister Esther again? I hoped for Esther's sake that wasn't the case.

Whoever it was creeping around the square in the early morning crossed the street and walked into the cemetery. If I didn't think the person was up to no good before, I certainly did now. Who ever had a good reason to step into a cemetery in the dark? Now, I will admit that I had gone into the cemetery at night before, but it was to save

Jethro, who had gotten lost. Juliet usually points to the moment I saved Jethro as the one that bonded the little pig and me forever. That's why she always leaves him with me to pig-sit, or so she says.

"Bailey, are you going to come into the shop and help us, or stand out there all morning?" Charlotte asked. She was standing in the doorway of Swissmen Sweets. "I thought I saw it was you standing outside." She yawned and held a cup a coffee. She handed it to me as soon as I stepped through the door.

"Charlotte, I'm surprised you're up. Today is supposed to be a day off."

She smiled. "Is it really a day off if we are in charge of setting up the dessert table at the village Thanksgiving? I know you will want everything to be perfect."

She had a point.

"Cousin Clara is in the kitchen too. We're up and ready to work. In any case, we knew you would be here early this morning to work. What could we do but help you?"

I put the strong mug of coffee under my nose. It had a lot of cream and sugar, which was just how I liked it.

Maami and Charlotte knew me well. "*Danki.*"

She chuckled. "Let's get to work."

Four hours later, Charlotte and I rolled carts full of candy across Main Street. Even though Margot told me to be there at nine in the morning, it looked as if most of the crew had been there for hours already. Volunteers were all over the square making sure every last detail was in place. There was no food on the grounds yet, but plenty of decorations, tables, and dishes.

"It looks like a scene out of a movie," Charlotte said in awe as she walked behind me.

She was right. After so many events on the village square, I thought I would be used to such a scene, but it was clear Thanksgiving was special. Everything sparkled and we had a gorgeous fifty-degree day with bright blue skies.

I recognized so many people there. I even saw my next-door neighbor Penny, who, as far as I knew, had never come to a square event before. Margot had been right that this event would bring even more people to the village center. She always seemed to be right about these things.

The plan after the meal was to decorate the square for Christmas and have a tree lighting. Thanksgiving officially rang in the holiday season in Harvest, and Margot hoped that this would be the biggest Christmas season Harvest had ever seen. Or at least, that was what she wanted until her mother and Blaze showed up.

"Everything is so shiny, and everyone is smiling." Charlotte paused. "Everyone but Margot." She lowered her voice. "What's wrong with her?"

I looked in the direction Charlotte indicated. Sure enough, Margot stood by the large Christmas tree that had been brought in from the Keim Christmas tree farm for the lighting ceremony, and she scowled at it.

"I don't think she's very happy about her mother being here today," I said.

"Why's that?" Charlotte asked.

I knew I shouldn't have said anything. Charlotte was just as curious as I was and would continue asking questions until she got what she thought were satisfactory answers.

"I'll tell you later. Let's get the dessert table set up. It's going to take a while."

She shrugged and followed me to the table.

One advantage I'd had from being stuck in charge of the square for so long the day before was that I'd claimed a prime spot for desserts. I had the table—or I should say *tables* because of the second one for the pies—in front of Apple Street, facing the gazebo. We had a clear view of the main dinner table and the spot where the tree lighting would be held. Margot and I both believed that people would continue to snack on my sweet treats during the ceremony. Also, when I was sitting at dinner, I would have a clear view of the candy table and could jump up and help anyone who had questions, although we were always careful to label everything.

I also put up my discreet disclaimer sign that said the candies had been made around gluten, nuts, and dairy. A candy maker could never be too careful when it came to allergies. With people of all ages joining the event, and so many people afflicted with various allergies, it was important to be very cautious about such disclaimers. Another reason that I wanted to expand the candy shop into a factory was because we could have different sections and dedicate one to making candies for those with allergies. Just because a person is allergic to gluten or nuts doesn't mean they should have to go through life without Amish fudge.

I had splurged and bought a half dozen multi-tiered glass trays of all sizes. It wasn't a very plain Amish purchase to make, but I thought the tiered dishes gave the tablescape height and depth, something that was typically lacking in our displays, which tended to consist of white plates and simple baskets.

Across the green, I saw Zara and her boyfriend Blaze walking arm in arm. Zara seemed to be taking everything in, and she was dressed to impress. She wore black high-heeled boots, a sleek silver trench coat, and black leather gloves. Her makeup was flawless. Her hair was perfectly in place.

My eyes searched the green for Margot. I spotted her on the opposite end of the square. She appeared to be in animated conversation with Juliet and Reverend Brook. Where her mother was elegant, Margot was, well, Margot. She was a woman who until this week I would have said was completely comfortable with herself. She wore her usual jeans, sweatshirt, and barn coat. It looked as though she might have put on a dab of makeup for Thanksgiving, but hadn't changed her appearance in any other way. She was who she was. I guessed that her exacting mother was the only one who was able to shake her confidence.

I looked back to Zara and Blaze. They stood by one of the long tables. Leon Hersh stood nearby, nodding at everything they had to say. Zara pointed at the table, and Leon jumped into action. He rearranged the seats and removed items from the table that I guessed Zara didn't approve of.

"Is that Margot's mom?" Charlotte asked.

I blinked. I had been so focused on watching Zara and Margot, I had forgotten that she was still at the candy table with me. "It is."

"She looks fancy. Way fancier than someone who grew up in Harvest."

"She is fancy," I said. My gaze traveled back to Margot, who had spotted her mother by now and didn't look a bit happy at the fact that Zara was there. "I'm thinking her fanciness is why she and Margot have so many issues. Her mother wanted something different for Margot than the life she chose."

A cloud covered Charlotte's face. "I think everyone wants to make her parents proud. I wanted that too, but I couldn't. I didn't want the life they wanted for me. I don't regret leaving my old district of the Amish church, but I wished their reaction could have been more accepting."

I touched her arm. "You did nothing wrong, and my guess is Margot did nothing wrong either. It may be in both cases that the parents are the ones who need to move on."

She shook her head. "My parents won't." She smiled. "But I hope for Margot's sake she and her mother can get past their differences this weekend."

"I hope so too," I said but from what I had heard about Zara and about Zara and Margot's mother-daughter relationship, it seemed like a far-fetched hope.

Charlotte smoothed the edge of the tablecloth. "This is the best display we have ever made. It's just so lovely, and I think adding the small pumpkins and fallen leaves was the perfect fall touch."

I understood her need to change the subject. "Why, thank you," I said, admiring it. "I'm quite happy with it as well." I bit my lip. "Do you think it will be too fancy for *Maami*?"

She tilted her head to one side. "Well, it's not very Amish, but I think she will still like it. I know it's not something she would have done herself."

I nodded. I thought the same.

"Oh, there's Luke," Charlotte said with pure joy in her voice. "I'm going to go say hello." She plucked a cellophane bag of buckeyes from the table. "Do you mind if I give him these right now? He likes them just as much as

Aiden does, and I have a feeling they are going to go fast. Don't worry about Aiden. Cousin Clara kept a large batch of them back at the shop just for him."

"Go ahead," I said with a smile. I kept that smile on my face as more and more buggies and cars rolled up to the square. The meal wouldn't be for another hour, but it seemed that people were eager to claim their spots. A few of them wandered over to my table and claimed their desserts as well.

"You're the television star that Margot introduced us to yesterday," Blaze said to me as he walked up with that bright smile on his face. He wore a gray wool sweater over freshly pressed chinos and dress shoes. He looked very much like a tennis pro off the court. He stopped in front of my table.

"I wouldn't say I'm a television star," I said.

"Don't be so modest. I looked you up after we left. You have one of the top-rated shows on Gourmet Television. You and that pig, I mean."

I suppressed a grimace. The pig was Jethro, of course. He had made a number of special appearances on *Bailey's Amish Sweets.* Juliet was convinced he would be the next Wilbur or Babe in the canon of world-famous swine.

Blaze ran his hand through his hair and it fell perfectly back into place. "I was very impressed by your show. You have a face for the camera."

I shifted my stance. "Can I interest you in some Amish candy?" When all else fails, turn the conversation to candy. That was my motto.

He stiffened ever so slightly."No, thank you. I just wondered if I could ask you a favor. Something special, just between us."

I didn't like the sound of that at all. And was he flirting

with me when his girlfriend was just a few yards away?

"I would love to see more of Amish Country. I don't know much at all about the Amish and am quite curious," Blaze said. "But Zara isn't interested in being my tour guide. I was wondering if you could make some time tomorrow and show me around."

I blinked at him, and I almost sighed with relief because I had the perfect excuse. "It's nice that you want to learn something about the area, but I'm sorry. Tomorrow is Black Friday. I will be working in my shop all day. We will be very busy all weekend long." I hoped that he would pick up the not too subtle hint that I wasn't interested, not even a little bit.

He smiled as if my answer didn't bother him in the slightest. "Oh, that's right. No one who works retail is off on Black Friday."

"That's usually the case," I agreed.

"Zara does have a sweet tooth. I know she will love all the offerings that you have here. She loves her chocolates. She has a piece of dark chocolate and a glass of red wine every night. She claims that's how she keeps her good health. Maybe tomorrow, you can take a break and we can chat."

"I don't know if it's possible," I said vaguely, becoming increasingly more uncomfortable.

I held one of the bags of buckeyes out to him. "Mr. Smith, would you care for some buckeyes? They're one of Ohio's native treats."

"Get those away from me!" he cried.

I dropped the bag on the table. It bounced off the tabletop and fell into the grass. I set the bag back on the table. "Are you all right?"

He tugged on his collar. "I'm sorry. I'm just very allergic to peanuts, so I don't want any of your buckeyes. My allergy is severe. If I even touch peanut butter to my skin, I have a reaction."

"Oh, I'm sorry." I glanced down at the dozens of bags of buckeyes on the table. "I know it can be a very serious allergy. There are peanuts in my candy shop, so it's probably not the best place for you to visit tomorrow."

"If that's the case, you're right. I can't be around peanuts at all." His face broke into a perfect white smile. "But it's good to hear that you are so understanding. Not everyone is, especially among the Amish."

I frowned. "Are you familiar with the Amish? I thought you said you knew very little about them."

"Oh." He shook his head as if clearing a conflicting thought away. "I don't know much about Ohio Amish. But there are Amish communities in Florida," he said quickly.

I nodded. *Maami* and Charlotte had gone on Amish vacations before in Florida.

"Pinecraft is not too far from where we live in south Florida. Zara and I have gone there and played tourist several times. You always feel like you're playing tourist in Florida because there are so many out-of-staters around. It's hard to know who's local, who's seasonal, and who is just there to high-five Mickey Mouse." He smiled again. "I'll be forgoing dessert today to play it safe." He smiled. "I always bring my own sweets to a meal anyway."

"Your own sweets?"

He grinned. "Marshmallow fluff. I put it on everything. I always bring my own jar to know it's safe. It's a good replacement for Amish church spread, which I could never have."

I nodded. Amish church spread was peanut butter mixed with marshmallow. It would be a death sentence for someone with a peanut allergy. I frowned. It seemed to me that someone who knew about Amish church spread was more aware of the Amish than was possible from a casual visit to Pinecraft for the day. Then again, maybe he'd noticed it because of his peanut allergy. With an allergy that serious, he would always have to be on high alert.

"But something tells me my marshmallow fluff is not nearly as sweet as you are. I would love to learn more about you." He winked.

I didn't know how to respond to that.

I watched him walk away with an icky feeling in the pit of my stomach. There were so many red flags about Blaze and Zara's relationship that had nothing to do with the age gap. I hoped for both their sakes they were happy.

CHAPTER FIVE

The turnout for the first village-wide Thanksgiving was excellent. Margot had been wise to plan for more than those who'd RSVP'd they would come, and I saw Bishop Yoder and his wife Ruth in attendance. It appeared her scheme to convince the bishop to ban his members from attending had failed. However, I was surprised to see Ruth there when she was so dead set on not being in the same place as Zara Bevan ever again. Maybe she was just there to keep an eye on everything. Ruth did like to know what was going on.

Of course, the bishop and his wife weren't the only familiar faces I saw. Everyone I knew in Harvest seemed to be there, from the owner of the market to Emily and her family of four. Even Esther Esh was present and sitting with Emily and her family. Maybe the kindness of the holidays was a real thing after all. I noted that Abel wasn't there, so maybe he hadn't been released from prison . . . yet. Margot stood at the top of the gazebo with a microphone. Usually, she just used a bullhorn. This was a special occasion indeed.

"Everyone," Margot said, "please take your seats. Reverend Brook and Bishop Yoder will be giving the blessing."

Finally, everyone was seated at the long tables around the square. Reverend Brook and Bishop Yoder stood side by side in the middle of the gazebo, so that everyone could see them. Reverend Brook held a microphone in his hand. "Bishop Yoder and I would like to thank everyone who made today possible. What a wonderful Thanksgiving it is that our two communities, the Amish and the English, can come together in Thanksgiving to the same God and set our differences aside as we share a meal. We are so grateful to everyone who prepared the meal and spent the countless hours of planning to make today possible.

"In particular," Reverend Brook went on, "we would like to thank Margot Rawlings for another wonderful event. Everyone in this village knows who Margot is and how much she cares about Harvest. We are grateful for all your hard work, not just today but all year long."

I stole a look at Margot. She sat rigid at the head of my table, which had a total of forty people at it. She looked nervous, as if she expected someone or something to jump out and tell her that she was being tricked. Her mother and Blaze sat to her right. In front of him was a blue squeeze bottle that I guessed held his precious marshmallow fluff. Although I saw church spread on the other tables, I noted that there wasn't any at Blaze's end of the table. That was a relief. Of course, he or Zara would have asked for it to be removed.

Blaze caught me staring and must have thought that I was looking at him. His face broke into a slow, and what I assumed he believed sexy, grin.

I looked away.

"Now, Bishop Yoder will lead us in an Amish blessing. Please bow your heads."

Everyone bowed their head and the bishop began to speak.

I took a peek at Blaze again, and he was staring across the green. I was facing the opposite direction. I didn't know what he saw, but it was clear that he wasn't happy about it. His eyes narrowed into angry slits.

As the bishop droned on in Pennsylvania Dutch, I risked looking at Blaze a third time. There was just something off about him. I couldn't put my finger it, but it went beyond the unwelcome flirting.

When I looked back at Blaze a fourth time, he had his eyes narrowed at me.

After what seemed like a very long time, the bishop said "Amen," and food was passed down the table.

"Isn't it just horrible that Aiden couldn't get away for a mere day to celebrate Thanksgiving with his village," Juliet said as she handed me a basket of rolls. "I knew when he took that job it would change everything. I'm proud of him for pushing himself, but to what end? He's away from home and has no time for a real life." She took a serving of green bean casserole. "It's just too much for a mother to bear. Have you heard from him, Bailey?"

"He texted late this morning while we were setting up. He hopes to be here by dessert. He said that he might be able to get away then. He can't promise anything, but he will try." Honestly, I wasn't expecting him, but I wasn't going to tell his mother that.

"By dessert everyone will be asleep from turkey overload or decorating the square for Christmas. He'll miss the whole meal. Maybe you should talk some sense into him about this new job. I'm sure the sheriff's department would take him back if he asked."

I wasn't nearly as sure about that. Sheriff Jackson Marshall and Aiden had barely tolerated each other when Aiden was a deputy, and since Aiden had left, Deputy Little had been promoted into his position. It wouldn't be fair to take the position away from Deputy Little, who was Aiden's friend and Charlotte's fiancé. I didn't voice any of this, of course, because I didn't want to be talking about it to Juliet or to anyone else.

Tink, tink, tink. There was the sound of someone hitting a knife on a glass. Zara stood up, holding Gator in her arms. "I have an announcement to make. I know that I have been away from Harvest and Holmes County for a long while, but I recognize many of the faces of those sitting here, some of which I saw in court." She chortled at this comment, but no one else found it amusing.

"Since I spent most of my life in Holmes County, it only seems right that this should be the place where I make our big announcement." She placed a hand on Blaze's shoulder. "Blaze and I are engaged, and we are getting married this Christmas!"

Margot paled.

The table fell silent.

Zara's eyes narrowed. "I would think that a *Christian* group like this would offer congratulations to the happy couple."

Congratulations were murmured down the table, and there was half-hearted clapping as well.

Zara looked to her daughter. "Margot?"

Margot blinked at her. "I—I just remembered I left my bullhorn in my car. I'll need it for the Christmas decorating." She jumped out of her seat so quickly that her chair toppled over. She set it back on its legs. "I'll be right back. Please continue to eat."

Zara and Blaze put their heads together and whispered. Gator snarled.

Charlotte, who sat between Deputy Little and me, whispered, "What's wrong with Margot?"

"I don't know," I whispered back. "I'm going to go check on her."

"I'll come," Charlotte said.

I placed a hand on her wrist. "No, stay here. It will draw attention if too many of us go."

She settled back into her seat. "Oh, all right."

I slipped out of my chair, hoping most of the guests at the table would assume I was headed to the ladies room.

I found Margot standing in front the Sunbeam Café, pacing back and forth. The café was closed for the holiday, and both Lois and Darcy were with everyone else from the village, eating on the green.

Margot spotted me through bloodshot eyes. She tugged at her curls as if they were growing out of her head just to torment her. "I should have known that you would come looking for me, Bailey. Did my mother send you?"

I shook my head. "Margot, what's going on? I don't think I have ever seen you this upset before."

She pointed at the square. "Why wouldn't I be upset? My mother just announced to the entire table that she's going to marry a man who is young enough to be my son."

"I can see why that would upset you, but they might be in love."

"You can't for a moment believe that. The only reason a washed-up middle-aged tennis pro would want to marry my mother is for her money. That's all that there is to it." She paused. "I hope for my mother's sake I'm wrong, but there is no way that I am. Anyone with eyes can see that."

"I had hoped that my daughter would support my decision," Zara said.

Margot and I turned around to see her mother standing on the sidewalk in front of the café. For the second time in less than an hour Margot's face completely paled. "Mother."

Zara pointed her manicured nail at her. "Don't you call me mother. You're no child of mine. How can you say such terrible things about Blaze?"

Margot stumbled around me, and I gladly hopped out of the way. I didn't want to be in the middle of this conversation. I inched away, knowing that I should go back to the table and let the two of them have a long mother-daughter chat without me.

Margot must have spotted me out of the corner of her eye because she said, "Bailey, stay here."

I froze in place because some of her usual Margot sternness was back.

"Should I not find happiness in my old age?" Zara said indignantly.

"No, Mother, I'm not saying that. You deserve every happiness. I just don't know that you will find it with Blaze. I don't believe he has the right intentions."

"You think the only reason that he has any interest in

me is because I'm old and have money. I will have you
know that we have a lot in common. We both love tennis."

I *really* should not be here for this conversation. Before Margot could stop me a second time, I slipped away.
I would be lying if I said that I didn't bolt across the street
and back onto the square.

When I was settled in my chair, Charlotte leaned over
to me. "What happened?"

I shook my head ever so slightly and tried to concen-
trate on my plate of food. I have to admit that a good bit
of my appetite was gone. I felt for both Margot and her
mother. I glanced down at the end of the table and saw
Blaze filling his plate for a second time while chatting
happily with those sitting close to him.

His eyes met mine and his face broke into a wide grin,
a grin that made me uncomfortable. I looked away.

Maami, who sat across from me, leaned over the table.
"Are you all right, Bailey?"

I smiled. "I'm just fine, *Maami.* I have a lot on my
mind like always."

She didn't look convinced.

Juliet and Reverend Brook sat to the right of my grandmother. Juliet broke off a piece of turkey and tucked it
under the table. I took a peek under my side of the table
and saw Jethro at her feet. Not only did he have that piece
of turkey, but he had a full plate of food.

He certainly was living high on the hog, as they say.

"It's Aiden, isn't it, Bailey?" She wiped her fingers on
a napkin and picked up her fork. "How can it not be? The
two of you have been apart so much in the last few
months. How is it even possible to carry on any relationship at all, let alone a romantic one?" She looked lovingly

at Reverend Brook, who had just taken a huge bite of stuffing; his cheeks were puffed out on either side of his face like a greedy chipmunk's.

"I don't know how I could be away from my Reverend Brook for that long. We rely on each other."

I hadn't been thinking of Aiden, but I didn't see that it would be worth contradicting Juliet. It would only make her talk about Aiden's absence from Thanksgiving more.

I concentrated on my meal instead.

Margot and Zara came back to the table, but it was clear the two of them weren't happy with each other. I shook my head. Everyone had their personal family drama.

I resumed eating and talking with my family and friends. Gradually, the mood seemed to lift, until there was a commotion at the end of the table.

Zara jumped up from the table and screamed. Next to her, Blaze's face was bright red and blotchy. He held onto his throat and collapsed forward, face first into his mashed potatoes.

There was another scream. I guessed it was Zara again.

Gator growled under the table. Juliet must have heard him because she scooped Jethro up into her arms, out of harm's way. Jethro was twice the size of little Gator, but no one would think he could stand up to the tiny dog if they came face to face.

Deputy Little ran to the end of the table and pulled Blaze's shoulders until he was sitting upright. Margot cleaned Blaze's face with a napkin.

"He's having an allergic reaction!" Zara cried. "Did he eat peanuts? Did someone give him something with peanuts?"

My heart stopped as I thought about the buckeyes on the dessert table that I had offered to Blaze. Had he taken one after all? He was so clear about his allergy. It was unlikely he'd knowingly eat anything with nuts in it. He had almost seemed scared of being close to the table. Seeing his allergic reaction now, I could understand why.

"Where's his shot? Where's his shot?" Zara was screaming. She dumped his satchel on the grass. "Where is it? He carries an allergy shot with him at all times." She rifled through the debris on the ground, but there was no shot. A flyer caught my eye. It was a handwritten advertisement for the Wittmer Poultry Farm. Why would Blaze have that in his bag? Was it a place he wanted to go while in Holmes County? It seemed to me to be an odd choice.

"Does anyone have an allergy shot on them?" I jumped on my chair. "A man is having an allergic reaction to peanuts."

I received blank stares.

"An ambulance is on the way," Charlotte said, holding up her new cell phone. It still seemed odd to me that she now carried the device.

Deputy Little and two other men knelt by Blaze's chair and turned him on his side.

"I have Benadryl." A young woman handed the bottle to Deputy Little. "Maybe it would help."

Deputy Little seemed to be unsure, and from what I could tell it was going to take a lot more than Benadryl to help Blaze.

In the distance, there was the sound of an ambulance. It would be here soon. Sooner than I expected even. Harvest didn't have its own police or EMTs. Everything came from the county, which covered a wide area. The ambulance must have been close when Charlotte made the call. This was very good news.

Surely, the ambulance would get here in time to give him a shot.

"He's not breathing," Deputy Little said.

Zara began to wail. Margot tried to comfort her mother and was pushed away.

Deputy Little and another deputy out of uniform moved Blaze from the chair to the ground. They laid him on his back and started CPR.

When the ambulance arrived, three EMTs jumped out of the vehicle and ran across the square. Deputy Little and the other officer moved out of their way.

The EMTs worked on Blaze for a few minutes while Deputy Little and the other officer ushered everyone away from the table.

I edged out of the way but remained in a spot where I still had a clear view of what was going on. The EMTs gave Blaze a shot. I guessed that it had to be for the allergic reaction. His face was covered with hives and so were his hands. Those were the only parts of his skin I could see. With such a reaction, I guessed he might even have hives in his mouth.

Over my shoulder, I looked at the dessert table. At the end was the buckeye display. *Maami* had been so proud of those buckeyes when she made them. Could they have led to this tragedy?

The EMTs' attempts at CPR slowed and the two technicians looked at each other over Blaze's prostrate body. One pressed his lips together in a line, and the other shook her head.

That's when I knew the truth. Blaze Smith was dead.

CHAPTER SIX

The EMTs carried Blaze away on a stretcher, but no one commented that he was dead. I believed the EMTs and I were the only ones who knew that. Zara and Margot hurried after them. They would both know the truth soon.

"What an awful thing to have happened," Juliet said.

"What do we do?" a woman asked no one in particular. "Do we go back to our meals as if nothing happened? That poor man. I hope they are able to help him."

"Please, please, everyone go back to your seats." It was Ruth Yoder speaking this time. With Margot out of commission, she had rushed in to take charge. "Bishop Yoder will lead us in a prayer for the ill man, and then we will continue giving thanks for the *gut* things that *Gott* has done for us."

Bishop Yoder said a prayer that was thankfully much

shorter than his meal blessing, and for the most part, every-one went back to their seats. Everyone except Deputy Little.

Quietly, the deputy cleared away Blaze's dishes. I noticed instead of taking them to the trash cans at the end of the square, he carried them to his department SUV. He put them in containers from the back and spoke with another deputy, who accepted the containers and drove away.

Next to me, Charlotte chewed on her lip. She had seen the same thing, and she had been around enough murder investigations to know what it meant.

"I think we are ready for dessert," Ruth said. "Bailey?"

I jumped in my seat when Ruth spoke my name. "Wh-what?"

"Dessert," she said in her customary sharp voice. "You were in charge of that, weren't you?"

I stood up. "Right." I began to clear away my plates. "Charlotte, can you tell the ladies who agreed to cut the pies for us that we're ready?"

She nodded and took the dirty dishes from my hands. "I've got these, Bailey."

I thanked her and went to the dessert tables across the green.

"Bailey." Deputy Little walked up to me. "I need to know which of your desserts have peanuts in them."

My shoulders fell. "Blaze is dead, isn't he?" It was something I already knew, but I still dreaded his answer.

"I'm afraid so. He went into anaphylactic shock. Because of what Zara said, we assume it was from eating something with peanuts."

"It didn't have to be from my desserts. It could have

been from any of the dishes that were served today," I said. "They were made by so many people. How are we to know that someone didn't use peanut oil on something? From the looks of it, Blaze's allergy was serious. If it was that bad, peanut oil could have been enough to cause a reaction.

"You're right, but we know that some of your desserts have peanuts in them." He eyed the buckeyes. "So this is the best place to start."

I closed my eyes and reminded myself that he was just doing his job. "Take the buckeyes then, and on the pie table there is a peanut butter pie. Don't forget the peanut butter church spread that will be on every table."

"Thank you. I *did* forget that. It's so ubiquitous to Amish dining, I don't even see it anymore."

In some ways, Amish church spread was like ketchup. Not that it was put on the same food, but because it could be found on every dining table in every Amish restaurant, whether you wanted it or not. It was a creamy mixture of peanut butter and marshmallow fluff that was a favorite for Amish yeast rolls before a meal. It was so sweet that it might rot your teeth right out of your head, and a diabetic might pass out at the sight of it. If Blaze accidentally ate any peanut butter, my money was on that spread and not my buckeyes. Especially because we'd talked about them, and he knew full well not to touch them.

"I'll have the lab test that too. Maybe they will be able to find the source of the peanuts in his system by testing the concentration of peanuts in the desserts and the church spread," he said.

"Little, be straight with me."

He sighed as if he didn't like what was coming next.

"How much trouble is Margot in?"

"You're assuming this is a homicide," he said. "It would be pretty difficult with everything Blaze ate today to prove that he didn't ingest something like peanut oil—as you already suggested—merely by accident."

"Okay, but assuming this is a homicide."

He sighed even louder this time.

"Assuming that, how much trouble is she in?"

"Well, I would say that she would be a strong person of interest. She made it no secret that she was upset with her mother's engagement. Then, less than an hour later, her mother's betrothed is dead? That will raise some questions."

"But she wasn't at the table when it happened. Neither she nor Zara were at the table then."

"That is true, but that doesn't mean she didn't have anything to do with it. Again, assuming it was a homicide, which I'm not."

"Oh, me either," I said.

He rolled his eyes.

"Bailey, do you need any more help with the desserts?" *Maami* joined us at the dessert table. She looked from me to Deputy Little and back again. "Oh dear, what is wrong? The two of you have such long faces." She clapped a hand to the side of her face. "*Nee*, don't tell me that poor man was murdered!"

Deputy Little frowned at me. "It's your fault that her mind would even go there."

I knew this was true.

"Blaze died from an allergic reaction," I told my grandmother. "There's no reason to suppose it was murder."

"No, there isn't," Deputy Little said as evenly as possible.

"Let's serve the dessert," suggested my grandmother,

who felt the best way to remedy any situation was to hand out candy. She picked up a tray of individual servings of pumpkin fudge. "Some people have already left their tables to start decorating the square for Christmas. It is best that we continue on and keep Blaze and his friends and family in our prayers. We must also think of a way that we can be a comfort to Zara during this time. It will be difficult for her to be away from home." She took the tray and walked back to the people who were milling around the table.

My grandmother was right; people were decorating the square. White twinkle lights were in the process of being wrapped around the gazebo's posts, and ornaments and velvet ribbon were being strung from the pine trees.

"That is good advice," Deputy Little said and gave me a pointed look.

It took everything in me to resist scowling at him. When I first met Deputy Little, he was a fresh-faced junior deputy in the department who hung onto Aiden's every word. It seemed now that he was no long working in Aiden's shadow, he had come into his own. I should be proud of him for that. He was engaged to my cousin so he would be family soon, but I didn't like having my questions shut down, no matter who was doing it.

At the next table, a line formed as people waited for their pieces of pie. Everyone seemed to be over the shock of a man falling into his mashed potatoes in the middle of the meal. I picked up my own tray of candy, peppermint bark in individual cellophane bags. I'd decided to include it in this meal because of the holiday decorating that was taking place today and as a nod to the start of the holiday season.

As villagers, both English and Amish, decorated the square and others cleaned up the meal, you wouldn't have suspected that anything ever went wrong in this little village. As I'd thought many times before, it looked like a Norman Rockwell postcard where everyone was smiling and giving their neighbor a hand.

But I knew otherwise. Murder and death happened in this place, and I knew that some of the smiling faces around me hid very dark secrets. That didn't just apply to the English either. There were many secrets in the Amish community as well.

"Earth to Bailey," a deep voice said.

I blinked and found I was standing in the middle of the square, holding out my tray of peppermint bark to no one.

I yelped and the peppermint bark tray went flying. "Aiden!"

He jumped back. "Well, that was not the greeting I was expecting. I had been hoping to surprise you, and it looks like I have done it."

"I'm surprised." I looked at the cellophane bags all over the grass. "Oh gosh. At least they're wrapped."

Aiden bent over and picked up four in one swoop, then put them on my tray. "We'll have them picked up in no time." He smiled at me. "Are you glad to see me?"

Was I glad to see him? Hundreds of emotions ran through me, but one pushed the rest aside: relief. I was glad to see him. I was very glad to see him indeed.

Aiden was tall and handsome. His blond hair caught the sunlight and the expression in his brown eyes, which always reminded me of milk chocolate, shifted from humor to concern. He wore jeans, a casual brown sweater that was the same color as his eyes, and sneakers on his feet. He was perfect.

I crushed him in a hug. "I'm so happy to see you." The peppermint bark fell off my tray again.

He laughed. "I'm glad to see you too. I've missed you. Now, let's pick up these candies and carry them to safety before you throw them on the ground again."

"I'm not throwing them on the ground," I said. "It's been a crazy day."

The corners of his eyes narrowed again. There must have been something in my voice that alerted him to the fact that it was more than the usual village gossip bothering me. It was much more. A man was dead.

I closed my eyes as if I could somehow block out the memory of Blaze struggling for breath. I opened them again. The closed eyes only made the memory that much more vivid.

Aiden took my hand. "Bailey, what's wrong?"

I looked into his chocolate-brown eyes. When we first met, it was his eyes that I noticed. Having been a chocolatier in New York City for the better part of a decade, chocolate was always on my mind.

"A man had an allergic reaction to peanuts. He didn't have his shot, and it was too late to save him by the time the ambulance arrived."

He stared at me. "What? But everyone on the square is going on as if it's business as usual."

I lowered my voice and hoped that he would follow suit. "I don't think they know that he died. I believe they think he just went to the hospital."

He nodded. "Who is he?"

"Margot's almost-stepfather, Blaze Smith."

Aiden stared at me. "Come again?"

We picked up the peppermint bark as I gave him the quick version of the day's events.

"Wow, Margot's mother sounds like she's really something. What kind of name is Blaze Smith?" Aiden asked. "Not an Amish one, I can tell you that."

"He was about as far from Amish as you can get," I said. "And I can't see Zara with someone connected to the Amish anyway. From what Ruth Yoder said, she was hard on the Amish when she was a judge in this county. She's not well liked by the community."

"You know, now that I hear her last name, I remember when I started in the sheriff's department, there were murmurings about Judge Bevan. I didn't know who she was or even that it was a 'she' since she had retired before I took the job. There haven't been that many female judges in Holmes County, so I assumed the judge was a man."

I nodded. I wasn't surprised. Holmes County wasn't the most progressive county in Ohio, and not all of that had to do with the high numbers of Amish living there.

"I see Little moving through the crowd. My guess is he's trying to find out if anyone saw anything suspicious. I know the death hasn't been ruled a murder as of yet, but it's best to act like it might be until you know for sure. If he waits until tomorrow or the next day to ask people what they saw, there's no telling what they'll remember, assuming that they remember anything at all. Why don't you keep passing out dessert, and I'll go check in with Little and see what's going on?"

I frowned. I didn't want just to pass out dessert. I wanted to know what was going on too, but I knew that Deputy Little would be much more likely to speak candidly to Aiden than he would to me. Aiden was his mentor and had taught him everything he knew about the job.

Since I couldn't go with Aiden, I went to look for Margot instead. As much as I wanted her to be innocent, only a fool wouldn't suspect her. I was no fool.

CHAPTER SEVEN

Usually when I was on the square, Margot was the easiest person to find. A lot of that had to do with her love of the bullhorn she kept constantly at her side. However, this afternoon, after the village Thanksgiving meal, Margot was MIA. I saw her go with her mother to the ambulance. The ambulance and Zara were both gone too. Had they all driven to the hospital together?

"Are you looking for someone, Bailey?" a kind voice asked.

I turned to see Millie Fisher smiling up at me. "I was looking for Margot. Have you seen her?"

She furrowed her brow. "Now that you mention it, I haven't seen her recently. Some of the men were looking for her to get directions on where they should set up the nativity scene this year. They claimed she'd said that she wanted it in a more prominent place. But she's nowhere to be found."

That didn't sound good or like Margot at all. Usually she loved setting up the square for the next event.

"If you find her, can you tell her I'm looking for her too?" I asked.

Millie smiled. "*Ya*, I will. I know you must be concerned about her after what happened at the meal. That poor man. I hope he's on the mend."

I bit my lip, knowing Deputy Little would not want me to be telling anyone that Blaze was dead. I'd told Aiden, of course, but that was different. Even Deputy Little would agree that his idol should know the full truth.

Charlotte and *Maami* were in the middle of packing up the desserts.

Charlotte smiled at me. "It's a *gut* thing that we made extras for tomorrow, Bailey. You were right not to be counting on there being any leftovers for us to sell at the shop. You just have that smart business instinct and always know the right move."

The expansion of Swissmen Sweets came to mind. Was it true? Did I really have the right instinct when it came to business? It seemed like such a risk and a giant leap to consider building a candy factory. At the same time, Swissmen Sweets could not grow any more where it was now. Confined by space limitations and what a staff of four could produce without lowering quality— and I would never offer lower-quality candy, and neither would *Maami*—our options were to stay where we were or to take some pretty big risks.

I took a rolling cart in each hand. "These are so easy to maneuver, I can take them back to the shop myself. You two stay here. It's starting to get dark. The tree lighting ceremony will start soon. I don't want you to miss it."

"Bailey, I can take those," Charlotte said. "I saw Aiden was here. You should spend as much time with him as possible."

"Ten minutes is not going to make a huge amount of difference." I waved her away.

Charlotte shook her head and said to *Maami*. "She is so stubborn."

Maami smiled. "This I know."

I left them on the square and headed across the street to Swissmen Sweets. It was just before dusk, and the gas streetlamps were coming to life one by one up Main Street. It seemed that every fall I forgot how quickly nightfall comes at this time of year.

I was crossing the street with my two nearly empty carts when someone on the square started to sing "Away in a Manger," and others joined in.

I reached Swissmen Sweets and was about to unlock the door when I heard a noise to my right, from the direction of the pretzel shop. I groaned to myself because I was more than half expecting to see creepy Abel Esh standing there with something awful to say to me. Abel made no secret of the fact that he hated me. His dislike of me went back to grade school when I came to Harvest to spend my summers with my Amish grandparents. Abel had a crush on me then and tried and failed to kiss me. Apparently his bruised tween ego never recovered from the rebuff.

However, when I glanced in that direction, it wasn't Abel I saw, but Margot.

Her curls stuck out from her head in every direction. "Bailey," she whispered.

"Margot?"

"Yes, it's me." She scurried behind me as if she thought she was going to be seen. The question in my mind was *seen by whom*?

"I thought you went to the hospital with your mother and Blaze's . . ." I trailed off. I had almost said, "Blaze's body."

"Why would I go to the hospital?"

Before I could answer, she asked. "Is there anyone in your shop?"

"No," I said and unlocked the door.

"Good. Let's go in."

Before I knew it, Margot had hustled my two carts and me through the front door of Swissmen Sweets. Nutmeg jumped up from his cat bed, where he must have been snoozing most of the day, arched his back, and hissed. Then he ran out of the room into the little hallway at the foot of the stairs. I knew he would hide under my grandmother's bed.

"Margot, what's going on?"

"What's going on? How can you ask me what's going on? You were there. You saw everything."

"You mean Blaze?"

She tugged on her hair. "What else would I be talking about? He's dead, Bailey. Blaze is dead, and you have to help me."

"I'm so sorry, Margot. I know this must be difficult for you and your mother."

"I don't know how it might be affecting my mother. A deputy drove her back to the hotel, and she isn't taking my calls."

"I'm sure she needs a little time to herself. Blaze's death must be a great shock; after all, she was going to marry him."

"I know she was going to marry him," she snapped.

I took a step back. Even when she was at her most irritated, Margot had never snapped at me before.

"I'm sorry." She fell into one of the paddle-back chair at the small café tables we had at the front of the shop. "I shouldn't have lashed out like that. Bailey, I need your help. I'm in a great deal of trouble."

I slowly lowered myself into the chair across the table from her. "What's going on?"

"The police are going to think I killed Blaze," she said barely above a whisper. "I know how this will go. Sheriff Marshall hates uncomfortable investigations. He will blame the most likely suspect just to make it all go away. That's me!"

"Why would you be a suspect? I know your mom was getting married and you weren't thrilled about it, but—"

"It's her will," she interrupted.

"Her will?" I asked.

"In my mother's will, it says that I get the entirety of her estate if she remains unmarried. However, if she were to marry, I would only get half of her money, and her husband would get the rest. I never worried about it much because my mother had made it clear to me that she didn't care for the institution of marriage. Even when I married my husband, she wasn't happy about it even though Rupert was a good, steady man. She told me I was throwing my potential away. It infuriated her even more that I wanted to be a stay-at-home mom. I have been a disappointment to her since day one."

"Why did she write that in her will before she was married? And why would she write it at all if it was unlikely she would ever marry?"

"Mom is a lawyer and a practical one at that. She didn't want to have to write her will over."

"How hard would it be for an attorney to write up a new will?" I asked. "Can't anyone really do that online nowadays?"

"That's beside the point."

But was it? I wondered.

"How much money does she have?" I knew it was a prying question, but the amount would affect how much motive Margot might have to ensure she got the full amount of her mother's estate.

She shook her head. "That's not something I'm privy to. I know she's comfortable, but we don't speak of finances. We never have."

"Then how do you even know you're in her will?" Honestly, given all the awkwardness and professed disappointment between Margot and Zara, it wouldn't have surprised me if Zara planned to use her money to erect a library or some other building that would bear her name. I didn't say this to Margot, though.

"She told me, and she made a point of telling me about what would happen if she were to get married." She let out a breath. "So can you see why I need your help? I can't go to jail!"

I bit the inside of my lower lip. Now I knew why Margot was so upset. If Blaze's death was ruled murder, she would be the prime suspect.

"We don't know that he was murdered. He could have ingested peanut butter in anything today. There was so much food."

She shook her head. "It was murder. I don't have any doubt in my mind about that."

"Why?"

She paled. "Bailey, I noticed the marshmallow fluff that Blaze slathered onto his sweet potatoes and dinner rolls seemed to have a hint of peanut color to it! I remembered thinking that I should say something just in case. Of course, I knew about his allergy. My mother had mentioned it several times to me. I was going to say something, I swear I was! But then my mother clinked her glass and stood up. She made the announcement about their engagement, and my mind just went blank. I can't even remember what happened next."

"You ran from the table," I said.

"That's right."

As Margot wrung her hands, a hundred thoughts crossed my mind, most of them not good. For one, had there been a hint of peanut in the marshmallow? And two, did Blaze eat it? How could he eat it and not notice the peanut taste? And the big one coming in at number three—where was his shot? People with severe allergies always carried their epinephrine pens, but when Zara looked in his bag, it was missing. Had someone stolen it to ensure his death? I shivered.

She folded her hands on the tabletop and looked down at her knuckles.

I remembered how Blaze had reacted to my buckeyes.

"If he was so averse to peanut butter, wouldn't he have tasted it?" I asked.

"Maybe not," she said. "You know how sweet marshmallow fluff is. The abundance of sugar knocks out any other flavor."

"If what you saw was real peanut, how'd it get into Blaze's marshmallow fluff? He told me that he brought it with him. He certainly wouldn't have tampered with it in that way."

"I don't know. There were so many people passing food back and forth. It was impossible to keep track of what came from where. I keep thinking back to that moment to see if I can remember exactly what happened, but I can't. It's like that game in which someone has three cups and puts a ball under one. They mix up the cups so fast, you can never hope to pick the right one with the ball in it. It was like that." She looked at me and gripped her hands together even more tightly. Her knuckles went white. "I wish that I hadn't let my mother's announcement throw me. I wish that I had said something to Blaze. Even if he and my mother had snapped at me about it, it would be better than his being dead." She put her head in her hands. "I pride myself on having a good head on my shoulders and being efficient. I always get the job done. But ever since I learned my mother was coming here, I have been a wreck. She's sent me into a complete tailspin."

I sat quietly and thought over what she'd said. I didn't need to tell Margot that if she had said something to Blaze, he might still be alive. I didn't need to tell her that the omission made her look even more like a prime suspect if the death was ruled a murder. I didn't need to tell her either of those things. She knew it all very well. That's why she was crying in my candy shop right now.

I had never seen Margot cry before. It was jolting.

"Bailey, will you help me?"

Margot had asked me for countless favors in the time I'd known her, but this one was different. It might be the biggest favor she'd ever asked of me.

I gave her the same answer I always did. "Yes, Margot, I will help you."

CHAPTER EIGHT

By the end of the tree lighting and the decorating of the square, most of the village had learned that Blaze was dead. Gossip in a small town such as ours spread quickly. It cast a somber cloud over the festivities, which would have been otherwise joyful.

Despite everything going to plan for the event—lavish food, decorations, the gathering of the entire community, both English and Amish—to mark the holiday, no one would reflect on these things. That Thanksgiving would go down in memory as the day a man lost his life. It was a sobering and deeply saddening thought.

I didn't think there was any hope that Margot would put on the same event next year, but of course, next Thanksgiving would be the furthest thing from her mind.

As terrible as it was that Margot hadn't warned Blaze that he was eating something with peanut butter in it,

given the shock of her mother's declaration, I think she
had a plausible reason for not mentioning it. My goodness, Zara's pronouncement had come as a surprise! Late
that afternoon, I'd heard through the "village news line"
aka *gossip*, that Blaze's death was not considered a murder. Millie heard it from Lois, who'd heard from Darcy,
and this came from the hospital nurse in Millersburg and
eventually trickled down to me. I was frustrated at not
having the information firsthand from Deputy Little. But
unlike in the days when Aiden was in charge, Deputy Little owed me no favors. Even Aiden had been careful only
to disclose what would have been released to the public;
he'd never been one to jeopardize the integrity of a case.

For the time being, Blaze's death was deemed a terrible accident. There could have been a myriad of ways
that the bit of church spread had gotten onto his sweet roll
with so many dishes and utensils and so much food on the
table.

It could have been an accident. It probably was an accident. Then why did I keep thinking that it wasn't?

It was close to nine at night when I walked through the
front door of my home on Thanksgiving. After the meal,
Aiden and I spent a little time together, but I told him to
visit with his mother and Reverend Brook while I worked
in the candy shop. Black Friday and Small Business Saturday were usually huge days for my business, and with
the success of my cable television show, I knew this year
would be even busier. I was nervous about tomorrow, and
I focused on doing everything possible before tomorrow
morning to get ready.

I finally quit when my grandmother practically chased
me out of the kitchen. It wasn't until I was slowly walking home that I realized Aiden had been gone much

longer than I'd expected, and I wondered now if he would have to go straight from his mother's house to Columbus. He might have gotten the afternoon of Thanksgiving Day off, but he had to work tomorrow.

Puff met me at the door. Her long white whiskers twitched in obvious irritation. I had been gone far too long and extra pieces of broccoli and carrots hadn't been enough to keep her happy.

I was surprised she was roaming loose in the house.

"Weren't you corralled in the kitchen?" I asked.

She twitched her whiskers again at me.

I walked through the living room to the threshold of the kitchen. Immediately, I saw how she'd done it. She'd pushed a low step stool in front of the baby gate, hopped on that, and from there was able to jump over the gate.

"You're a clever girl," I said. "And I think you have spent too much time with Jethro lately. He's teaching you all of his bad behaviors." I removed the gate, and Puff hopped straight to her empty food bowl.

"I don't usually feed you this late at night, but it is Thanksgiving." I put some pellets in her dish and added a stalk of celery from the fridge.

While Puff ate her late dinner, I texted Aiden to tell him I was home and if he couldn't come over before he went back to Columbus, I would see him Saturday evening.

After sending the message, I stared down at my phone. It would be odd for Aiden to head back to Columbus without at least saying goodbye to me. But maybe not so odd . . . One thing that I'd realized over the last few months was that our relationship was more disconnected than ever. The fact that I could envision him potentially leaving without coming to say goodbye only further emphasized the distance between us. It was something I would have to address with him. If we were going to live two hours away from each other for at least another year, we had to discuss what effort each of us would have to put into our relationship to make it work.

I knew that many couples managed long-distance relationships and thrived. I knew it was possible, but it would take some effort. If Aiden left Harvest without saying goodbye to me, it made me wonder if he really wanted to put the work into us.

I shook my head and turned off the kitchen light. I checked the windows and doors. It was close to nine thirty now, and Aiden would know that I was headed to bed.

I had to be at the shop at four in the morning. I would have to go to bed now if I had any hope of getting the rest I needed to make it through the busiest days of our entire work year.

Puff kept on eating with the light off. Nothing got between that girl and a meal. You could tell from her round shape. I had a feeling the next time she went to the vet for a checkup, I was going to get a stern warning about her weight.

I had just reached the stairs when my phone rang. I assumed it was Aiden, and relief flooded into my veins. I really did want him to say goodbye, even if it was just a quick phone call.

But I was wrong. When I looked at the screen, I saw that it was a phone number I didn't recognize. Normally, I would just let it ring over to voicemail, but I answered the call. It could be an Amish friend calling from a shed phone who needed a ride or help. "Hello?"

"Bailey King?"

"May I ask who is calling?" I had no idea who this person was, but I could safely say that they didn't sound like they were Amish.

"Ahh, so you are a woman of the world, and don't readily admit that you are available." There was a smile in the voice on the other end of the line. "I respect a woman who has her guard up. If we don't take care of ourselves, who will? We can't trust men to do it. It's a lesson that unfortunately needs to be learned over and over again."

"Zara?"

"I'm flattered that you recognize my voice. It must be true what everyone in the village says—you are a detective."

"I'm not a detective," I said.

"How many murders have you solved now?" she asked.

I didn't reply.

"Exactly. You might not be a trained detective, but you have done the legwork. That's good enough in my book. I have a job for you."

A job? If she was going to ask me to make a hit, this conversation was over. What could the former judge possibly need of me?

"Tomorrow, I would like you to meet me at the Sunbeam Café for a little chat. Be there at nine a.m."

"Tomorrow is Black Friday. It's going to be a very busy day at the shop, and we are opening at eight. That's two hours earlier than normal. I can't just leave."

"Sure you can," Zara said, undaunted.

Now I knew where Margot got her gift of getting people to do things they didn't want to do.

"I really can't," I said.

"I promise not to take more than an hour of your

time," Zara said. Her voice was a little less cheerful now. "Unless you want my daughter to be framed for Blaze's murder."

As she spoke, I noted that she didn't seem to be upset that her fiancé had just died. There were no tears in her voice. "I don't want that. Margot is a friend."

"Neither do I. It's bad enough that I have lost Blaze. I don't want to lose my daughter too. That's why I need your help. You need to find out who killed Blaze."

I wish I could say that this was a request I hadn't heard before, but it would be a lie. Since moving to Holmes County I had garnered a bit of a reputation as a sleuth. I had the unique ability to move in both the Amish and English communities. I knew most of that trust was built on the reputation of my grandparents.

So many questions ran through my head. Blaze's death had not been ruled a homicide. Why was everyone so eager to make it one? Did Zara know her daughter had seen a trace of peanut in Blaze's marshmallow fluff?

Feeling like a broken record, I said, "Why do you think Margot is in trouble? Blaze's death could have been an accident."

"Oh, I know it wasn't an accident, and I know someone Amish was behind it."

"Amish?" I asked. "That's a very strong statement."

"It may be a strong statement, but that doesn't make it any less true. The Amish may claim to be forgiving people, but they hold grudges. While I sat on the bench here in Holmes County, I was not a popular judge, especially with those people."

Those people?

"I had heard that," I said.

"I'm sure you have. However, it was my belief that

everyone in the county should be treated in the same way. Just because someone was Amish didn't make them better than the rest of the community. They may have claimed I was harsh, but I wasn't. I was tough, and what the Amish seemed to forget was that I was tough on everyone. I wasn't singling them out." She paused. "Now, I need you to meet me at nine in the morning tomorrow at the Sunbeam Café. I will expect you to be there. Don't be late." She ended the call.

I stared at my cell phone. "What just happened, Puff?" I asked the rabbit, who had finished her dinner and settled into her bunny bed in the corner of the living room for the night.

I wondered if I would go to the meeting tomorrow. I knew I was kidding myself, thinking for a second that I wouldn't go. I wanted to hear what Zara had to say. Did she know who'd killed her fiancé? How could she be so sure that it was murder before the sheriff's department ruled it as such? I was happy to hear that she didn't believe the killer was Margot, considering their rocky relationship. I doubted that Margot had confessed to her mother what she'd told me about seeing Blaze eat the church spread. However, it was a great leap to assume there was a murder and that the killer was Amish just because Zara had frustrated some plain folks over a decade ago.

"I'm going to bed, Puff. It's been a long day and my brain just can't take in any more information." I planned to set my alarm for two in the morning. I guessed that I would have a fitful night's sleep and the sooner I could arrive at Swissmen Sweets, the better.

Honestly, I would have left my house right then to go to the candy shop and work the whole night through. But if I did, I would wake up *Maami* and Charlotte, who were sleeping upstairs. Knowing the two of them, they would feel obligated to work the whole night long with me, and then we all would be zombies in the morning.

Moving slowly, I'd gotten halfway up the stairs, when I stopped at the sound of a knock on the front door.

Looking behind me, I could tell Puff heard it too. By the light of the one lamp that I left on all the time, I could see her lift her white head from her bed. Her long ears twitched.

The knock on the door came again. It wasn't terribly late. It was before ten, but I wasn't a person who got unexpected knocks on her door at night, unless it was my nosy next door neighbor, Penny, and I seriously doubted that she would be out this late at night.

I walked over to the door and peered through the peephole. Aiden stood on my doorstep holding a duffel bag. I opened the door. "Aiden, what are you doing here?"

He came into the house, dropped his duffel bag on the floor, and kissed me on the lips. "That's what I wanted to do when I saw you on the square, but it didn't seem right under the circumstances."

I stepped out of his embrace and asked again, "What are you doing here? I thought you had to get back to Columbus."

He frowned. "I didn't tell you I was leaving."

"But when I didn't see you . . ." I trailed off.

"You thought I would leave the village without saying goodbye?" His brow furrowed.

I hugged him. "I'm glad you're here."

He studied my face as if he didn't believe me. In the last few months Aiden and I had seen very little of each other. It seemed every time he could come home to Harvest, I was called away to New York for the show. Texting and talking on the phone weren't enough. I just had to admit that. I didn't want him to feel bad about taking the BCI job any more than I should feel bad about making the show in New York.

"I'm happy you're here. I always want to see you. I just thought you were working a case in Columbus and had to get back tonight. I'm sure your mother kept you at their house as long as possible."

"It doesn't matter how long Mom kept me there. I would always say goodbye to you, Bailey."

I looked away. "I know that." I swallowed and was unsure why I was feeling shy around Aiden. I blamed it on the events of the day, most notably Blaze's death and the odd conversations I'd had with Margot and her mother. I also had worries about the weekend. The first weekend of holiday shopping was always exciting, but also nerve wracking.

He closed the front door and locked it, then walked over to my sofa and sat. The couch was still the same one I'd bought for two hundred dollars in a tag sale at a local furniture store. It was terribly uncomfortable. With the success of the show and the shop, I could afford something much nicer now, but never seemed to be able to find the time to look, not even online.

"Besides," Aiden said. "Most of my visit with Mom and Reverend Brook was my mother asking where you were and why weren't you with us. I told her you were getting ready for tomorrow, but I don't think she thought that was a satisfactory answer. I would not be surprised if she stopped by the candy shop tomorrow looking for a better explanation."

"It wouldn't surprise me either." I followed him to the

couch and curled up crossed-legged on the cushion facing him. "What are you doing here? And what's with the duffel bag?"

He laughed. "I shouldn't be surprised that you want an explanation."

When I didn't say anything, he went on, "My superior assigned my case to another agent. They want me to stay here and see if I can improve relations between BCI and the Holmes County Sheriff's Department by assisting on this case."

"This case? Do you mean Blaze's death?"

He nodded.

"Is it a homicide?" I asked.

"Right now, it's a suspicious death. We should know tomorrow if it's a homicide."

I guess the town gossip mill had been premature in its information. On the heels of that thought, I realized Margot might indeed have cause for alarm. Lastly, my mind was still trying to work its way around the notion that Aiden would be assisting with a case here. "Do they really think it's a good idea for you to help the sheriff's department? Sheriff Marshall, to put it mildly, is not your biggest fan."

"BCI hired me because they thought I could be a bridge between the Amish and English communities, not just in Holmes County, but in all of Ohio. This is my first chance to prove to them that they made the right choice."

"I'm not questioning your ability, Aiden. I would never do that."

He took my hand in his. "I know that. I'm just tired and that's making me short-tempered. Also, I know you're right that Sheriff Marshall is not going to make it easy."

I held his hand and was quiet for a moment, and then I added, "You said you're on this case because the Amish are involved. Who are the Amish? Blaze was from Florida. Zara's not Amish and neither is Margot. Who else is involved?"

He pressed his lips together, and I knew there was something he wasn't telling me. Was it because he was with BCI now? Had I lost his trust? He used to share more about cases with me.

I considered telling him what Margot had said and that Zara had asked me to meet her at the Sunbeam Café the next day, but then I decided against it. I felt I needed to hear Zara out first, and then I would tell Aiden. I wasn't going to keep information from him. I was just waiting. That was different. Even as I rationalized the decision to myself, I knew it wasn't different. Not really.

Aiden was watching me again, and his shoulders sagged. It seemed to me that he wasn't up to having the conversation we so desperately needed to have. I knew it was just a matter of time. But it was still Thanksgiving, a Thanksgiving that had gone terribly wrong. I wasn't in the mood to add more hurt to a troublesome day.

"So you are working this case, and need a place to stay?" I gestured to the duffel bag by the door.

He nodded. "The bureau offered to get me a room at one of the local hotels, but I said it wasn't necessary. I hoped that I could bunk with you." He took my right hand in both of his.

Bunk with me? He made it sound like a kids' sleepover party.

"I'm sure your mom would want you to stay with her," I said, not sure why I was so hesitant. It wasn't as if Aiden hadn't spent the night in this house before.

He smiled as if he were expecting that answer from me. "I know she would, but while I'm here in Harvest, I want to spend as much time with you as I can. I know I've been absent these last few months." He held onto my hand more tightly. "I think in our heads we knew it would be like that, but in our hearts, we had no idea how hard it would be."

I gave a sigh of relief. Even if we weren't ready to have a deep conversation about it, I was grateful that he had acknowledged how hard it had been to have him away from the village. It made me a little more hopeful about the conversation I knew was coming.

"I'm not asking for anything other than to spend time with you. I'll sleep on the sofa." He patted the hard seat. "It will be perfect."

I gave him a look. "This couch is no better than sleeping on a concrete floor."

"It's a nice concrete floor," he said with shining chocolate-brown eyes, and I had a glimpse of the man I had fallen in love with.

"Aiden, you barely fit on the couch. At least let me get the air mattress out. I use it when Cass is visiting here from New York."

He cocked his head. "It's kind of hard for me to imagine Cass sleeping on an air mattress."

"Are you crazy? She doesn't. I sleep on the air mattress and she sleeps in my bed."

"That sounds about right."

I went to get the air mattress, sheets, blankets, and a pillow to give him. The activity kept my mind off everything that had been preoccupying me just an hour before. "Sorry that the air mattress has to be in the living room. It's the only place where it will fit. It's a queen-sized bed, and the two bedrooms upstairs are both too small for it. I know I've talked about converting the other room from an office back into a bedroom. And, truly, I will."

He smoothed the sheets and blankets over the air mattress. "This is perfect. Plus, I will be closer to the floor. Puff might like that."

She might also nibble on his toes the way she did mine when I slept on the air mattress, but I thought better of telling him that.

I nodded. "Well, I have to be out the door by three a.m. tomorrow. It's Black Friday and the shop will be crazy. I'll try not to wake you when I leave."

"Three a.m. That's early even for you."

"It's a big day."

He looked up at me from the mattress. "Are you nervous about tomorrow?"

I nodded. "It's an important day for the shop." But I didn't tell him that wasn't the only reason I was nervous. I had no idea what Zara had in store for me.

I couldn't ignore the fact that Blaze's death was much closer to being ruled a murder than it had been an hour ago. If BCI wanted Aiden in Holmes County to help, the bureau must have a good reason for it. I just wished I knew what it was. Part of me wanted to ask Aiden outright, but in my heart, I knew that if he didn't tell me, I would be disappointed. And that wasn't fair. Aiden was a man of the law, and he had to maintain his moral integrity. Just because I liked to snoop and had been known to be successful following up on leads, it didn't mean I had a right to insert myself into an active investigation. Amateur sleuthing required a great deal of balance, I realized. Enough meddling to get the answers, but not so much as to obstruct justice or negatively impact the prosecution of a criminal.

"The shop will do great," Aiden said, dragging my thoughts back to the present. "And so will you. You always do well, Bai." Sitting on the air mattress, Aiden reminded me of a little boy. He looked up at me with innocent hope in his eyes, but I didn't know what the hope was for.

"Good night, Aiden." I leaned over and kissed him.

"Good night, Bailey."

As I walked upstairs, I felt like I could cry.

CHAPTER NINE

The next morning, I woke up long before my alarm went off and didn't feel rested in the least. I'd tossed and turned all night. There was just so much on my mind. I felt I was on the cusp of making some monumental decisions, but I didn't know what those decisions were. I didn't know if they were about the future of Swissmen Sweets, about Aiden and me, or something else entirely.

By one thirty in the morning, I gave up trying to sleep. I got up, showered and dressed, and set about preparing for my day. When I arrived at Swissmen Sweets, I would have to make the coffee for the day. *Maami* never made it strong enough to suit me, and I would need the strong stuff today.

Honestly, if there was a coffee house in Harvest, I would have gone there and asked if I could chew on their coffee beans.

I didn't want to make coffee at home because there was too great a risk of waking Aiden. He was splayed on his stomach on the air mattress. The blanket I'd given him was balled up on the floor, and Puff was tucked up under his arm like a teddy bear.

Puff's red eyes were bright when I came down the stairs, and she shimmied out from under his arm. Aiden sighed in his sleep and rolled over onto his side. As quietly as I dared, I picked the blanket up from the floor and covered him with it.

He snuggled under it, and I fought back the urge to touch him. He looked so adorable in his sleep.

I went into the kitchen, and Puff followed me. It was a tad early for her breakfast, but I knew she was thinking, "Hey, she's awake. Let's eat."

I liked to eat right when I got up too, so she was a bunny after my own heart.

"Wait here," I told the rabbit. "I'm going to get you a special treat."

Her white cotton ball of a tail wiggled in anticipation. The treat was the least I could do since I didn't plan to take Puff to the shop for the next two days. It would be just too crowded, and I didn't want her getting stepped on by tourists in desperate need of Amish fudge.

I went outside to gather some leafy greens from the garden for Puff. As of yet, we had not had a hard frost. I knew it was coming any day. It was just a few days from December, after all. Until then, I was happy to see that the lettuce I grew specifically for Puff was limping along until winter. There would be just enough to make her happy, but I would supplement it with some fresh cabbage from the fridge as well.

I only had the back porch light to guide my way to the

garden. There was a chill in the air as I pinched off what was left of the greens.

"Bailey King, is that you?" a woman asked.

I threw the lettuce and spinach in the air and grabbed my chest. I spun around and looked directly into the porch light. I had to blink a few times to make out the form in my driveway.

"Penny?" I asked.

My neighbor opened the gate and came into the yard. Penny looked like she was Amish, but she wasn't. She was conservative Mennonite, which meant she dressed plainly but could drive a car. She also went to church in a church building on Sundays instead of inside someone's home as the Amish did.

"Penny, what are you doing outside at this time of night?" The question came out more harshly than I wanted it to, but she'd startled me.

"I could be asking you the same thing."

I shook my head and began picking up the pieces of lettuce and spinach that I could find in the dark. Admittedly, I didn't find many of them.

"I got up in the middle of the night to fetch a glass of water and came over because I heard some activity in the backyard and I noticed a strange car in your driveway. I just wanted to make sure you were all right," she said hotly. "Neighbors should keep their eyes on their neighbors."

Penny did a very good job at that.

Aiden stepped out the back door in his sweatpants and no shirt. He had a gun in his hand. "What's going on out here?"

Penny stared at him open-mouthed. "Oh my. Deputy

Brody. I didn't know it was you who was over at Bailey's home. I should have known better. I'm so sorry to interrupt."

"Penny, you're not interrupting anything," I said. "Aiden just needed a place to stay for a few days."

"Yes, yes, I'm sure that's it," she said, but her tone said she didn't believe me for a second.

Aiden lowered his gun. "Why are you both up so early?" His voice still sounded a little groggy.

"Penny was just being a kind neighbor and making sure I was all right. She saw the BCI car in my driveway," I said.

Penny was looking at her feet. Maybe she was afraid to look at Aiden.

"All right," Aiden said. Then he looked down and must have realized for the first time that he wasn't wearing a shirt. He leaned through the open door and grabbed something. I realized that he held one of my hoodies over his chest for cover. It didn't help much.

I turned back to Penny, who was still staring at her feet. "Thank you for your concern, Penny. You're a very kind neighbor to come over and check on me. As you can see, everything is just fine here."

"Yes, I can see that. I'll leave you be." She shuffled back through the gate and headed in the direction of her house.

I scooped up the last bit of lettuce I could find and shooed Aiden back into the house. I closed and locked the door behind us. "What's with the hoodie?"

"It was the closest thing to the kitchen door. I didn't want to leave you out there too long with Penny. Unfortunately, it doesn't fit so I settled for holding it over me."

I rolled my eyes. "What do you think she was going to do? Penny wasn't going to hurt me. I don't know which scared her more: your gun or your shirtless chest."

"If I hear you scream outside in the middle of the night, I'm going to grab my gun and protect you."

I hugged him. "I appreciate that. All is well. Go back to bed. I need to head to the shop."

"It's two thirty in the morning. Are you walking there?"

"I was planning on it. I don't want to take up any parking spots on Black Friday."

"Let me grab a shirt and my wallet. I'm driving you."

"Aiden, you don't have to do that."

He folded his arms over his chest. It was a very nice chest. "Yes, I do. Someone died yesterday in broad daylight on Thanksgiving. Until we know for sure that it was an accident, I want you to be careful."

I pressed my lips together because there was no point in arguing with him about this. "Okay, then let's go. I have a lot of work to do."

I finished feeding Puff and gathered up my coat and bag while Aiden found a shirt.

"Aiden will be back to spend a bit more time with you," I told the rabbit as we left.

As I climbed in Aiden's departmental car in the driveway, I saw the curtain move in a second-story window of Penny's house. I groaned as I buckled my seatbelt. "I think Penny is going to have a lot to talk about when the sun rises."

Aiden backed up out of the driveway. "What do you mean?"

"I mean everyone in the village is going to know you spent the night at my house."

"We didn't do anything," he said, exasperated.

"That doesn't make a difference. The village talks, and honestly, I don't care what they think. I just don't want it to reflect badly on *Maami* or the shop. I don't want to be the prime subject matter for gossip. I feel like I am too often already."

"I don't think you are in danger of that with the events of yesterday."

"Trust me. Some people will think this is more interesting than the murder—er, suspicious death—was."

Aiden and I were both quiet on the very short drive to Swissmen Sweets. I reached over and took his right hand in both of my own and held it in my lap. It felt warm and strong. I hadn't realized in the time we were apart how much I had missed just holding his hand. It was the physical connection without words. He smiled at me and squeezed my fingers. I wished we could just keep driving. I wished we'd drive straight out of Harvest together and into the sunset as if we were in an old black-and-white film.

However, I would never leave like that—neither of us would, actually. We were far too responsible. I felt my responsibilities weighing heavily on my shoulders. Those responsibilities ruined our little moment, and I pulled my hand away.

In my head, I went over the list of things that I needed to do when I got to the shop before my meeting with Zara. Honestly, I was a bit surprised that she'd called me. From what everyone said, she didn't have much use for anyone in Harvest. Why would she want to talk to me? I had a bad feeling about seeing her.

It also made me wonder why she'd come back for Thanksgiving. If she and Margot had a tense relationship and Zara hated everything about Holmes County, why would she come back? Was it just to make the announcement about her engagement, and to what end? To rub the romance in her daughter's face?

I didn't have the best relationship with my mother either. We got along well, but we'd never been close. The same went for my father. It was my Amish grandparents I had always gravitated to, so I guessed it shouldn't be much of a surprise that I ended up living in Holmes County.

The square was quiet. All the gas lampposts were lit, and the Christmas lights shimmered all over the square. All we needed was a fresh layer of snow, and Harvest would look like a holiday postcard.

I frowned when I thought I saw someone walking through the square. This was the second early morning I'd seen the mysterious figure. When I looked again, I didn't see anyone. I shook my head and wrote it off as sleep deprivation. I really needed to make that extra-strong pot of coffee. I thought about mentioning the figure to Aiden, then thought better of it. He had already pulled his gun out once that morning on my behalf.

Whoever it was, if there was even someone there, was clearly gone.

Aiden stopped the car in front of the shop. I could see the lights were already on inside. I wasn't surprised. I knew *Maami* and Charlotte were nervous about the busy day ahead too, especially since we were opening two hours earlier than normal.

"Be careful today," Aiden said. "I have a feeling something very strange is going on in the village. Today we will know if Blaze's death was a murder, but I'm thinking that it will be. I don't want you to be caught up in this as you have in past cases. What happened to Blaze should be none of your concern."

He had no idea that two people had already reached out to me about the case for help. I would tell him, but I would wait until after I met with Zara. Maybe something she said would change my mind and make me not want to help. Probably not.

I leaned over the seat and gave him a quick kiss on the lips. "I have to run. You be careful today too."

"I'm always careful, Bailey."

"I know you are, just like me."

He snorted a laugh. "You're one of a kind, Bailey King. It's one of the things I love most about you."

My heart fluttered with hope as I got out of the car. It was the first feeling of hope I'd had in a while.

CHAPTER TEN

As expected, Black Friday at Swissmen Sweets was *busy*. What I hadn't expected was that there would be a line outside the shop as early as seven in the morning, even though we weren't to open until eight.

Emily looked out the window. "It's the Jethro bars. That's what's got them coming."

I finished loading the front domed candy counter with fifteen different kinds of fudge. We had even more in the back ready to refill at a moment's notice. It looked as if we might need it too. "It could be the quality of our candy," I said.

As part of our promotion to encourage people to stop by on Black Friday, the first customers would receive a custom Jethro chocolate bar. The bars were a mix of white and milk chocolate shaped in the image of Jethro. In addition to getting one of the most popular candies in the shop, they had a chance of a photo op with Jethro in person. Aiden's mom was particularly excited about this.

Jethro had shot to stardom by appearing on my television show. The Jethro episodes were the most popular and the most difficult to film because he knocked over or ate many of the ingredients. I think maybe that's why viewers liked the episodes so much. They featured a lot of mishaps, and even I'd found myself laughing at Jethro's antics. He sure did *ham* it up for the cameras.

"You really think it's just the candies?" Emily asked. "Not all things Jethro? Because I don't think the people standing in line would agree with you."

There was clapping and cheering outside. It seemed that the pig of the hour had arrived. From my spot at the counter, I could see Juliet in a blue and purple polka-dotted trench coat and large tortoise shell sunglasses. She held Jethro and waved to all of Jethro's admiring fans.

The front door opened and the bell on the door rang.

"Yes, yes, we will take time to meet all of you. Jethro has been waiting to spend time with his public." Juliet blew kisses to the crowd.

Jethro held up his snout in a regal way.

The door closed behind Juliet. She set Jethro on the floor and whipped off her sunglasses. "Did you see the crowd? They're all here for Jethro. I knew he was meant for great things! This could really be the event that changes the course of his career." She pointed at me with the hand now holding her sunglasses. "I told you, Bailey, time and time before, that Jethro is the heart of *Bailey's Amish Sweets*. Everyone outside is proof of that. You'll have to ask your producer to give Jethro a larger role this season. The show will end up with an Emmy if you do."

Jethro waddled over to the cat bed, where Nutmeg was resting. The two animals touched noses.

"Where do you want us to set up? Jethro is going to be in a lot of pictures today," Juliet said excitedly. "Do you think we should make it a kissing booth?"

Emily looked from me back to Juliet. "A kissing booth?"

Juliet's eyes sparkled. "Yes, Jethro can kiss people on the cheek and they can get a picture with him. It's a wonderful idea."

"Why don't we start with the candy bars and go from there?" I suggested.

"Bailey, you're right. I'm getting too far ahead of myself, aren't I?" She beamed. "I'm just so glad you chose to make Jethro a part of this special day at Swissmen Sweets."

"Thank you for bringing him. You're right that he's well-beloved on the show, and I know there must be many people here early for a chance to meet him."

I looked around the room. We were going to open in ten minutes, so I had to make some decisions. The front of the shop held three café tables and chairs, and the walls were lined with jars of peppermints, hard candy, and butterscotch drops. When we had over ten people in the shop, it felt tight. There were a lot more than ten waiting outside. The line stretched all the way past the pretzel shop to the corner.

"We'll give them their Jethro chocolate bars when they come inside. I think you and Jethro greeting people just outside of Swissmen Sweets will draw lots of the people who are shopping in the village. It will also help prevent the shop from becoming overcrowded."

Juliet clapped her hands. "Bailey, that is a lovely idea,

and I think you're right that it will draw a crowd. Who wouldn't stop and look if they have a celebrity in their midst?" She smiled. "You always seem to know the best solution."

I turned to Emily. "Can you go and grab Charlotte from the kitchen? Can the two of you move one of the café tables and chairs outside for Juliet and Jethro to sit at? I'll go out and see if I can move the crowd back a bit to make space in front of the window." To Juliet, I said, "Can you and Jethro wait here while we set up?"

She scooped up the pig, which had been happily snoozing next to Nutmeg in the cat bed. Jethro kicked his legs in protest, but Nutmeg didn't so much as twitch a whisker in his sleep. With all the commotion and noise that we got in the shop, the cat had become a pro at sleeping in noisy situations.

"Of course." Juliet sat at one of the café tables. "We'll wait right here until you have everything just so." She held up Jethro's right foreleg and shook his hoof at me. "Isn't that right, Jethro?"

The pig gave me a look that said sometimes, even he, pampered pig that he was, needed a break from Juliet's affection.

I slipped out of the candy shop.

"Oh my gosh!" a woman shouted. "It's Bailey King!"

Cell phones were held up in my face, and people tried to get a photo of me. I could only guess how awful those pictures would turn out with my mouth hanging open in surprise.

My friend Cass had sent me a whole package of cosmetics a few months ago. It was the same kind of stuff they glopped on me before filming. While I didn't take the time to use it most days, this morning I had dabbled, mainly because I knew Aiden would be home. Now I was glad for the extra few minutes I'd spent getting ready for the day. Of course, even a bit of blush wouldn't overcome my openmouthed expression of shock. If any of those cell phone photos wound up on the Internet, I suspected I'd look like a goldfish.

I clapped my hands and the excitement quieted down. "Thank you, everyone, for being here so early on Black Friday. I realize that you had many places to shop today, so it means a great deal that you're here. Now, I know many of you have come to see Jethro."

A cheer rose up. I blinked. Perhaps Juliet was right and Jethro was a real celebrity. It seemed to me at least this crowd thought so.

I cleared my throat. "To do that, I just have to ask you to back up about five feet. Two of the girls from the shop are going to bring out a table, and that's where you can visit with Jethro and get all the selfies you want. Afterward, come inside and we'll give you your Jethro bar treat." As I said this, I hoped I had made enough. In all our Black Friday promotions, I said that everyone who came to Swissmen Sweets within the first hour and half of opening would get a free Jethro bar. I had a feeling we would have to break into some of the orders that we already had ready to ship to other stores for the holiday season. We could make new Jethro bars for those orders. As a last resort, I figured we could ship some Jethro bars to the fans who were in attendance.

"Inside the shop, we ask you not to take photos out of respect to the Amish working there. It is Amish custom not to pose for pictures. If you would like to take a photo with me, we can step outside for a moment. Thank you so much for understanding."

The crowd stepped back just as Emily and Charlotte came through the door carrying one of the café tables on its side. I held the door for them. They ran back inside and came out again with one chair, a burnt orange tablecloth, and bouquet of mums for decoration. With the table all ready, Juliet, who had put her sunglasses back on for the occasion, strolled outside carrying Jethro.

The crowd cheered and called Jethro's name, hoping to get the little pig to look in their direction for a picture. I did notice that the shouts and cheers for the little bacon bundle were a tad more jubilant than they had been for me. I understood. I wasn't an adorable little comfort pig. It was difficult to compete with such cuteness.

Juliet sat at the table. "Jethro is excited to be seeing so many friends," she said, and the crowd immediately grew quiet to hear what else she might say. "I'm his manager, Juliet Brook, so any bookings that you might want to make with Jethro for an event—he's available for anniversaries, birthdays, and class reunions—I'm the one you want to talk to."

I raised my brow. I hadn't known that Jethro was out for hire for birthday parties. Juliet knew how to maximize Jethro's audience.

"Okay, everyone," I said. "We open in a few minutes, but you can begin chatting with Juliet and Jethro."

The line re-formed along the sidewalk as shoppers queued to meet the famous pig. In the time that it had taken to set up the table, the line had grown by a third. I could feel the excitement of those waiting. Maybe Juliet was right, and I needed to call my producer to increase the number of Jethro episodes this coming season.

I stepped back from the line and was about to go into the candy shop to greet customers when I saw a tall blond

Amish man leaning against the side of the pretzel shop just inside the alley that divided my building from theirs.

I sucked in a breath. It was Abel Esh.

He scowled at me. I knew that was because I had been the reason he was arrested in the first place. I figured out what he and his gambling partner were doing to rig races at the track. Needless to say, Abel was not my number one fan.

I spun around and saw that Juliet and Jethro were holding their own at the meet-and-greet table. I went into the shop. It was time to open.

The next hour passed in a blink.

When I removed my apron so I could meet with Zara at the Sunbeam Café, Charlotte shot me a nervous look.

"Bailey, what are you doing?" she asked as she buzzed by me to refill the display case for what would be the second time since we'd opened at eight.

There had been a steady stream of customers as soon as we opened our door that morning. They just kept coming and coming and coming. Outside, Jethro and Juliet were basking in all the attention, and it didn't look like that attention would stop any time soon either.

"I have to run to the café just for a few minutes," I told Charlotte.

She stared at me with exasperation on her face. "The café? Now? Can't it at least wait until we are done handing out Jethro bars?"

"It can't," I said. "I know that it's a terrible time, but I have to go."

She slid a tray of pumpkin fudge into the display case and asked under her breath, "Are you meeting someone about Blaze?"

I wrinkled my nose.

She straightened up. "I knew it! I knew it!"

"Shh. Now, I really have to go or I'll be late."

"Fine! Go! But you'd better tell me everything when you get back."

I slipped into the empty kitchen. For once, everyone was at the front of the shop selling candies instead of two people upfront selling and two people in back making.

I went out the back door into the alley behind the shop. Here there was a small horse shed where *Maami* kept her horse and buggy. Although the horse shed was technically hers, she let other Amish park their horses and buggies there to keep them out of the wind and rain in bad weather. Esther's horse was in the shed next to my grandmother's.

I glanced at the back door of the pretzel shop. If I had more time, I would have asked her what was going on with Abel, but there was no time. Even if I asked, I didn't know that she would tell me. Esther and I had reached a truce for Emily's sake, but I would never say we were friends. We were more like civil acquaintances.

I slipped between the buildings and was able to make it across Main Street while the crowd in front of my shop was distracted by Jethro. That pig really knew how to hold a crowd.

The square was busy too. Shoppers sat on the benches, and children ran around doing cartwheels in the grass. It was hard to believe that there was a promise of snow before the weekend was over.

The Sunbeam Café was the newest business around the village square, and it was the first one completely owned and operated by a non-Amish family. Until I came to the village, only Amish worked on the square. As to be expected, Ruth Yoder blamed me for starting this non-

Amish trend on the square. She often pointed out that my arrival in Harvest had led to a lot of changes in the makeup of the community. There were more English businesses and more English working in Amish-owned businesses. However, most of the buildings and businesses in the small downtown area of Harvest were Amish-owned and operated. Ruth wanted them all to be.

To the right of the Sunbeam Café was Juliet's church, the small cemetery next to it, and the playground. The playground had received a facelift last year with money raised from events held on the village square and organized by Margot.

A dozen children, both Amish and English, locals and tourists, played on the new swing set, jungle gym, and teeter-totters while their parents and grandparents looked on. It was a perfect example of some of the good that Margot was doing in the village. I made a mental note to point that out to her mother. As of yet, Zara seemed underwhelmed with Margot's accomplishments.

On the side of the café that faced the playground there was a giant yellow sun mural. It made me smile. A brightly colored mural wasn't something you'd typically see in Amish Country, but for Darcy Woodin's business it was a perfect fit.

I stepped into the café and saw it was packed. I should have expected as much. All the restaurants and cafés around the county would be busy today with the beginning of the holiday shopping season. Also, the village of Sugarcreek, which wasn't that far away, always held its annual Christmas parade on Black Friday. There would be a lot of visitors in the area just for that, and they all were hungry. The main tourist activity when coming to

Amish Country was eating the food, and even though Darcy didn't serve Amish fare, her business still did very well, especially when tourists were in Holmes County for a long stay and wanted a break from the heavy Amish food.

To my left there was a blue shelf filled with brightly colored teapots and teacups. Ahead of me was the counter. The three stools at the counter were full and behind it, Lois refilled a coffee pot from a massive machine. A small, open window allowed me to look into the back kitchen. I saw Darcy's blond curls move rapidly around the kitchen as she did her very best to fill the orders for the breakfast rush.

I realized this was the worst possible time for Zara and me to meet in the café. It would be crowded and loud, and Lois and Darcy couldn't afford to lose a table if we stayed too long.

To my right was the main dining area. There were three small tables by the large front window, and the rest were peppered around the room. There were at least two people at every table I could see. Coming here had been a very bad idea.

"Bailey!" Lois pointed a stack of menus at me. "She's in the back corner."

I didn't bother to ask Lois how she knew who I was looking for. I wove through the tables, apologizing to the people I bumped. In the very back corner, Zara sat with a cup of black coffee, petting her tiny puffball of a dog. I immediately got the image of Cruella De Vil.

"Bailey, you're late," she said, looking up at me.

"I'm sorry. It was difficult to break away from the shop. It's a busy day."

"Yes, you've told me that before." She frowned. "Don't just stand there staring at me. Have a seat. I don't care for being loomed over."

I slipped into the wooden chair.

She set her purse with the dog inside it on the chair between us. Her nondescript puffball of a dog stuck his head out of the bag. I started to pet him but he nipped at me. Well, I supposed it was nice to know where I stood with Gator. He certainly had the perfect name.

"Gator," Zara said. "Don't go trying to bite people. I don't want to be sued."

It was interesting that she was concerned about possible lawsuits rather than someone being hurt. However, I imagined that Gator would bite if he felt the urge so it didn't matter what Zara said to him.

"I took the liberty of ordering us both coffees. I told the waitress that you were coming and to bring whatever you usually order."

At that moment, Lois appeared at the side of the table with a coffee loaded with cream and sugar for me and another black coffee for Zara. As she stepped away with her empty tray, she raised her brow at me as if to ask what was going on.

I wished I knew. I gave the slightest shrug. "Thank you for the coffee, Zara. That was nice of you." I wrapped my cold fingers around the warm mug.

"That's the least I can do since you are going to find the person who killed my Blaze."

The coffee mug was a millimeter from my lips. I lowered it. "I'm what?"

"Don't play coy with me. I know you must have already put feelers out about the case, and I know that you're friendly with my daughter. I assume she asked for your help as well."

I didn't say anything because, yes, Margot had asked. She'd pleaded, actually. I knew I had no choice but to help Margot, not just because I knew her, but because I honestly believed that she hadn't committed this crime. But I didn't say anything like that to her mother.

"Why do you think your fiancé was killed when his death hasn't yet been ruled as a murder?"

"Oh, but it has."

I stared at her.

She smiled. "I thought you would have known since you are supposed to be such a talented sleuth, but it seems I will just have to take the time to tell you."

I wrapped my hands around my mug again to keep them warm and safely away from Gator, who was eyeing my right pinkie with worrisome intensity.

"The lab tested Blaze's food. There were small traces of peanut on his plate. Now before you ask, there were no peanuts in anyone else's food. Someone added the peanut to Blaze's food on purpose."

This was news to me. But with hindsight, I could envision Deputy Little going over to the church to retrieve samples from all of the serving dishes to test the food for the allergen.

"What were the dishes that contained peanuts?" I asked.

She ticked them off on her fingers. "The sweet potatoes and the sweet roll. Blaze had put marshmallow on both of those."

When she mentioned the sweet roll, I immediately thought about what Margot had told me. She had seen traces of peanut butter spread on Blaze's sweet roll. I also noted that the two dishes Zara mentioned were very sweet. Add to that the sweetness of the marshmallow, and it was possible all that sugar had masked the peanut flavor. If Blaze's allergy was as severe as he'd told me, it wouldn't take much to cause a deadly reaction in him."

"That doesn't sound coincidental."

"It wasn't," Zara said, leaving no room for argument. "Whoever did this was thorough. They were determined that Blaze would have a reaction. I would even go as far as to say that it was premeditated murder."

I shivered.

"So I have asked the sheriff to declare it a homicide case." She frowned. "It's quite unfortunate that the county has too little foresight to stop electing Jackson Marshall as the county sheriff. I knew him when he was a new deputy. He was incompetent then, and I can't see much changing in that regard. Since I don't trust the man, I have also called in some favors from the local BCI office. I asked if they would be willing to assist on the case."

Now I knew why Aiden was asked to stay in Harvest to assist with the case. Normally, this case would fall under the jurisdiction of the Holmes County Sheriff Department; BCI would only be involved if the investigation crossed county lines or if the sheriff's department requested assistance. Sheriff Marshall would never have asked for help, and must have been livid at the idea of BCI's involvement. To make matters worse, it was Aiden they'd assigned to the case.

She eyed me. "I assume that you know the BCI agent on the case." She raised her brow. "There was talk that he spent last night with you."

I felt my skin flush, but I wasn't surprised Penny had already gotten my private life onto the village grapevine. The best way to deal with such gossip was to ignore it.

"If you have the sheriff's department and BCI on the case, why do you want my help? It seems to me you have it covered."

She set her mug back on the table. "I am a firm believer in working every angle. There are things that only you can find out, especially when reaching out to the Amish. You must remember I was an attorney and judge in Holmes County for a very long time. I know how this place works. If the Amish don't want to tell you something, they won't. They clam up as soon as a person in uniform knocks on their door." She sat back in her seat. "But you are different. With your sweet face, bright eyes, and Amish grandmother to back you up, you can go places law enforcement can't.

"I'm not a fool," she said. "The case is going to be solved in those places where law enforcement can't go, which is why I'm asking you to intervene."

"This makes me think you believe that someone Amish is involved in Blaze's death."

"I don't think it. I know it."

"How?" I asked. "He didn't have any connection to the Amish."

"Oh, Blaze's death had nothing to do with who he was. He was killed to hurt me."

CHAPTER ELEVEN

"To hurt you?" I asked.

Gator growled under his breath as if to say, "How dare you question my mistress?"

As far as guard dogs went, he was the fiercest I had ever come across, and I'd much rather be sitting next to a pit bull right now than Gator, the indecipherable fluff ball.

She sniffed, and I thought for a moment I saw an actual tear in her eye. Just as quickly as it came, that moment passed. "It's revenge for the many times I sentenced Amish men while I was on the bench. Everyone that I sent to prison was guilty and deserved the punishment they received. But when I came back to the village, it was time to get their revenge. They took it. In a way, I can appreciate the Amish ability to hold a grudge."

"Why not kill you then?" I asked.

She snorted a laugh. "Would that really hurt me? I'm eighty-six years old. I'm in good health for my age, but I don't kid myself into thinking that I have decades left to live. So killing me wouldn't hurt me. Not like taking something I loved away from me. Now I will have to live the rest of my life without Blaze."

I wanted to ask her if she really loved Blaze, but that seemed rude. Even though Zara had been nothing but rude to me, I couldn't return the favor.

"Okay. Why do the Amish want to hurt you? I know you believe it's because you were a judge, but do you have specifics? Are there names of people you believe were the angriest at you?" I asked the question in a low voice. Even though most of the diners looked like tourists, you could never be too careful. There was nothing a villager, either English or Amish, liked more than to listen to gossip. Whatever was overheard would be news in the village in a matter of minutes. The fact that Penny had seen Aiden at my house very early this morning and that Zara already knew about it was proof of that.

Which made me think that perhaps Zara was sending a message by having me meet her here. Hmmm.

"I heard you were tougher on the Amish in court than you were on the English."

"I wasn't. I was tough on everyone. I had to be. I was the first woman judge in the county. Everyone was expecting me to be soft. It was a different time than it is now. The only way to advance was to prove you could be as strong as any man, stronger really. You had to make up for being female, which immediately put your abilities in question. You had to be tough back then to make it in a man's world. Women today complain and whine over how bad they have it. They have no idea. None." She slapped her hand on the table. "They would curl up and die if they knew the sacrifices women before them had to make to give them the privilege to whine about the tough lives they lead now. They need to learn self-reliance. As for the Amish and their arcane and juvenile beliefs, I have no use for them."

I believed in self-reliance too. I was self-made in my way, but I didn't believe in stepping on others to reach the top. I didn't believe in belittling someone's belief system and calling it arcane and juvenile just because I didn't agree with it. I didn't agree with everything the Amish taught. Parts of their doctrine made me uncomfortable. I didn't like that women couldn't hold leadership roles. I didn't like that one man got to make the decisions for the group. But I did respect them. I respected the fact that every Amish person had the choice to leave their faith. I respected how hard that must be. I had just witnessed Charlotte navigate that struggle and it had been painful to watch her feel torn between the life she had always known and the life she wanted to gain her own independence and the man she loved.

"I was married at eighteen," she went on. "Pregnant at twenty. By twenty-one, I knew that was not the life I wanted. In truth, I knew at eighteen. I left Margot's father. She should be happy I didn't leave her with him. I could have. He was a terrible man."

If Margot's father was so terrible, why would Zara even entertain the thought of leaving her child with him? Inwardly, I filed away these details. My opinion of Zara wasn't terribly high, and while I'd tried to stay objective when the other villagers had spoken negatively about her, it was hard not to have an unpleasant view of the woman despite all her accomplishments. She wasn't particularly kind.

"Trying to put myself through college and law school as a single mother was near impossible, but it was my firm belief that I could do it. No one cares more about your career than you do. No one. Not your mother. Not your partner. Not the God the Amish speak about so often. If you want to go anywhere, you have to take your-self there. I'm living proof of that. Do you think anyone helped me along the way?"

I could certainly see how the difficulties of her life had made Zara hard, and maybe it was the reason she was so tough on her daughter too. She knew that to advance she needed to be strong, so she wanted Margot to be strong. I could see the signs of that childrearing in Margot today. She was certainly able to manage a crowd with confi-dence and she made her voice heard, but Margot didn't have the hard edges that her mother did.

I wondered if that was because of their different life experiences. Zara went into the world of law, and Margot chose family and the world of a community organizer.

"As for the Amish," Zara went on. "It may appear that I was tougher on them because I went into each case as-suming that they were not saints. Too many people think they are automatically good because they are Christian and are so pious. There are a lot of pious people in this world who do terrible things. The Amish are no different. In my opinion, saints are a myth. I have seen too many Amish cases that involve domestic abuse, drugs, drunk driving . . . you name it. It makes you believe there is no good left in the world."

I could see how she would feel jaded, but that made

me sad for her too. If you saw absolutely no good in the world, then what would be the point of living at all? Why on earth would you think that your small life could make a difference?

I had seen the dark underbelly of the Amish and the English too in recent years. I knew murderers. I had looked them in the eye and seen no light there, but I still saw good everywhere else. I had to believe in the good to keep my sanity and know that, by helping everyone I could, my own life wasn't being wasted.

Some of her tough veneer began to crack. "It's why I got out. I was old enough to retire, and I am good at investing. I had created a nice little nest egg for myself by taking the right amount of risk. After my last term was up, I didn't run for judge again. I packed up my bags and moved to Florida. I didn't expect to find good people there either, but I found sunshine and snowless winters. That was enough for me for my twilight years." She took a breath. "And then I met Blaze, and things changed. I thought I'd finally found someone who cared about me." She looked away.

I made a gesture to reach out and touch her hand, but Gator jumped up on his chair and growled at me. He bared his pointy little white teeth. The image of a fluffy piranha in a feeding frenzy came to mind.

I pulled my hand back. "I'm very sorry for your loss."

She shook her head, and when she looked back at me again, her eyes were clear. "I should have anticipated something like this." She opened her purse and pulled out a piece of paper. "But since I was a fool for not seeing what was coming, I won't be a fool now and let Sheriff Marshall fumble through this investigation. I trust that you and your BCI boyfriend can find the killer."

I bit the inside of my lip. I couldn't promise her I'd succeed, but I could promise that we would try. "We will try."

"Good." She handed over the piece of paper from her purse. "Here's what you need to get started." She slid it across the table to me.

I didn't move to pick up the paper. "What is it?"

"If you unfold it and read it, you'll find out."

Gator snarled next to me.

I scooted away from him and unfolded the piece of paper to find a list of names.

I read them to myself. "Allen Shirk. Levi Wittmer. Clyde Klem."

I looked up from the paper. "Who are these men?"

"They are the three most likely suspects, those who might still be upset that I brought them to justice."

"You want me to talk to these people?"

"My daughter seems to think you're the best at these things. I suppose this is one time I have to take her word for it. I also did my own research. It seems you have had quite a bit of luck at infiltrating the Amish community in Holmes County in a very short matter of time."

"I don't infiltrate. The Amish are real people and they are my friends," I said.

"Call it what you will, but we both want the same thing. We don't want my daughter to be framed for this murder."

"No, we don't," I said. On that, we could agree.

Her lips curled into a smile as she realized that she had me right where she wanted me. Of course, I would help Margot. She frustrated me and twisted my arm to volunteer at just about every event she held on the village square, but she was a good person.

Zara waved her hand and the fluorescent lights overhead caught in her engagement ring. The ring was stunning and as big as the gems I had seen on the fingers of the socialites on the Upper East Side who came into JP Chocolates looking for a chocolate feature sculpture for their weddings. I guessed that it easily cost as much as the value of Swissmen Sweets.

"Can I ask you one more question?" I said.

She narrowed her eyes. "Fine."

"Why were you going to marry Blaze?" I asked.

"You think he wanted to marry me for my money." She smiled.

I didn't say anything.

"Of course that's why he was marrying me. I might be old, but I can assure you that my brain is in perfect working order. I never miss a beat and I never lose my keys. My mind is a steel trap." She sipped her black coffee. "So yes, I knew that he was marrying me for money. And do you know what?"

I shook my head.

"I didn't care. Blaze was a kind man, a man of his word. I knew what I was getting. In exchange for my money, I would have companionship and someone to care for me when I am too old to care for myself. That's what I was buying. Do you know how many of my friends have died old and alone in a nursing home? The nursing home takes all the money they have left and their loneliness takes all their dignity. I'm not stupid. Maybe I will live to one hundred. If anyone can, it's certainly me, so I didn't take any chances. I had the world's best prenup, and part of it stated that if I were to be incapacitated, Blaze had to care for me at home. If he wanted my money, he didn't have a choice. If he opted not to, and I was placed in a nursing home, then the home got it all and he'd receive nothing. He wouldn't have made that that decision. Blaze liked his creature comforts. He wouldn't put them at risk when he knew he would probably have forty years with my money—without me. We were both solidifying our futures."

I noted that even as Zara spelled out her logic, her daughter, her only living heir, was completely left out of the arrangements.

"I know you suspect someone from your past is the killer, but what about Blaze? Did he have any jealous ex-girlfriends or anything like that?"

"I'm sure he did, but the question is would they come all the way to Ohio to kill him when they had plenty of opportunity in Florida? His girlfriend now is short-tempered."

"His girlfriend now? But he's engaged to you."

She shrugged. "He is, but we had an open relationship. I didn't care if he fell in love with another. Love was not my goal here. Security and safety were my goals. When you get to be close to my age, you will understand. You might look for a man now because of his looks, his humor, or his passion. But will he feed you soup when you're ill? That's what I was looking for. That's what I found in Blaze."

"If that's what you wanted and you have money, why didn't you just hire someone to care for you? Such as a companion?" I asked.

"Employees quit, and they expect things like health insurance and time off. This wasn't a job I was offering. This was a *life* I was offering."

Oh-kay.

"What about Margot?" The question popped out of my mouth before I could stop it.

"What do you mean, what about Margot?"

"Didn't you believe that your daughter would care for you when the time came?"

"I wish that I could believe it." She looked me right in the eye. "However, in my experience, Margot has never done one thing right. I wasn't going to take chances with my welfare."

"She's a very important person who has done so much for Harvest. That new playground right next door is because of her, and that's just one of the many things she's done for this village."

"She's done for the village," Zara said. "What has she done for her mother?"

CHAPTER TWELVE

After I left Zara at the café, I was torn about what to do next. Poor Margot. She hadn't been lying when she'd said that her mother was disappointed in her. What had happened between her and Zara that would lead to such a rift that Zara was willing to marry a man who didn't love her?

I knew what that felt like, to have disappointed parents. My parents had not been happy when I skipped college and went to culinary school with a concentration in chocolate. They were even more unhappy when I up and moved to New York City to pursue my dream of being a world-renowned chocolatier at JP Chocolates. However, as I rose in the ranks of NYC's chocolate society, their opinion changed. They realized this was something I really cared about. They were proud of my success until I threw them for a loop again.

When I left that career to move to Ohio and help my grandmother in her Amish candy shop, they had been disappointed all over again. My father, in particular, claimed I was taking a step back. He grew up in that candy shop; my mother, who was English, also grew up in Holmes County. Both of them wanted to escape rural Ohio and see the rest of the world as soon as they could. And when they could, they left and did what they'd always wanted.

Now, their only child had gone back. For my father, it felt like a failure of sorts. I don't think it was until they saw me in the village that they realized this was where I really belonged. I was truly happy for the first time.

As I thought of being happy, my musings traveled to Aiden. The idea of his living in my house while he worked this case made me feel even worse about our relationship. I'd never thought I would be the kind of woman who would wait around for a man to propose to her, but that's where I was. I didn't know if I would be able to stand the next few days of his being around and not knowing where our relationship stood. I sensed things were about to come to a head and that terrified me.

As I walked across the square, I texted Aiden, not to talk about our relationship but to discuss the case.

"Is Blaze's death a homicide?" I typed.

The text came back immediately. "Yes."

I frowned at the screen. When I looked up to cross Main Street to return to Swissmen Sweets, my jaw dropped. The line to get into the shop was even longer than before we opened. I waited for a minivan to drive by, then crossed the road.

Jethro was now standing on the café table, posing for photos with his adoring fans. A handwritten sign pointed to the candy shop from the corner: "Photos with a Television Star!" Juliet stood to the side with a proud mom smile on her face.

She glanced behind her and saw me standing there with my mouth hanging open. "Bailey, can you believe this? People love Jethro so much. I really think he's having his big break."

If his big break was taking a picture with every tourist who rolled through Harvest, then yes, I guessed that he was.

"It's amazing," I said.

She clapped her hands. "I don't know when I have been so proud." She paused. "Of my pig. I'm always proud of my son Aiden, as you know."

I nodded in astonishment. "Well, I had better go back inside and help with the candy."

Juliet patted my arm. "You do that, dear. I have everything under control out here." She sighed happily.

I shook my head and realized I couldn't enter through the front door. There wasn't enough room to squeeze past all the customers going in and out. And even as I stood there, people were snapping cell phone pictures and calling my name. I smiled and waved. "Have to check on the chocolates," I said and hurried toward the alley.

Esther Esh stood in the doorway of her pretzel shop, scowling at me. "Bailey King, your pig table is blocking customers from getting into my shop. How is anyone able to see my store, much less come inside and buy a pretzel?" As usual, there was a sharpness to her voice. I was happy that Emily and Esther had made up, but Esther still wasn't my biggest fan. Letting Jethro's fans block her front door would only make that worse.

"I'm so sorry, Esther. I'll ask them to move."

She sniffed and disappeared back into the pretzel shop

before I could ask her the question I really wanted to: whether or not her brother was there.

It took Juliet and me about ten minutes to move the line.

When everyone was settled and happy that they could still see Jethro from where they stood, I hurried down the alley to the back door of Swissmen Sweets. Much to my surprise, I found Abel Esh behind the pretzel shop smoking.

It seemed that I didn't have to ask Esther at all if Abel was back. It was clear he was.

"If it isn't the famous candy maker, Bailey King." He stepped in front of me.

I frowned at Abel. "I have work to do, Abel. Move out of my way."

"I know. All you do is work." He smiled. "Perhaps that is why Aiden Brody lost interest and moved away. I can't say I blame him. There are more dutiful women out there who know how to take care of a man."

I had the urge to punch him in the stomach to force him to move, but I resisted. Also, he was a lot bigger than I was, so I doubted that a fistfight would end well for me. "Please move," I said through clenched teeth.

He stepped to the side, and I walked past him.

"Don't you have some work to do?" I asked. "The pretzel shop is busy, and I know Esther would be happy for some help."

"Esther is doing fine on her own. She always has."

"I would have thought that you'd come out of prison with a new attitude. That you would want to change yourself for the better."

He laughed. "If you thought that, you didn't know me very well."

I didn't say anything more but went into the shop. As much as I wanted to know what Abel was up to, I had other things that were more pressing, like selling candy and solving Blaze Smith's murder. When I did those two things, then I might try to see what Abel was up to.

We were so busy, the rest of the day at the candy shop went by in a blur. I'd suspected it would be a Black Friday to remember, but this was one for the record book. Having Jethro sit outside the candy shop to gather attention had really done the trick. I just might have to give that pig a special treat. He loved chocolate. Unlike dogs, pigs could eat chocolate, and Jethro certainly had consumed his fair share over the years at the candy shop. He was especially fond of buckeyes. I had quite a few of those left over from Thanksgiving.

At the end of the day, I made up two bags of buckeyes and gave them to Juliet.

"It's a special treat for when you get home. I really can't thank you enough for staying all day. All I asked was for a couple of hours."

"How could we do that? It would be a great disappointment to Jethro's fans." She cradled the pig in her arms and kissed his snout.

She took the buckeyes with her free hand.

She sighed. "I wish we could be here tomorrow too, but Reverend Brook needs my help at the church. We're starting practices for the Christmas programs and discussing new decorations for the sanctuary this year. The place could use a fresh look, and since this is now my second Christmas as the pastor's wife I finally feel comfortable enough to say that." She held up the bag. "Thank you, Bailey." She went out the door, and I locked it after her.

In the kitchen, I found Charlotte and *Maami* sitting silently on stools around the island. Both of them looked exhausted. It was shortly after five, and there was still a ton of work to be done. We'd sold so much that it would be another long night of candy making for me, But not for them.

"You two should go upstairs, have dinner, and put your feet up," I said.

"Bailey, we aren't going to leave you to do all the work yourself. You can't possibly make everything that is needed for tomorrow without our help. You have to make over a hundred Jethro bars alone to make up the ones from store orders we gave away, and the buckeyes have been a popular item too. I think it must be because you included them in your last episode of *Bailey's Amish Sweets*. I never witnessed such a run on buckeyes in all my life."

"She won't have to do all the work alone," a deep voice said.

The three of us would have jumped at a male voice in the shop after hours if we hadn't been so tired.

"I can be Bailey's assistant tonight," Aiden said.

"How'd you get in here?" I asked, and then I rubbed my forehead. "That came out the wrong way. I just remember locking the door after letting your mother and Jethro out."

He frowned. "The lock must not have caught because it was unlocked. I did lock and bolt it when I came in."

I sighed. "Maybe I forgot to double-check it. There's been so much going on."

"We had over five hundred customers today," Charlotte told Aiden. "When the number hit five hundred I just stopped counting. We have never had that many before."

"And tomorrow will be more of the same," *Maami* said.

"It will be busy, but I don't expect it will be anything like today. Jethro and Juliet will be at the church."

"I bet Juliet would let you borrow Jethro for the day," Charlotte said.

"I'm not sure I can handle that crowd two days in a row." I glanced at my grandmother. "If we had more space and a bigger staff, things would be different."

A brief frown crossed my usually cheerful grandmother's face. That didn't bode well for discussing an expansion of the business with her.

Aiden smiled. "Just call my mom tomorrow if it gets slow and you need Jethro to come to the rescue. Knowing her, she'll send him over right away. There's nothing she loves more than helping Jethro spend time with his adoring public."

This was true.

It took a few minutes more, but Aiden and I were finally able to shoo Charlotte and my grandmother upstairs for the night. It was very early by New York standards, but I guessed that both of them would be asleep before their heads even hit their pillows.

After they were gone, I turned to Aiden. "So you want to learn to make candy."

"I just want to help. Show me what to do and I will do my best."

I smiled. "Thank you. Even if you do the nonskilled jobs, you'll make my life a lot easier by helping out. I might even get some sleep tonight."

"You're just giving me the nonskilled jobs?" he asked in a teasing voice.

I cocked my head. "When was the last time you made candy?"

"Never, but I'm an excellent student, Teach."

My heart did a little flip as I remembered the closeness that Aiden and I used to share. It was still there. I knew we could get it back. It would take some work, but we would adjust to living apart. It wasn't forever, right?

After we washed up and donned gloves, I put Aiden on the job of dipping the chilled peanut butter balls into the melted chocolate to create the buckeyes.

Aiden stared at the hot glass bowl of melted chocolate in front of him. "How do I do this without burning my fingers off?"

I laughed and grabbed a box of toothpicks. "Use a toothpick." I poked the center of one of the peanut butter balls with the toothpick and dipped it two thirds into the chocolate. I then pulled it out and set it aside on a tray lined with waxed paper to dry.

"It's easy." I kissed his cheek.

"Easy for you." He smiled at me, and my heart felt like it might melt right into the chocolate. "Do I get docked for all the peanut butter balls I lose in the chocolate?"

"Definitely. It won't hurt much though, since you're working for free."

He laughed. Aiden worked in silence, trying to master the perfect buckeye dip while I gathered the ingredients for the next batch of fudge I was going to make.

"Lost one!" he cried in dismay when I sat back on my stool.

I chuckled. "It's okay. We can always make more."

He poked another peanut butter ball. "You are always so kind to me, Bailey. I need more chocolate."

I smiled. "There is another bowl warming on the stove."

"How did you hear that Blaze's death was a homicide?" His tone was much more serious now.

"I had a brief coffee date with Zara this morning at the Sunbeam Café."

Aiden almost dropped the glass bowl of melted chocolate that he was holding between two oven mitts. I had never seen him wear oven mitts before, or an apron. He looked adorable.

"Careful with the chocolate," I warned. "You could burn yourself."

"Why on earth were you meeting with Zara?" He settled back onto his stool without spilling any chocolate.

As I whipped up the recipe for peppermint fudge, I told him about the meeting, including the list that Zara gave me.

"Who's on the list?" he asked.

I told him the names. "Allen Shirk. Levi Wittmer. Clyde Klem. The only one I know is Levi Wittmer. He owns the poultry farm that supplied the turkeys for Thanksgiving. I don't know him well at all. I met him briefly when Margot was discussing the turkeys with him. They met on the square one morning earlier in the fall. The exact date eludes me."

"I know those names. I know all three of them."

"You do?"

Aiden had lived in Holmes County since he was a child, and he had been a sheriff's deputy for many years. I was certain he knew more people, both English and Amish, than I did, but there was something about the way he spoke of these men that felt was different.

"How do you know them?" I asked.

"They are all convicted criminals. I've seen their names on cases or on lists when prisoners were released."

"That makes sense since Zara said these men were the ones who were most likely to want to hurt her. She must have sentenced them to prison."

He nodded.

"Do you remember what their cases were?" I asked.

"No, but that won't be too hard to find out."

I nodded. "She wants me to talk to them."

He shook his head. "You're not talking to them without me."

"Aiden, they will never talk to you. You're from law enforcement. If they've been in prison, then it's not much of a stretch to think they aren't too keen on cops."

Aiden finished dipping his peanut butter balls. "Bailey, these men have been in prison. It's not like they are a group of elderly Amish ladies sharing gossip with you at a quilting bee."

I frowned. "I've helped you before."

He sighed. "I know, and you've been a great help. I'm not going to tell you not to help Margot because I know that you wouldn't abandon her. All I am asking is that you let me go with you when you talk to them. I don't think that's unreasonable."

I frowned. It wasn't, but I would be lying if I said I liked being told what to do.

I shook my head. "I asked Zara if Blaze had anyone who might want to hurt him. She was pretty insistent that the motive was to hurt her. I guess she must be right. What ties would Blaze have to the Amish?"

"Not any that we know of," Aiden said. "But we are looking into it. It had to be someone who knew of his allergy."

"Zara and Margot knew."

He nodded. "We can't discount them completely. It

seems that we could come up with a motive for both of them, but would either be good enough to kill for?"

"Do you think these three men have stronger motives?" I asked.

"Hate is a very strong motive, but I don't know. If Zara was the one dead, I would lean more that way. It's a confusing case. Also with an allergy as severe as the one that Blaze had, we still have to consider the possibility that it was an accident."

"Zara said that she got the sheriff to call it a homicide."

He frowned. "I know."

I started a recipe for peanut butter fudge. I wondered if it was wrong to make such a peanut buttery dessert while talking about Blaze.

I changed the subject. "Did you know Abel Esh is out of prison?"

Aiden's jaw tensed. "How did he get out?"

"Emily said it had something to do with overcrowding in the prison system."

Aiden blew out a breath. "Abel isn't the kind of convict you want to let out."

"It seems the powers that be didn't agree with you." I paused. "Do you think he was involved in this at all?"

"In the murder? I don't see how. We can't blame him just because we don't like him. Abel is conniving, but he assesses risk. I can't see him doing anything that could send him back to prison so soon without making him money. His crimes in the past have involved moonshine and gambling. Those are both ventures that he could use to make money."

"We need to talk to him." I mentally added Abel to the list that Zara had given me.

"*I* need to talk to him. You know Abel has no use for you, and he will be even less helpful if you talk to him."

He had a point, but I was dying to learn what Abel knew about Blaze. Did he know about his peanut allergy? I thought back to the day of the Thanksgiving festival. It had seemed like everyone in the village was there, but had Abel been there? I didn't think so. He wouldn't want to bring attention to the fact that he was back in Harvest. Assuming that was true, why did he reveal himself to me? Was that just to torment me and put me on edge? I could see Abel doing such a thing. He was spiteful that way.

"Let's finish making up these candies and plan how we're going to talk to the men on your list," Aiden said.

I nodded dumbly. My brain was still juggling the murder with everything that I wanted to talk to Aiden about—not the least of which was our relationship. However, that conversation would have to wait until after the investigation. I just didn't think I could handle both at the same time.

CHAPTER THIRTEEN

Small Business Saturday was another busy day at the shop. We had well over two hundred shoppers come and go from Swissmen Sweets, but it was a much more manageable number than the day before. Without Jethro out front making everyone in the village stop and look, we were able to keep up with sales and even finish packing up the online orders that needed to be shipped on Monday. Charlotte, Emily, *Maami*, and I worked like a well-oiled machine. When we worked so well together like this, it made me wonder why I would want to expand the business. Wasn't this enough?

If I were Amish, I would have been told to learn contentment. It was a useful lesson for an Amish or non-Amish person to receive, but I had never been any good at it.

We got through the day without incident. At six, I left

the candy shop and walked home. It was already dark out. The square was quiet. It seemed that everyone in Harvest was ready to take a break from the activities of the weekend.

I was itching to talk to one of the men on my list, but I'd promised Aiden I wouldn't do that without him. I texted him that I was on my way home.

I had just finished the text when my phone rang, and I tapped the screen hoping to see that it was Aiden. No such luck. Instead, I saw the smiling face of my best friend Cass on my phone screen. I almost didn't answer the call. The only thing that made me pick up was knowing Cass would continue to hound me until I did.

"Has there been another murder in Holmes County?" Cass asked without preamble.

"Umm."

"OMG, it *is* true?" she shouted in my ear. "I was really hoping that it wasn't."

"Shouldn't you be working at JP Chocolates?" I asked.

"I am. We close at eight and I cannot wait. It's been a long weekend. Thanksgiving is nice. The two days after are exhausting if you work in retail."

I agreed with her. I knew I was exhausted from the last two days.

"How did you hear about the murder?"

"I have an alert on my e-mail to send me updates on any murders in Holmes County. This is one way for me to know that you are okay when you won't tell me what's going on."

"Cass, I always tell you what is going on," I said.

"Oh, you do, do you? When did the murder happen?"

I didn't say anything.

"It was Thanksgiving," she answered her own question. "You know, two days ago. I'd still be in the dark waiting for you to call me. . . ."

"It looked like a suspicious death. I didn't even know it was a murder until late last night."

She snorted. "Well, you can make up for it now. Tell me everything, from start to finish, but be quick about it. I have to get back to the front of the shop. I have a good team around me, but they're tired and their fuses are short. One more Upper East Side snob comes in here and yells at them for being sold out of her favorite truffle, they just might snap."

I gave her the quick version of what was going on.

When I finished my summary, she clicked her tongue. "You know, on a scale of one to ten in crazy Thanksgivings, I'm going to give this one a fifteen. You have family drama, a huge group of people, and a retired cabana boy dies in a plate of mashed potatoes. I don't know if my wacky Calbera family has a single hope of topping this one, and my relatives have been to prison."

I rubbed my forehead. "For your sake and for the sake of everyone in your family, I hope they do not."

"I wish I could come out there and help you. Maybe I should ask Jean Pierre if I could borrow his plane and fly out for a few days."

"You don't have to do that," I said. "Aiden's here."

She was silent on the other end of the line.

I increased my pace as I drew closer to my house. My goal was to get inside without being stopped by Penny. I knew if I asked whether she'd told anyone that Aiden had been spending the night at my home, she would deny it. I really didn't have anything else to say to her.

"Hot Cop is there?" She didn't sound that excited about it. At the beginning of our relationship, Cass had been very much pro-Aiden. The longer he was away, the more lukewarm she grew, even though I had never told her I was worried about our relationship. She was my best friend. I didn't have to tell her—she knew.

"Is he home for Thanksgiving?"

"Not exactly. BCI put him on this case."

After a beat she said, "Well, I, for one, think this is a good thing. It will give the two of you time to talk."

How she knew that Aiden and I needed time to talk, I would never know. More of that BFF instinct, I guess.

"Now I'm really tempted to fly out there and see you."

"To help with the case?" I asked.

"No, to ask Aiden when he's planning to pop the question. I have to say I'm tired of waiting."

That made two of us, but I would never say so to anyone, not even my best friend.

Cass got called back into JP Chocolates, and, given the shrill voices in the background, the threshold for snobby shoppers might have been reached. She ended the call quickly, with promises to call back for "all the answers" and I made it into my house without being spotted by Penny. I knew I couldn't avoid her forever; she was my next-door neighbor and a very attentive one at that. But I counted my blessings for tonight.

I wished that I didn't care what she thought. If I had still been in New York, I knew I wouldn't have. That was because the gossip would have only affected me. Harvest was a very different place, where everything I did also reflected on my conservative Amish grandmother. So, yes, while I wouldn't have given a second thought to having my boyfriend spend the night in my home in New York, it was a problem in Harvest.

I went into the house, fed Puff, changed my clothes,

and paced. Aiden wasn't answering my text messages. I wasn't the kind of woman who sat around and waited for someone else to show up. However, I also knew going to an Amish farm where I wasn't known on a Saturday night probably wasn't the best idea I'd ever had.

The Sabbath was strictly for worship in the district, so talking to any Amish suspects on Sunday was out of the question. If I didn't speak to at least one of the three Amish men on Zara's list that night, I would have to wait another whole day. I sighed. There was always Margot.

I called Margot, but there was no answer. I chewed on my lip. I was antsy. I had to do something. Sitting and waiting for Aiden to show up and give me direction was never going to fly. He knew that. In fact, he would be surprised that I had sat at home and waited for him this long.

"Puff, I need to go out again." I grabbed my coat.

She didn't even look up from her bowl of cabbage.

Margot lived on the outskirts of Harvest in a planned neighborhood. It was twelve or so large homes that seemed to be set right in the middle of a fallow field. All the trees were young and the sidewalks were spotless.

Despite the manicured identical lawns, I knew something was off as soon as I turned into the neighborhood.

Blue and red flashing lights reflected off the windows of the large houses. As my car rolled up Margot's street, I saw why.

There were three sheriff department cars in front of her two-story home. My heart sank. Was she all right? Was she . . . dead? Zara wholeheartedly believed that Blaze had been killed to hurt her, and what better way to truly terrorize Zara than to harm her only daughter?

Along with the sheriff's department SUVs, I spotted Aiden's BCI vehicle. That put my mind at ease just a little. *No, no she couldn't be dead. Aiden would have told me right away.*

Neighbors stood on their front porches, watching the spectacle. It wouldn't be long before the whole village—if not the whole county—knew that the police had been to Margot's home. I parked on the street behind Aiden's SUV. As soon as I got out of the car, I heard, "Bailey, what are you doing here?"

It was Deputy Little. He stood by his car, holding an evidence bag. It was too dark to see what was inside the bag.

"Hi, Little," I said in my most upbeat voice.

"Bailey King, how did you hear about this already?" he asked.

I had no idea what *this* was, but I wasn't about to let him know that until I figured it out. I shrugged. "You know, this town talks."

His eyes were wide. "But it just happened. Even for the Harvest grapevine, that is extra fast."

I shrugged. "Margot is my friend, well, mostly."

"What does this have to do with Margot?"

I frowned. "This is her house, isn't it?"

He looked back over his shoulder at the scene. "It's her house, but we aren't here to talk to Margot." He narrowed his eyes as if he was beginning to suspect that I had no clue as to what was happening, and of course, I didn't.

"Oh?" I asked, afraid that I was letting on that I really had no idea what he was talking about.

"We are here to talk to her husband. He's the suspect."

"Suspect for the murder?" I asked.

"You know that it's a murder too." He rubbed the side of his temple. "No one is supposed to know that yet. The sheriff was very clear on that."

"I know he doesn't like bad press. Zara told me it was a murder. I guessed that she would know," I said, relieved that I could say I had learned the news from Zara and not Aiden. The less trouble Aiden was in with the sheriff, the better.

Deputy Little pressed his lips together. "The sheriff asked her not to share that with anyone. Not that I thought she would follow his orders. There is definitely some bad blood between them."

I was just going to ask him what he meant by that when the front door of Margot's house opened and her husband, Rupert, was escorted out by another deputy. I noted that Rupert's hands weren't cuffed. I gave a sigh of relief. He wasn't arrested, at least not yet.

Margot was a few paces behind him. "This is outrageous. My husband wouldn't kill anyone. He didn't even know Blaze. He had never even met him."

Aiden stepped out of the house. "Margot, we are just taking Rupert to the sheriff's department to ask him a few questions. He should be home tonight."

"Can't this wait until the morning?" she asked. "I promise you neither of us did anything wrong."

"Time is of the essence in a case like this. The sooner we interview your husband, the sooner he can come home."

Rupert looked over his shoulder. "He's right, Margot. Go back into the house. I'll be home soon."

Margot looked as if she might cry.

The deputy and Rupert got into the department SUV and drove away.

Aiden walked to his SUV and stopped short when he saw me standing there with Deputy Little. "Bailey, what are you doing here? How did you know we wanted to talk to Rupert?"

I glanced at Deputy Little. "I didn't know. I only came here tonight to see how Margot was."

Aiden looked over his shoulder at Margot, who stood in the doorway of her house glaring at the deputies as they drove away. She was angry, and anger was an emotion that I was used to when it came to Margot. In a way, it was comforting.

Margot walked over to us. "Did you see that, Bailey? Did you see how they treated my husband? They marched him out of my house like he was a common criminal. It was disgraceful. Rupert didn't have anything to do with Blaze's death. He wasn't even here on Thanksgiving. He arrived home that night. Blaze was already dead!"

"We know that, Margot," Aiden said calmly.

"Where was he?" I asked, realizing that I hadn't seen Margot's husband at the meal. In fact, I thought this was the first time I had ever seen Margot's husband. That was odd to me because of how much time I'd spent with Margot since I'd moved to Harvest.

"He was coming home from a long-distance drive. He's a truck driver and got caught in a snowstorm in northern Michigan. He had to wait at a truck stop for a day before he could get back on the road. He didn't return home until Thanksgiving night." She put her hands on her hips.

"We know all this Margot. However, we still want to speak with him since he has threatened Zara in the past," Aiden said.

"Threatened her? That's ridiculous. Rupert doesn't care for my mother, but that's just because he's my husband and wants to defend me." She held up her hand. "He doesn't think that she would hurt me physically, but she has a sharp tongue and no fear of using it. He's just being a good husband."

"If Rupert has an alibi, why question him at the station? What's wrong with doing it here?" I asked.

Aiden looked at me out of the corner of his eye. "We had planned to talk to him at home, but he was being less than cooperative."

Margot put her hands on her hips. "That's because you came to our home in the middle of the night and peppered us with questions. I know that Rupert can have a short fuse, but he's harmless."

"He threw a remote control at Deputy Little."

"That was an accident. He was waving his hands and it slipped out."

I bit my lip. Warning bells went off. If Rupert would throw a remote control at a sheriff's deputy, what was he like when no one was around? I'd never for a moment thought Margot could be in a bad marriage. In fact, I can't say that I had ever thought of her marriage at all. It wasn't something she talked about. Occasionally, she mentioned her grown children, but most of our conversation centered on events at the square. I wondered what else I didn't know about her.

"The truth is"—she dropped her arms at her sides— "my mother never liked Rupert. She never liked any choice I made for my own life. She was the one who pointed to my husband as a suspect, wasn't she? No one else would have even thought of him."

Deputy Little and Aiden shared a look.

Margot shook her head. "I knew it would be bad for me when she came back to Harvest, but I honestly never thought it would be this bad. I never thought she would stoop so low as to hurt my husband, and me by association."

If Zara thought Rupert was behind her fiancé's death, why had she met with me that morning? Why had she given me that list of names?

"If you see my mother again, tell her we are done. I don't care what happens to her money. I don't want it or need it. Rupert and I are fine. Our children are grown and happy. No one here needs her. She should remember that. The break with the family and with me was her fault, and now she has to live with it." Margot went back into the house and slammed the door closed.

"I guess she won't be talking to us again tonight," Deputy Little said.

That was a safe guess.

CHAPTER FOURTEEN

After we left Margot's house, Deputy Little and Aiden went to the sheriff's department to talk to Rupert, and I headed home. I tried my best to stay up until Aiden came back to the house after finishing his interrogation, but the evening hours ticked by. With each passing minute, I grew more and more exhausted. Ten turned to eleven, which turned to twelve. When it was almost one in the morning, I gave up. I had gotten up for Small Business Saturday at four in the morning. I couldn't keep my eyes open any longer.

The next morning, I woke up at six, which, for me, was sleeping in. Sunday was the one day a week that sleeping in was actually possible. It was the only day that Swissmen Sweets was closed. Usually, I loved Sundays, because for me they were long and lazy. However, the Sunday after Thanksgiving I felt impatient, knowing it would be next to impossible to get any new information about the case.

Holmes County was mostly shut down on this day, and the Amish men that Zara had suggested I speak to would not talk to me on Sunday because it was the day of rest. I didn't think they would consider discussions about murder as resting.

That being said, staying in bed much past six never worked for me. I had to get up, if only to solidify my ideas about the case and my plans for expanding Swissmen Sweets. I decided that I would speak to my grandmother just after Christmas. I wouldn't move forward without her blessing, but I hoped she would give it to me.

I hoped she would see the potential in Swissmen Sweets that I saw and see how expansion could help her. However, I wasn't sure about her being willing to accept that help. The Amish believed pride was a sin, but they were proud of being hard working for their whole lives. Real retirement from work was a foreign concept to them.

My drive to expand the business wasn't about the monetary potential. It was about creating something lasting. Something larger than ourselves that honored *Maami,* and my late *Grossdaadi*, and the Amish community whose traditions were reflected in the recipes for our sweets. Sharing those sweets with the world . . . that was quite a privilege, indeed.

I got ready for the day and tiptoed down the stairs. I didn't want to wake Aiden, who I thought would be asleep on the air mattress in the living room. He wasn't there, and the bed was made up just as I had left it for him the night before. He had never come back to my house.

My heart sank. I didn't know exactly what was going

on with Aiden, but there was something, and murder investigation or not, we'd soon have to address it.

Since I didn't have to be quiet, I said good morning to Puff and asked her if she was ready for breakfast. She gave me a look that was the rabbit equivalent of *that's the dumbest question I ever heard.*

After I fed Puff, I sat down at the dining table, which was in the corner of the living room near the kitchen. I got pen and paper and started to make a list of everyone I wanted to speak to about Blaze. It wasn't a terribly long list. There were the three men Zara had told me to speak to: Allen Shirk, Levi Wittmer, and Clyde Klem. I didn't know Allen at all, but I had at least met Levi Wittmer and Clyde Klem. Levi had the poultry farm and Clyde worked at the Harvest Market. Both would be closed today.

I tapped my pen on the notepad and then stood up. "Puff, I can't talk to these men today, but that doesn't mean I can't do some recon."

The rabbit looked up at me and twitched her nose. I had every suspicion that she knew what I was speaking about. She was a very smart rabbit.

My cell phone rang. When I looked down at the screen, I saw a photo of Jethro taken last Easter in a pair of bunny ears. It was my photo ID to tell me that Juliet was calling. Usually the only times she called me were Jethro-related, so I found the picture appropriate. The odd thing was her calling me on a Sunday morning. She was the pastor's wife, after all. She had so many responsibilities on this day.

"Hell—?" I couldn't even get out the greeting before Juliet interrupted me.

"Bailey, thank goodness. I need your help!"

"Juliet, what's wrong?" I asked.

She took a breath. "Jethro is sick!" There were tears in her voice.

There was a sharp pain in my chest. Until that moment, I hadn't realized how much I cared about the little bacon bundle. The pig and I had been through a lot together. No one would dispute that. We'd faced down killers together. "What happened?"

"Oh, Bailey, I don't know how it happened, but there was a turkey bone on the floor in the church kitchen. It must have been missed during the rush of cleaning up after Thanksgiving, and you know everyone was all a twitter over that poor man's death. Jethro and I went to the church last night to make sure everything was just so for church this morning—we're having a ladies' tea in the afternoon—so we needed the kitchen to be perfect. I turned my back for one second and Jethro gobbled up the turkey bone."

I grimaced, not liking where this was going.

"It wasn't very big, but it got stuck in his throat. Thank goodness, I was able to get him to the emergency vet. Reverend Brook was a dream through it all. I cried like a baby."

"Juliet, I'm so sorry. How's Jethro now?" I asked.

"Much better. It wasn't that far down his throat and the vet was able to remove it without surgery. Poor Jethro has a sore throat and is just not himself at all. I don't want to stress him by taking him to the church today."

Without missing a beat, I said, "So you want me to watch him today while you're at church."

"Could you? Oh, you are the best almost daughter-in-law that anyone could have."

I made no response to the almost daughter-in-law comment. "Are you home or at the church?"

"We're already at the church. Reverend Brook always likes to be the first one here on Sundays. As the leader of his flock, he knows how important it is to be there to greet all of his parishioners. He takes his job so seriously." She sighed. "I just don't think there is a more caring man on the planet. I know that he would love to take care of Jethro today himself or let me do it, but we have a duty to the congregation. It is God's call, you see."

"I'll be there in about twenty minutes," I said before she could go into any more details.

"Bless your heart, Bailey. Bless your heart."

I said goodbye to Puff and went out the door. It was a short walk from my house to the church. Since it was still early, the church parking lot was empty except for Reverend Brook's sensible sedan, which was parked in the spot reserved for the pastor.

I was just about to walk up the church steps to go inside when I heard someone call my name.

I turned around to see Juliet walking around the side of the building pushing a baby stroller. "Oh, Bailey, thank you for coming so quickly. I really don't know what I would do without your help. I'm in such a bind, and I want Jethro to get the best care possible."

"Where's Jethro?" I asked. Typically, she carried the pig or walked him on a leash.

She nudged the stroller closer to me. "He's in here. I took this from the nursery. I know the nursery teachers will understand that Jethro needed this stroller a lot more today than the toddlers would. Besides, most of the parents come with their own strollers."

I peeked into the stroller. Jethro was snuggled in a bed of pink and blue blankets, also taken from the church nursery, I guessed. There was a stuffed white rabbit in the stroller with him. He had his right front foreleg over it as if he was giving it a hug. Perhaps it reminded him of Puff. Poor Jethro. He was adorable and pathetic all at the same time.

He lifted his head just a fraction of an inch and blinked at me. I reached in and scratched him between the ears. "Jethro, what have you done?"

He set his chin back on the pile of baby blankets and expelled a deep breath—a piggy sigh, if ever I'd heard one. It was as if he couldn't even talk about it.

"The vet told me that Jethro likely has some abrasions in his throat from trying to swallow the bone. Because of that, he's not very interested in eating right now." Juliet put a jar of honey in my hand. "The vet said to use this to soothe his throat. Also, he's supposed to drink a lot of water."

I stared at the jar in my hand. It said, "Grade A Amish honey."

Only the good stuff for Jethro. It seemed taking care of Jethro today would be a lot more work than usual. I'd never been instructed to spoon-feed him honey before.

"I have to get back inside the church. The ladies' auxiliary will be here soon. We're setting up for the ladies' tea that will be held after morning services." She pressed her lips together. "Bailey, when you marry, you're welcome to join the auxiliary as well."

I tucked the honey into the back pocket of the stroller. "The ladies' auxiliary is only for married women?"

"Well no, it's for all the ladies in the church, but since

Aiden is a member, I imagine you will join the congregation after the wedding."

Oh, I should have known it was something like that. Even when her pig was under the weather, Juliet could turn the conversation back to the subject of when Aiden and I were getting married. I didn't have the heart to tell her it would be a very long time before that happened, if ever. Aiden and I certainly needed to have a discussion about our future before any ring was purchased.

It was time to end this conversation before it became even more uncomfortable. "I will take good care of Jethro."

She clasped her hands together and held them under her chin. "I know you will." She bent over the stroller and gave Jethro a kiss on the top of his head. "You be a good little pig for Bailey. No more turkey bones." She shook her finger at him.

I took hold of the stroller handles and carefully turned Jethro in the direction of Swissmen Sweets. A sick pig would certainly put a damper on my plan to do recon that day. I would stand out too much if I rolled up somewhere pushing a pig in a stroller.

The front door of Swissmen Sweets opened just as I was crossing the street and Charlotte stepped out.

Today, my cousin wore a blue T-shirt under a denim jacket and a long khaki skirt. Her hair was in a long red-gold braid that glowed in the sunlight. She wasn't exactly dressed like a liberated Amish woman. She wore no makeup or jewelry. She seemed to be taking it slow assimilating to non-Amish life. I respected that. It must have been hard to go from being told what to wear and how to style your hair every day to dressing however you wanted.

She stopped in her tracks. "Bailey, do you have a baby with you?" Her voice had so much disbelief in it that I realized my younger cousin would be utterly shocked if anyone chose to leave their child with me.

I pushed the stroller over to her. "Take a look."

She peered into the stroller and hopped back. "That's Jethro! Why are you pushing Jethro in a stroller?"

"First of all, your reaction is a little much. I will have you know, in NYC, pushing your pet around the city in a stroller is the thing to do. I have seen dogs, cats, chinchillas—you name it—being pushed around Central Park on a nice spring day."

She wrinkled her brow. "What's a chinchilla?"

I sighed and shook my head. "That's beside the point. The point is Jethro is just being very urban today. You know he's a famous pig."

She cocked her head. "Are you teasing me, Bailey King?"

I smiled. "Maybe a little. The real story is that Jethro tried to eat a turkey bone and had an emergency vet visit last night. Juliet asked me to piggy-sit since he isn't feeling well today."

"I should have known. Juliet always asks you to watch her pig."

"Not always."

She gave me a look.

"Okay, you're right. Almost always." I rolled the stroller back and forth because I had seen people do that with their babies and animals while stopping to chat in Central Park. I guessed whatever those Upper East Side nannies and pet sitters chose to do must be the right thing. "Are you going to church today?" I asked.

Charlotte wrinkled her nose. "I don't think so. I'm not

playing the organ today. The church's regular organist is on the bench, and Luke is on duty, so he's not there to sit with me in the congregation. I still feel a little out of place in an *Englisch* church. Everything is so different. I feel better when Luke is there to guide me on what to do. I always feel like I'm standing when I should be sitting and vice versa."

"I know I'm not the most religious one in the family, but I don't think you can do anything wrong when it comes to Sunday worship."

She twisted her mouth as if she wasn't so sure about that. "What are you and Jethro up to today?"

"Well . . ."

"You're going to investigate the murder, aren't you?"

I sighed. "I can't do that now. Just look at Jethro."

We both looked down at the pathetic pig at the same time. His chin was on the stuffed white rabbit, and he blew hot air out of his nostrils. He really was a sorry sight.

"Jethro does look under the weather, but you can still snoop," she said. "I will go with you and take care of Jethro while you root out the bad guy."

"Root out the bad guy?" I asked.

"Luke and I have been watching this show called *Murder, She Wrote*. He says it's an older show, but I love it. Have you heard of it?"

"Umm, yes, I have." I raised my brow. "You and Deputy Little have been watching it together?"

"Sure. I only see it when I'm visiting him. I don't have a TV here. It's really good." She cocked her head. "You have a lot in common with Jessica Fletcher."

"Please don't remind me," I said. "Are you sure this is how you want to spend your Sunday?"

"What else am I going to do? Cousin Clara is at church today, and she wouldn't like it if I spent my time working. Luke is on duty, and I suspect that he will remain that way until the murder is solved. And all my other friends . . ." She trailed off.

"All your other friends what?"

"Let's just say even though I was never baptized into the Amish church and so I wasn't officially shunned by the district, they're keeping their distance. They're leery. Maybe they think my *Englischness* is catching."

"I'm sorry, Charlotte."

She smiled, but it was forced. "There is nothing to be sorry for. I knew this would happen. It's the choice I made and now I must live with it. I'm hopeful that when time passes, my old friends will want to spend time with me again. Until then, I'm just giving them their space."

I pressed my lips together. Charlotte was handling the loss of so many of her friendships with a lot more grace and maturity than I would have. What's more, we both knew that if an official shunning came down by order of the bishop, then none of her former friends would break with their bishop's orders. Charlotte was not unaware of any of this. She'd known all the risks, had acknowledged all the losses she might suffer when faced with her decision to leave the Amish way. Her eyes lost their shine almost as if her thoughts were mirroring mine.

"Hey," I said. "How about on our mission today, you be Jessica Fletcher, and I'll just be the backup."

"Really?" She beamed at me.

"Sure," I said with a smile.

CHAPTER FIFTEEN

Charlotte and I walked back to my house to pick up my car. Penny stepped out of her house as we came up the walk and put a hand over her heart. "Bailey King, do you have a baby now?"

I suppressed a grimace. This was definitely one rumor I had to squash. "No, it's Jethro. Charlotte and I just took him out for a little walk."

Charlotte wiggled her fingers at Penny.

"You are walking a pig in a stroller?" She stood there with her mouth hanging open.

"It's a nice day for a walk," I said with a shrug.

She shook her head and hurried to her car, which was parked on the street.

As she drove away, Charlotte said, "Your neighbor thinks you're crazy."

"That's not all she thinks of me."

Charlotte turned her innocent face to me. "What do you mean by that?"

I shook my head. "Is Levi Wittmer in the same district as *Maami*?"

Charlotte nodded.

"Do you know where they're holding church today?" I asked.

"I think it's at the bishop's house. Ruth Yoder would like to have it at her farm every time, but the bishop won't allow it. It does end up there every other time though."

"And Levi attends services?"

She wrinkled her nose. "I guess so. I never spoke to him, but I think he's been there in the past. His kids were. They're closer to my age."

"We'll give it a try. We are going to see some turkeys."

Jethro lifted his head up off the pillow in the stroller for half a second as if he was excited by the prospect of a turkey visit, but then he put his head back down.

"He's really not feeling like himself," Charlotte said.

"I have half a mind to leave him here with Puff, but I want to keep an eye on him."

She grinned. "You have a soft spot for Jethro, don't you?"

I pointed at her. "Don't go and tell Juliet that."

She laughed.

Wittmer Poultry Farm was on the border between Holmes and Tuscarawas counties, so it was on the far eastern side of Harvest. The farm was back off the main road on what I would call at best a dirt and gravel path.

My car bounced up and down as we went along the

track. Every time we hit a rut, Charlotte put one hand in the air as if to stop herself from hitting the roof of the sedan. Her other hand rested protectively over Jethro's flank. He lay across her lap like a sack of potatoes. It could be my imagination, but he was looking a little green. Had I known how rough the road was, I would have insisted Charlotte stay with him in the car, and I would've tackled this stretch of road on foot.

"The ruts are made by buggies and wagons," Charlotte said as we rocked and rolled over another one. "I don't think many cars come back here. It's a lot like many of the roads in the conservative district where I grew up before I came to stay with Cousin Clara. We never saw a snowplow much less a road crew."

"How does Levi get his chickens and turkeys to market then? Wouldn't trucks have to have access to his farm?"

Charlotte shrugged.

We came around a bend in the winding road, and a mailbox seemed to pop out right in front of us. Stuck in the ground next to the mailbox was a hand-painted sign that read, "Wittmer Chickens and Turkeys."

A hidden driveway was just beyond the sign. The driveway appeared to be in better shape than the road, so I turned down it. The farmhouse was maybe four hundred feet from the mailbox. Two large barns stood another five hundred feet beyond that. I parked the car at the end of the driveway. "I think we should get out and walk."

Charlotte looked down at Jethro. "What about him?"

I scratched Jethro under the chin, and he perked up. "Let's take him with us. I have his leash. Maybe walking around a bit will help him."

She shrugged as if it made perfect sense to walk a pig

around a poultry farm. "I've done some pretty odd things since I met you, cousin."

"Don't remind me."

We got out of the car, and I clipped the leash on Jethro's pink and white polka-dotted collar.

He looked up at me.

"If you get tired of walking, just let us know, and we will carry you."

Charlotte looked around at the gravel driveway. "*Ya*, the stroller would not work here."

The farmhouse was quiet, which made me believe that Charlotte had guessed rightly that Levi and his family had gone to church at the Yoders' farm that morning. Amish church could last well into the afternoon, so I wasn't worried about Levi or another family member coming home to find us snooping around.

We could smell the birds before we reached the barns. The air was full of the scent of meal, hay, and scat. Since moving to Amish Country, I had spent enough time on farms that I wasn't immediately repulsed by the smell, but I knew it would be ten times worse inside either of the barns.

The aroma seemed to be just the ticket to revive Jethro though. He put his snout in the air and inhaled deeply. His tail appeared to be a bit more curled and he had a spring in his step.

"Well, if nothing else, coming out here has been a big help to Jethro." I watched as the pig pranced ahead of me.

"Why are we here?" Charlotte asked. "Don't you want to talk to Levi about Blaze? You can't do that on a Sunday."

"I know. I guess I just want to get the lay of the land before I speak to Levi."

"That means you'll have to drive down that bumpy road on another day. You can count me out on that. I almost got sick to my stomach from all the jostling."

Next to the barns there was an open area and I guessed there were sixty to seventy chickens and turkeys roaming around and pecking at the ground. I was happy to see the birds had space to roam and weren't trapped in little cages inside the two barns. From what I could tell, they were healthy. However, seeing them running about and scratching at the grass did make me feel a tad guilty for eating turkey on Thanksgiving. Just as I'd stopped eating pork and bacon when I met Jethro, I guessed that these birds were going to convert me closer to becoming a vegetarian as well.

A young Amish man came out of the closest barn. He whistled to the chickens and turkeys as he threw a mix of corn and feed pellets on the ground for them.

"That's Leon Hersh," Charlotte said. "Hey, Leon!" she called.

Leon jumped and the feed pail flew into the air, barely missing a brown hen that was minding her own business. The birds didn't seem to be upset about Leon's mishap at all. They rushed him and pecked at the ground. He ran from the frenzy and jumped onto the top rung of the fence between us.

"You okay?" I asked.

Gathering what dignity he could, he climbed over the fence to join us.

The turkeys bulldozed the hens out of the way, so they could reach the overturned pail of feed first.

"I'm fine." He was breathing heavily. "You just startled me is all, and those turkeys can always smell weakness, can't they?"

"You seemed to know how to get out of their way," Charlotte said as she shielded her eyes from the sun. "I don't think I have ever seen anyone jump that high in my life."

"It's not the first time I've been chased by poultry. It probably won't be the last either," he added in a forlorn voice.

Leon adjusted his glasses, which had gone askew on his nose. "What are you doing here?"

"We could ask you the same. Shouldn't you be at Bishop Yoder's house for church?" Charlotte asked.

I raised my eyebrows at her. Since my cousin had left the Amish way, she'd certainly grown more assertive. I didn't mind at all. It saved me from having to ask all the questions.

Leon brushed dust from the front of his trousers and removed a feather from his hair. "I plan to head to church later. I promised Levi that I'd finish up the chores here first. I just cleaned out the chicken and turkey barns. I was in the process of giving them an extra snack for being so good while I cleaned the pens and cages. Then you scared me." His tone was accusatory as he looked at me.

I held up my hands. "It wasn't me. It was Charlotte."

She frowned at me. "Thanks."

Leon swallowed. "Levi wanted to have the barns cleaned because he has a state inspection tomorrow. He offered to pay me extra to do it on a Sunday. I couldn't turn the offer down—I need the money. Now that I'm done, I'll run home, get cleaned up, and go to church."

I wanted to ask him why he needed the money so much. For a devout Amish person to work on Sunday was very unusual. However, I didn't really know how dedicated Leon was to his faith. Before I could ask that, though, Leon looked down at Jethro at our feet.

The little pig was in much better spirits. He wiggled his tail and had his snout pressed up against the ground as he inhaled all the delicious scents of a new farm.

"You brought Jethro with you?" he asked as if it was a very bad idea.

I supposed most locals in Harvest thought bringing Jethro anywhere was a bad idea.

"Sure," I said as if the pig's presence was perfectly normal.

"You brought him to see the turkeys?" Leon was thoroughly confused.

"We just wanted to see where the Thanksgiving turkeys came from. You brought the turkeys from Wittmers' for Thanksgiving, didn't you?"

He paled slightly when I mentioned Thanksgiving, and I wasn't the only one to notice. Charlotte leaned forward as if taking a closer look at his face. "Are you all right?"

Leon blinked behind his glasses. "*Ya*, I'm sorry. I was just thinking of that man who died. It was awful. I can't get his face out of my head."

I nodded. "It was." My heart softened to Leon. He was still very young. At fifteen, he might have been considered an adult in the Amish world, but to me he was still very much a kid—in this case, a scared kid. "How long have you been working for Levi?" I asked, hoping to get his mind off the dead man.

Leon twisted his mouth. "For a year or so. Since I finished school. He's not the only person I work for. I do odd jobs all over the county."

"Like for Margot."

Sweat began to form along his hairline. "*Ya*, the village square needs a new caretaker and I would like the job. The position would pay me what I need, and it would be so nice to work in just one place instead of scraping together odd jobs, hoping I can make rent."

I wanted to ask him what he meant when he said "make rent." Did he not live with his family, or did his parents make him pay for room and board?

Before I could ask any of those questions, Leon said, "Margot is letting me try out being caretaker but hasn't decided for sure if she wants to give me the job. Ever since Uriah Schrock went back home to Indiana, she's been on the hunt for the perfect replacement. I don't think this week's events helped my case. It was my job to make sure Thanksgiving Day went well. . . ."

"It's not looking good then," Charlotte said.

He hung his head. "It's not."

"But it's not your fault Blaze is dead," I said.

He wouldn't look at me. "I know."

I frowned. "Did you meet Zara, Margot's mother, on Thanksgiving?"

He nodded. "Margot asked me to take care of her. That was my main job for the day. She said if her mother had everything she needed, the day would go perfectly. I didn't want to do it. Zara is even more intimidating than Margot, but I agreed to it because she said she'd give me the caretaker job if her mother had a nice time. I didn't know then that Zara was the kind of person who could have a terrible time just about anywhere. She complained about everything, even when it was done just as she liked it. She found fault with just about everything I did."

That was an interesting observation and one that I didn't necessarily disagree with.

"What does it mean when you say 'take care of her'?" Charlotte asked.

"Nothing bad. I was just supposed to give her whatever she needed while she was in the village. That way Margot didn't have to deal with her mother. I don't think the two of them like each other all that much."

That was a serious understatement.

"Mostly, I was supposed to keep Zara away from Margot."

"Were you told to do the same for Blaze?"

"Blaze?" he squeaked.

I felt some sympathy for him. I truly got the feeling that he wanted to do a good job at everything he undertook. Unfortunately, he was s skittish young man. I couldn't help but wonder about what might have transpired in his life to make him so jumpy and unsure of himself.

I felt my forehead crease. Why hadn't Margot told me that she'd had Leon babysitting her mother? Did she think it wasn't important? It stood to reason that if Leon was keeping such a close eye on Zara—and Blaze, by extension—he might have seen something related to the murder, including someone putting church spread on Blaze's marshmallow fluff.

"You probably want to leave before Levi gets home. I don't know if he would take kindly to you being on his farm when he's not here." Leon looked this way and that. He removed his black felt hat and twisted the brim in his calloused hands. "He probably will talk to you if you come back, but he'd be mad that you were here on a Sunday."

I didn't read much into the last statement because I knew how important the day of rest was to most Amish. Levi would be angry if I interrupted his family's Sabbath day.

There was a loud bang as the side gate at the end of the large chicken and turkey pen flew open.

"How did the gate get open?" Leon cried, hurrying in that direction.

At first, the turkeys and chickens just stared at the open gate in confusion. However, that confusion didn't last long. Just as Levi reached the gate to close it, they charged.

The biggest of the turkeys flapped his wings and ran full tilt at Charlotte, Jethro, and me. He had blood in his eyes. Three other turkeys and at least a dozen chickens were in hot pursuit.

Screaming, Charlotte scooped up Jethro and ran for the car. She was fast. I had no idea that she could run so fast, and in a skirt too. I was right behind her. I wasn't a runner by any stretch, but the threat of being pecked to death by an angry turkey was a great motivator.

Charlotte threw open the car door leaped inside with Jethro. Taking a few precious seconds, I ran around to the other side of the car and jumped into the driver's side, just as the lead turkey hopped onto the hood of the car and flapped his wings.

Charlotte stared at the turkey as it angrily squawked and gobbled at us. She pointed at the claws scratching the paint on the hood. "That's going to leave a mark."

I grimaced.

The turkey jumped off the car, and he and his gang ran back to the poultry barns. From where we sat, we could see Leon chasing the birds back through the gate. I considered getting out of the car again to help but thought better of it. That lead turkey had it out for me.

"Bailey," Charlotte said, out of breath. "It seems like every time I'm with you something new happens. I have never been chased by turkeys before while carrying a sick pig."

"Few people have, Charlotte. Few people have." I started the car and backed out of the driveway.

CHAPTER SIXTEEN

After the turkey episode, Charlotte and I thought it was best to call it a day. She went back to Swissmen Sweets, and I took Jethro to my house. He and Puff reunited. The pig grunted at the rabbit, and I imagined that he was telling her about his insane morning. Within an hour the two were asleep side by side in Puff's bunny bed.

In the meantime, I was in the process of breaking my grandmother's rule again about working on Sunday. However, since she never went on the shop's website, I wasn't worried she would find out about it. In theory, I understood the idea of Sabbath. Rest was important. In my mind, rest could be different things for different people. Updating a website was restful to me. It was quiet and peaceful. It distracted me from worries about Aiden and about Blaze Smith's death.

I had been working on the website for over an hour when my phone rang. I picked it up and saw the caller ID read, "Yoder shed phone." I grimaced. The only person I could imagine calling me from that phone was Ruth Yoder. That couldn't be good. Something would have to be very seriously wrong for Ruth to call me on a Sunday.

I put the phone to my ear and winced as I said, "Hello."

"Bailey, it's your *maami*." My grandmother's voice was in my ear.

I sat up straight. "*Maami,* is everything okay?"

"*Ya*, I'm fine. I came to church today with a friend, and she and her husband had to leave early because their goats got loose back on their farm. Could you come pick me up? Normally, I would ask the bishop himself, but he had to take the Yoder family buggy out to call on a sick church member, so Ruth can't run me home. I don't want to ask anyone else to go out of their way for me."

Relief flooded me. Even though I had lived in Harvest for over two years now, I could count on one hand the number of times my grandmother had called my cell phone. Because of that, I had expected the worst. Picking her up from the Yoder Farm was the least I could do.

"I'm happy to come get you," I said.

"I knew you would be, my dear."

"I'll be there in thirty minutes."

"*Danki*, don't rush, dear, especially if you are spending time with Aiden."

I bit my lip. I hadn't seen Aiden all day. "I'll be there soon." I stepped over to the bunny bed and shook Jethro's shoulder. "Wake up. We have to go get my grandmother from the Yoder farm. We'll drop you off at the church after."

Jethro twitched his ears but didn't open his eyes.

I put my hands on my hips. "Jethro. We have to go. *Maami* needs our help."

He lifted his head half an inch and looked at me. He did look incredibly comfortable curled up next to his best bunny friend, Puff.

I sighed and picked up the pig. He squealed in protest and then became a dead weight in my arms. "When you want to, you can weigh as much as a sack of bricks."

Puff rolled over and went back to sleep. It seemed she didn't mind having her bunny bed back to herself at all.

On the drive to the Yoder farm, Jethro seemed to get a second wind. He sat up in the passenger seat and looked out the window. I wondered what my neighbors thought when I drove by with a polka-dotted pig riding shotgun. I had a pretty good idea what Penny would think. I sighed. I needed to find a way to smooth things over with her. I didn't want to feel that I needed to avoid my next-door neighbor. At the same time, I hadn't done anything wrong, so I was frustrated for being judged. Aiden wasn't embarrassed by what Penny might think or gossip about, but he didn't live in Harvest anymore. What could rumors really do to him? Honestly, I didn't care what they might to do me either. I was thinking of *Maami*.

Bishop and Ruth Yoder had one of the largest farms in the village of Harvest. The house had once been a simple farmhouse, but over the generations had grown into a monstrous thing that covered nearly one hundred fifty feet of farmland. From what I had been told, the reason was that Ruth liked to keep her family close. As the family grew, the house was expanded. Most of their children had their own farms or homes now though, so from what I heard, it was just Ruth and her bishop husband alone in the giant house, with family moving in and out as they needed support from the bishop and his wife.

I had overheard Ruth telling my grandmother once that she thought church meetings should always be held at the Yoder farm because they had so much space, especially when it came to winter services that had to be inside because of the cold and snow. However, the bishop had only agreed to host the meeting every other church Sunday. Because Amish church services alternated with visiting Sundays, the district met at Ruth's home once a month. The bishop's wife was not satisfied with that setup.

I turned into the driveway of the farm. There was a line of Amish buggies going the opposite way on the wide driveway. Church and the meal after services were over. The district members were headed home. However, when I parked my car on the edge of the driveway, I saw there were still at least two dozen members milling about. Women carried dishes and leftovers inside the large rambling house, while men folded the tables and chairs to be stored in an outbuilding until the next gathering.

I stepped out of the car, and Jethro followed. That was going to be a problem. It was always better if the pig stayed in the car. He pressed his snout into the grass and began inhaling all the scents of the farm. He seemed happy and mostly recovered from the turkey bone incident of the day before. I didn't have the heart to put him back in the car.

I pointed at him. "Stay by the car and out of trouble this one time, okay?"

He didn't even lift his head, which wasn't the best sign of compliance.

There were many times when I stuck out like a sore

thumb in Holmes County. Standing there in my leather coat, jeans, boots, and spiral earrings, I definitely had the feeling again. I also was on the lookout for Ruth. Knowing her, she wouldn't be very keen on seeing me at her farm on a Sunday.

"Bailey King, what are you doing here?"

Millie Fisher walked over to me with a smile on her face.

I let out a sigh of relief to be welcomed by a friend instead of by Ruth. I wouldn't go as far as to call Ruth a foe, but she definitely wasn't my biggest fan.

"My grandmother called to say that she needed a ride home."

"Oh, I could have taken her home in my buggy. You didn't have to come all the way out here," Millie said.

"That would be completely out of your way, and *Maami* didn't want to impose on her friends."

Millie shook her head. "No one would have minded."

I smiled. "I know that's true, but to be honest, it was nice to get out of my house."

"Hmm," she murmured. "I thought you would be looking into the death of that man on the square at Thanksgiving."

"Me?" I asked.

She laughed as if she knew all too well that I was interested in the murder.

"Your *grossmaami* just took some dishes into the house a moment ago. She will be out soon."

I nodded and thanked her.

"Did I see Jethro here with you?" Millie asked.

"Yes, he's by the car."

Millie shook her head. "He's not by your car now. I think he just waltzed into Bishop Yoder's barn."

I slapped my hand in the middle of my forehead. Why did I ever think bringing Jethro along was a good idea? "I'll go get him. Can you tell my grandmother I'm here?"

"Of course," she said with a smile.

The Yoder family barn was actually roughly the same size as the house. It was primarily a dairy farm, and Guernsey cows were munching on grass out in the fields around the property.

I stepped into the dark barn. "Jethro?"

There was no answer. I hadn't really expected the pig to oink in return. There was a large window in the hay loft to my right. However, it created more shadows than light in the large space.

Something large and soft bumped my shoulder. I jumped.

A cow mooed in my face.

I gasped and then took a deep breath.

"Sorry," I muttered.

She went back to chewing her cud.

Now that my eyes had adjusted to the dim light, I stepped farther into the room. "Jethro? Come on. You have to come out. If Ruth Yoder finds out you're running loose on her farm, I will never hear the end of it."

The barn was large, and I went through a gate that led into a second small room. By the open door at the back of the room, Ruth stood with her hands on her hips, speaking sternly to a man in Pennsylvania Dutch. Not for the first time, I wished I had been a better student when my grandmother had tried to teach me the basics of the language.

I didn't know what Ruth was saying, but it was clear she wasn't happy with him. Knowing Ruth, I thought it could be something as simple as his hair being too long.

"*Bruder*!" Ruth snapped and continued to speak.

I perked up. Was this the brother whose life had been ruined by Zara as Ruth had claimed the day before Thanksgiving?

He said something in return and pushed her aside before stomping out the door. Ruth left as well. It was clear that she wanted to follow her brother, who was stomping across the cow pasture, but a woman from the congregation called her. Ruth looked at her brother's back and then at the woman again. She turned in the direction of the woman.

Before I could change my mind, I followed her brother. I knew full well that Ruth would be furious if she knew what I was up to, and I still had to find Jethro before she stumbled upon him. If she found him first, that wasn't going to end well for me.

There was a small feed shed in the middle of the pasture. Ruth's brother stopped beside it. He pulled a pack of cigarettes and a book of matches from his pants pocket. He ran a match along the concrete foundation of the barn and ignited it. He held the flame to the cigarette in his mouth and inhaled.

I wasn't completely surprised to see an Amish man smoking. It depended on the district, but tobacco wasn't forbidden in most Amish communities. Actually, if an Amish man was a tobacco user, he was more likely to use chew than smoke. What did surprise me was that it was Ruth's brother who was doing this, and on a Sunday to boot. I knew without a doubt that his sister would not approve of such behavior.

Now that I could see his face, the first thing I noticed about Ruth's brother was that he must have been at least ten years younger than she was and his red hair was just going gray. In all the time that I had known her, Ruth's hair had always been steel gray, but now I wondered if she had been a redhead in her youth.

He was also cleanly shaven, which meant that he had never been married. Just as Ruth had said, he was the end of the line for her father's name.

"I see you standing over there staring at me. You might as well come over. You are standing in the middle of a cow pasture; it's not like you can hide." His voice was a deep baritone.

I waved. "Have you seen a polka-dotted pig around here?"

He removed the cigarette from his mouth and looked at me. "A polka-dotted pig. Is Jethro here?"

"You know Jethro?" I asked.

"Name one person in Holmes County who doesn't know Jethro." He put the cigarette back in his mouth.

He had me there. I couldn't.

"I'm sure he will turn up. That pig tends to stand out in a crowd."

"He has to. Juliet Brook would never recover if something happened to him."

"And as her son's girlfriend, you must know how Juliet would react." He eyed me.

"You know who I am."

"Bailey King." He dropped the stub of his cigarette in the grass and ground it out with the toe of his boot. "The granddaughter of Jebidiah and Clara King. Now owner of Swissmen Sweets and cable television star."

I blinked at him.

"Don't look so surprised. You are a popular topic with my sister Ruth. She finds you particularly annoying.

Since Ruth is annoyed by just about everyone she has ever met, being particularly annoying gives you special status."

"I don't know that that's something to be proud of."

"You should be. I'm in the group too."

"You might know who I am, but I don't know your name." I tucked my cold hands into the pockets of my coat. Other than the small feed shed, there was nothing to break the cold wind that was picking up, bringing with it the warning of the freezing rain and snow that was in the forecast for the next few days.

"Christopher Lapp, Ruth's tragic *bruder*."

"Why do you say that?"

He studied me. "I'm sure you heard the stories that I went to prison, never married, and was generally a failure in the eyes of my family, most especially the eyes of my parents and older sister."

"What did you go to prison for?"

"I got a DUI." He said it in such a matter of fact way that it took me aback.

I stared at him. "In a buggy?"

He frowned. "*Nee*. It was in a car. I was in *rumspringa* and an *Englisch* friend lent me his car for the night. I was taking an *Englisch* girl out on a date, and I didn't want to reveal to her that I was Amish. At that time, I was certain I was going to leave the Amish faith. Being nervous about the date, I drank a little too much cheap wine that I had hidden in the family barn. I got into an accident even before I reached her house to pick her up. I remain grateful for that because I wouldn't have been able to live with myself if anyone had been hurt."

"No one was hurt? You weren't?"

He shook his head. "The lamppost in the village that I

ran into had to be replaced, but that was the worst of it. I was charged for DUI and for driving without a license and destroying property. I served three years in prison for the crime. I had been sentenced to seven but got out for good behavior. When I was released, I recommitted myself to the Amish church. Of course, I will never be as dedicated as my sister, but I do my best. I chose not to court anyone or marry because I believe that is part of my punishment from *Gott* for what I did."

"Don't you believe in God's forgiveness?"

"For other people, I do . . ." He trailed off.

"Zara Bevan was the judge on your case."

"She was, and knowing what my sister has said about you in the past, I guess that is the reason you are here speaking with me today."

"I came to the Yoder farm to give my grandmother a ride home, and I'm out here looking for Jethro."

"That may be true, but you won't let an opportunity to speak to a suspect go by."

"Are you saying you are a suspect in the death of Blaze Smith?"

"I'm not, but you might think that I am."

"Why should I believe you? Zara gave you a harsh sentence and was known for being tough on the Amish who came in front of her in the courtroom. Maybe you killed her fiancé to retaliate."

"That would be a very long time to hold a grudge, don't you think?" he asked with a chuckle. "I would hope that I wouldn't dwell on something that happened to me twenty years ago for that long."

I opened my mouth to argue, but he went on. "I wasn't at the Harvest Village Thanksgiving. I spent my Thanksgiving with *Englisch* friends who have two runaway

Amish teens from New York living with them. My friends wanted me to talk to the boys about my experience in a less strict Amish district, so they can make an informed decision as to whether they want to leave the Amish church completely or just their restrictive New York community. If you don't believe me, you can check with Deputy Little. I gave him the names and phone numbers of everyone who was at the meal."

"Deputy Little spoke to you already?" I asked.

He studied me. "My guess is the sheriff's department is speaking to every Amish man that Zara was unfair to in court. It's no secret that Sheriff Marshall would be delighted if this murder was pinned on an Amish man."

"Bailey King!" Ruth Yoder cried as she stomped across the pasture.

Uh-huh. I was in trouble.

"What are you doing out here with my *bruder*?" she asked as if Christopher and I were up to no good.

"Ruth, sister, we were just having a chat about my *gut* old days." Christopher pulled another cigarette from his pack, struck a match on the shed's foundation, and lit up.

"Christopher," Ruth snapped. "I told you that I would not abide smoking on my farm."

He inhaled deeply and then dropped the barely smoked cigarette in the grass, stubbing it out with his boot as well. "Whatever you want, sister. It's time for me to go home. It was nice to finally meet you, Bailey King, after all the stories I've heard." He set out in the direction of the barn.

"What did the two of you speak about?" Ruth demanded.

"I just told him I was here to pick up my grandmother."

"You felt you needed to follow him out to the pasture to tell him that? Why would he care?" She narrowed her eyes. "How stupid do you think I am?"

"I don't think you're stupid, Ruth. I came to your farm to pick up my grandmother. I saw Christopher, so yes, I took the opportunity to speak to him about Zara. You were the one who told me that she ruined his life."

"I told you that to have her removed from the Thanksgiving feast, but you, Margot, and even my husband were too cowardly to do that. Now, look what has happened. A man is dead, and the police are speaking to my *bruder* again. I blame you for this. You must have told them what I said about Zara."

I held up my hands. "I didn't."

She looked as if she wanted to argue with me more, but there was a loud moo, and Jethro shot out of the barn like his curly tail was on fire. He ran straight for me and leapt into my arms.

I caught him, but it was like being hit with a bag of sand in the middle of my chest. I stumbled backward into the shed yet managed to remain upright.

A huge Guernsey cow stood in the back barn door, blowing steam from her nostrils.

"He must have irritated Matilda. She's pregnant and not in the best mood," Ruth said.

"I thought most calves were born in spring."

Ruth glared at me. "Tell that to the neighbor's bull who escaped into our pasture."

Yikes. I wouldn't want to be in that bull's hooves. It seemed to me that Ruth was still a wee bit upset by the invasion.

"I'd better get both *Maami* and Jethro home." I took her irritation with the cow situation as a chance to escape.

"I know what you are up to, Bailey King," she called after me. "And you won't pin this murder on the Amish in Harvest. I won't allow it."

I didn't even bother to turn around. I would pin the murder on whoever was guilty, Amish or not.

CHAPTER SEVENTEEN

While I drove *Maami* back to Swissmen Sweets, she held Jethro in her lap in the passenger seat. If I had the nerve, this would have been the perfect time to pitch her my ideas for expanding the business. It was one of the few times that we were completely alone, not counting Jethro, of course. Even knowing that, I couldn't do it. I told myself it was because it would be kinder to my grandmother to wait to have this conversation until after the holiday rush. I told myself I wasn't delaying because I was a coward.

Instead, we chatted about church and the coming week at the candy shop.

Outside Swissmen Sweets, my grandmother got out of the car. "I will see you tomorrow, Bailey. I hope you have stopped working on the shop website for the day."

I blushed. *Maami* always found out.

I drove the very short distance to the other side of the square and parked in the church parking lot. Jethro had his hooves up on the dashboard, and he wiggled his tail. He knew that he was going home soon.

I let us both out of the car, and he ran for the church's front steps. I followed at a much slower pace. There were only a few cars in the lot. I recognized Reverend Brook's as one of them. I hoped that even if Juliet wasn't here, the reverend would take the pig off my hands.

Jethro galloped up the front steps to the large double doors, which were painted purple. There was a green wreath with a red bow in the middle of each door. It was yet another sign that Christmas was just around the corner.

The doors opened, and Reverend Brook and Zara stepped out. "Again, I am very sorry for your loss, Ms. Bevan," the reverend said in somber tones. "The whole congregation will continue to pray for you during this time."

"Thank you, Reverend Brook," Zara said. "I do thank you for that." She turned around and saw me standing on the steps with Jethro just a few steps ahead of me. "Bailey, I hope that you are here to tell me some good news."

"I—I . . ." I was just so surprised to see her coming out of the church with the reverend that I didn't know what to say. I shook the muddled thoughts from my head. "I was returning Jethro to Juliet."

Reverend Brook slapped his thigh, and Jethro ran up the last few steps to sit as sweet as could be at his feet.

I frowned and wondered how I could learn that trick. Jethro never came when I called.

"Juliet is just inside. I'll make sure that Jethro gets back to her." He nodded at Zara. "Please don't hesitate to call or stop by the church. We are here to help."

"Thank you, Reverend Brook."

The reverend went back into the church, and Zara made her way down the steps. After she passed me, I followed her.

She stopped on the sidewalk. "Have you spoken to any of the men I told you about?" She studied my face.

"Not yet. I went to the Wittmer farm today, but it is a Sunday. It's not a good day to speak to the Amish."

She scowled. "I'm sorry to inconvenience the Amish with my fiancé's death."

I swallowed. "It's just difficult to speak to them on Sundays. You should know that from your time in Holmes County."

She made a face.

Something that bothered me came to mind. "Have the police spoken to you about Blaze's death?"

She folded her arms. "Of course, they have. I was going to marry the man."

"Did you tell them the same thing you told me—that he had another girlfriend and you weren't marrying him for love?"

"I don't know what that had to do with anything."

"I'm just surprised that they don't suspect you."

"Suspect me? Why would I hurt the man whom I wanted to care for me the rest of my life? It's ludicrous."

I opened my mouth to argue.

"As for the other girlfriend, Deputy Little has already spoken to her. She's not a suspect because she's still in Florida. However, I gave the deputy her name and number so that he could verify that I knew about the relationship and I didn't care. Love had nothing to do with Blaze and me."

I blinked. "You told the sheriff's department about the girlfriend?"

"Of course, I did. I'm an attorney and judge. I know the worst thing I can do is withhold information. I was as open and upfront with them as I was with you."

I didn't say anything.

"You think *I* killed my fiancé?"

"I don't know," I replied honestly. "You have as much motive as anyone else involved, perhaps even more."

She unlocked a rental car with the key fob in her hand. "If I'd done something wrong, wouldn't I have already left town?" She climbed into the car and drove away.

I kind of wished that I would have that much confidence when I was in my eighties, but since I couldn't muster it up in my thirties, I had serious doubts.

I didn't see Aiden until he came back to my house to crash around nine that night. I knew he was not only working on Blaze's murder case, but on other BCI cases that he couldn't even tell me about. He was exhausted, and it made me wonder how he would be able to keep up this pace after he went back to Columbus. How would our relationship be able to withstand it?

The next day was Cyber Monday, and we would have lots of sales because of the popularity of *Bailey's Amish Sweets*. However, it was manageable because foot traffic in the shop was low. Both Charlotte and Emily could work on fulfilling orders. Growing up Amish, neither one of them had computer experience. Charlotte was starting to learn since she'd left the church. But to make everything easier for all of us, I printed off all the online orders and checked the computer every hour as new orders came in. Emily and Charlotte worked off the printed sheets while *Maami* watched the front of the shop.

It was midmorning when Emily said, "Oh!"

Charlotte and I spun around. I think after being chased by turkeys—which we'd decided not to tell Emily or *Maami* to save them worry—we were both on edge.

"What?" we asked in unison.

"We are out of powdered sugar. I was in charge of ordering last weekend, and it looks like I left it off the list. We need it for so many recipes."

I let out a sigh of relief. "That's no reason to panic. We've been under a lot of pressure these last several weeks. If we make a small mistake or forget something, that's all right. Business is booming . . . we can hire more help."

"But we can't have more people working in here at the same time," Emily said. "We are already on top of each other."

I bit my lip to hold back my idea of building an auxiliary candy factory that would support Swissmen Sweets. I thought the girls would be behind the idea, but it would not be an easy decision for my grandmother. Bringing the expansion up now, amid so much work and such high stress . . . I didn't think that was best.

I just had to get past Christmas; then, I promised myself, I would talk to *Maami*. It was less than a month away. I had held the idea in for this long—what were another few weeks?

"Do not worry about it," I told Emily. "I can have powdered sugar overnighted to us. In the meantime, I will run to the market and buy enough to get us by today."

Emily started to remove her apron. "I should be the one to go. I was the one who made the mistake."

I waved away her suggestion. "Keep your apron on. It would be good for me to get out."

And it would give me a chance to slip away and speak

to Clyde Klem. I just hoped he was working at the market that day.

"Emily," Charlotte said. "Don't you know that Bailey wants to sleuth?"

"*And* buy powdered sugar."

"Right," Charlotte snorted.

I shook my head. Sometimes this new English version of Charlotte was all sass.

CHAPTER EIGHTEEN

Before leaving the shop, I grabbed my coat and a scarf. The weather had changed overnight. Wednesday would be the first day of December. I probably should have put on gloves and a hat as well, but I was going to fight that for as long as possible, which wouldn't be too long. Freezing rain and snow were predicted for later in the day as temperatures dropped.

I suspected after the long holiday weekend and with the poor forecast, the shop was going to be slow that day. I didn't think any of us would be sorry for that. Anyone who worked in retail of any sort had to recover from working over the Thanksgiving holiday weekend. It was the most profitable of the year but also the most exhausting.

The market was a street over from the square. It was in a long, one-story building that had been in the same place since my grandfather was a boy. Little had changed inside either. It was an old-fashioned Amish grocer that sold items in bulk and carried just the bare necessities. If you were in need of ten pounds of flour or a cheap toothbrush, it was the place to go. If you wanted fancy premade meals or exotic spices, it was best to make the forty-minute drive to Canton to go shopping there. I guessed Ansel, the store manager, wouldn't even know how to get those items if you asked him to order them for you.

One thing that they did have was powdered sugar, and the five-pound bag that it came in would be perfect for our needs at the shop for one day.

I stepped inside the market and grabbed a small shopping cart. It wasn't like the shopping cart you could get at an English supermarket. It was half the size and looked as if it was made for a child. However, it was perfect for the market since the aisles were narrow and the corners were tight.

I pushed it to the baking aisle and grabbed the powdered sugar. All the while I was on the lookout for Clyde Klem. He wasn't in the baking aisle, so I took a lap around the small store and found him stocking Amish noodles in the back.

"Excuse me?" I asked.

He looked up from his task with a scowl. Clyde wasn't what you would call a friendly Amish man. He was the type of Amish guy that most tourists who came to the county expected. He was quiet, reserved, and spent a good amount of time scowling over his Amish beard.

"Can I help you?" he asked in a tone that clearly said he hoped the answer was no.

"Maybe, I'm Bailey King, and—"

"I know who you are," he interrupted me. "But I don't know what your name has to do with helping you find something in the market."

"It doesn't. I actually wanted to talk to you about Zara Bevan."

He sat up with a jolt and muttered in Pennsylvania Dutch. I didn't know many words in the language but since moving to Holmes County, I had picked up on the less than flattering ones. He said a good number of those.

"Are you upset because she was the judge on your case and sent you to prison?"

He glared at me. "Leave me be. I did my time. There is nothing more I have to say."

"Did you know Zara was here for Thanksgiving?"

His jaw twitched, and I was convinced he wasn't going to answer me. Instead, he surprised me by saying, "I saw her at the community Thanksgiving feast. As soon as I did, I gathered up my wife and children and we left. I would not attend the same function as that woman. She is worse than a snake."

"There was plenty of seating away from Zara, or you could have eaten inside the church. Why did you think that you had to leave?"

He straightened up to his full height, which was half a head taller than me. "What I do or what I have my family do is none of your concern." He picked up the box of noodles and stomped in the direction of the storage room.

"Do you know her fiancé was killed at Thanksgiving?"

He stopped and looked at me. His jaw was tense. I thought if he clenched it any harder, he might just crack his teeth. "Then I would say that he was lucky. He is much better off dead than married to that horrible woman."

His tone was so furious and sharp that I found myself taking a step back.

"You have very strong feelings about Zara, don't you?"

He glowered at me. "If she had done to you or someone you loved what happened to me, you'd have very strong feelings too."

"What did she do?" I asked.

"She didn't give me a second chance. Even *Gott* gives a man a second chance."

"You mean she sent you to prison. What were you in prison for anyway?"

"Why should I tell you?"

"You're right. It wouldn't be hard for me to find out, but it would be a lot faster if you just told me."

He glared at me.

I waited.

After a long moment in which he didn't speak, I asked, "Were you arrested because you hurt someone?"

He held a package of noodles in his hand, and I could hear the noodles snap as he ever so slowly tightened his grip. Crack, crack, crack, the noodles went.

I grimaced, hoping that Clyde wasn't imagining my head as he crushed those noodles.

"*Nee*," he said.

"No to what?" I asked.

"I never hurt anyone. I have never hurt anyone. I took a lawn mower."

I blinked. "A lawn mower?"

He dropped the noodles back in the box. I was grateful to see that. I hoped no one bought them unless they liked their noodles pre-crushed.

"*Ya*, and I was going to put it back. I was seventeen and my *daed* told me to mow the lawn. In my district, we are not allowed to use gas-powered mowers. We were just supposed to use push mowers, but I saw my neighbor had left his gas mower out. He wasn't home, and I borrowed it to mow the lawn."

I didn't like the direction that this story was going.

"The neighbor came home, saw what I was doing, and called the police. He told them I stole his mower. When I said that I was borrowing it and planned to take it back, no one listened to me, not the neighbor, the police, or my *daed*. My father was just so ashamed that I would break district rules and cut corners when I should have been using a push mower. I was arrested."

"They convicted you and sent you to prison for that?"

"It was for six months, but it was enough. My family would have nothing to do with me after that. Luckily, I had an aunt who took me in. Without her I would be lost." He narrowed his eyes. "So if you ask me if I care that the judge who sent me to prison for borrowing a lawnmower is having a hard time, I do not."

"What's going on back here?" asked Ansel Beachy, the manager of the Harvest Market. Ansel was a heavyset man with a mostly bald head except for a few gray tufts that didn't seem to want to lie down. His salt-and-pepper beard was coarse. He loved to talk and had always been kind to me when I came into the market, even early on when the other Amish residents of Harvest weren't sure what to make of me. "Oh, Bailey," Ansel said. "Can I help you with something?"

I nodded to my cart. "After a busy weekend, I just stopped in to restock."

He smiled. "The market was packed all weekend too. I was happy for the business, but I would be lying if I didn't say I'm happy for a quiet Monday." He glanced at Clyde, who hadn't moved since Ansel arrived. "Clyde, where are you going with that box? Shouldn't those noodles be on the shelf already? I gave you that task well over an hour ago." Ansel's tone was kind but firm.

Clyde's jaw twitched. It seemed to me that he didn't care for being questioned by anyone, not even his boss.

Ansel said something to Clyde in their language.

Frowning, Clyde carried his box back to the spot he had been in just a moment before and went back to stocking. He didn't even look at me.

Ansel looked back in my direction, and his forehead creased. "Is that all you need, Bailey?"

I glanced at Clyde. There was no way he was going to speak to me now. "This is it."

"Let's go up front, and I will check you out so you can be on your way."

It might have just been me, but I felt I was being shuffled out of the market. I followed Ansel to the front of the store. An Amish mother and four children came inside, and Ansel greeted them in their language. The mother gave me a shy smile before ushering her children into an aisle.

I set the bag of powdered sugar onto the counter, and Ansel rang me up.

"You had a busy weekend too, you said?"

He nodded. "Very busy. Since last Wednesday. It was nice to have yesterday to refresh."

"You were busy on Wednesday and Thanksgiving Day too?"

He nodded. "We were closed on Thanksgiving, but I kept finding myself running in and out of the store as people needed things for the community meal. Since my store is so close to the square, many times it was easier to ask me to grab any forgotten items than having whoever forgot the item go all the way back home to get it."

"Did Clyde help you with any of that?" I asked.

"Clyde?" Ansel asked, his brow wrinkling again. "*Nee*, the market was officially closed that day, so I was the only one who went in and out of the store."

"Did you see the man collapse during the meal?" I asked.

"*Ya*, the *Englischer* at the head table? I did see that. I heard hours later that he died. Was he ill?"

"Peanut allergy."

Ansel's eyes went wide. "If he had a peanut allergy, then why was he asking for church spread?"

I stared at him. "Blaze *asked* for church spread?"

"Blaze? Is that's someone's dog?"

I shook my head. "It was the name of the *Englischer* who toppled over."

Ansel shook his head. "It seems that more and more *Englischers* are giving their children names that are better suited for pets."

"When did Blaze ask for church spread?" I asked.

"He didn't ask directly, but someone came to the market as I was leaving and said that the man from Florida—Blaze I guess—would like church spread."

"Who was it?"

"I didn't see."

"You didn't see who it was?"

He shook his head. "I had a huge stack of boxes in front of me to take to the square. They covered my face and I couldn't peek around them to see who was asking. I know it was a young Amish man from his voice, and I could see his plain black shoes. I needed to get the items to the square, so I told him where the church spread was and to go in and grab it. My hands were full. I had a few more items to come back for, so I knew I would return to lock up the market."

I stared at Ansel. What he was telling me was that he'd probably spoken to the killer just as he was collecting the murder weapon.

"That will be $7.45 for the powdered sugar," Ansel said, not knowing what part he had played in Blaze's death. I wasn't going to tell him.

I handed him a ten-dollar bill and collected the powdered sugar and my change. I turned just before I reached the door. "Ansel?"

He looked up from the counter, which he was now wiping with water and vinegar. "*Ya?*"

"If you heard that young man's voice again, would you recognize it?"

He folded his cleaning cloth. "I don't know that I would. He sounded just like every other Amish young man to me."

That was no help at all.

CHAPTER NINETEEN

Instead of going back to Swissmen Sweets, I decided to walk over to the square and take a look around. Maybe if I went back to the scene of the crime, something would jog my memory. I was trying to remember if I'd seen anyone, especially a young Amish man, carrying a container of church spread at any point before, during, or after the meal. Nothing came to mind.

Midday on Monday, the square was deserted. After the holiday weekend people were back at work and school. Also the quick drop in temperature might have kept away anyone who might be out for a walk.

I was certainly regretting my decision not to wear a hat.

The Christmas decorations that sparkled at night were all off and hung forlornly from the trees and the gazebo until they would be called on to brighten the square that evening.

I tucked the bag of sugar in the crook of my arm and texted Aiden. I told him what I had learned from Ansel at the market. I knew that he or Deputy Little would want to talk to Ansel about the young man collecting church spread.

There was no evidence other than the holiday decorations that had been put up directly after the meal that a Thanksgiving gathering had ever happened on the square.

I thought of everyone who was at the table with Blaze and Zara. Of the forty sitting there, there wasn't an Amish young man.

I knew there had been many Amish at the meal, but the only young man I had taken any note of was Leon Hersh. Leon had said that he was told to keep an eye on Blaze and Zara for the entire meal. I do remember Leon pacing around the square before the meal, but I'd thought he was just nervous about following Margot's orders for the day. Could it be possible he was the one who went to the market and got the church spread?

My brow wrinkled as I walked by the gazebo. Just as I came around to the gazebo steps, there was a squeal and a blur leaped at me. I screamed and squeezed the powdered sugar bag so hard, it burst open and I was enveloped in a white cloud. I started coughing.

When the cloud of sugar dissipated, I looked down to see Jethro, who was also coated in white sugar. He gazed up at me with concern on his piggy face.

"Oh dear." Juliet came running down the gazebo steps. "Jethro was just so excited to see you that he got a bit carried away."

Margot came down the same steps at a much slower

pace. She didn't look nearly as excited to be there as Juliet and Jethro.

Juliet picked up Jethro and began wiping powdered sugar from his face. The pig stuck out his tongue and licked himself. To be honest, he didn't seem to be all that upset about the sweet predicament he found himself in.

I brushed sugar from my eyebrows.

"I think Jethro is extra bonded with you since you took care of him when he wasn't feeling well. What happened to the two of you yesterday? Jethro was covered in dust when he got home."

Dust kicked up by the turkey run, I would guess. I thought it was best not to confess to being chased by turkeys.

"I'm so sorry," Juliet said. "You have powdered sugar in your hair." She tried to dust it away from the top of my head.

"It's all right. This isn't the first time I've been covered in sugar. I'm a candy maker, after all." I looked at the burst bag. There was still at least two-thirds of the sugar in the bag. It would be enough to get us by in the shop until the new order of powdered sugar came in the next day.

Juliet gave a sigh of relief. "Bailey, you are so sweet. It seems that nothing upsets you."

That wasn't true. I just didn't wear my emotions on my sleeve the way Juliet did, or her pig for that matter. I patted Jethro on the head, and he looked up at me with a happy expression on his little face. "What are you all doing in the gazebo on a chilly morning?"

Margot spoke for the first time. "We are putting finishing touches on the plans for the Christmas parade. December begins tomorrow, so it's all hands on deck to get ready for Christmas."

"You still want to put on a big event after what happened at Thanksgiving?" I asked.

"Yes," Margot said, leaving no room for argument. "Blaze's death is tragic, but the village and the world can't stop because he died."

I supposed the world never came to a complete halt when death happened. People died every day.

"I think we are all set with the plans we've made, Margot. Most of them have been in place for the better part of half a year. This year's Christmas parade will be more wonderful than ever. I'll look into the elephant rental. Don't you worry."

Elephant rental. Now, I *was* a little worried. Also, who said there were elephants at the first Christmas?

Juliet wiped sugar from Jethro's cheek. "I had better take Jethro home and give him a bath. He is the sort-of mascot of Harvest, so he has to look his best during this busy holiday season. Many people come to the village to meet him. Do you know he has over five hundred thousand followers on Instagram? He's a sensation." She paused. "Bailey, I think that's more than your television show has."

"I'm sure it is," I said, not feeling offended at all. There wasn't much on the Internet that could compete with a cute polka-dotted pig.

Juliet and Jethro headed across the lawn in the direction of the church.

"Did Rupert get home last night?" I asked.

Margot pressed her lips together. "He did. They only kept him at the station for an hour. That's because they shouldn't have taken him there in the first place. He wasn't even here at the time of the murder."

"I'm glad to hear it."

She shook her head. "I'm just sorry that he was put through such questioning. It's humiliating. Not that my mother cares in the least about embarrassing my husband and, by extension, embarrassing me."

"Have you seen Zara since Thanksgiving?"

"No, and I don't plan to see her until it's time to drive her to the airport."

"When is she leaving?" I asked.

"Just as soon she can make arrangements for Blaze's burial. His body has not yet been released by the sheriff's department."

"It seems they've had it a long time when there is no question about how he died."

She shrugged. "Sheriff Marshall blamed the holiday weekend, but you never know with him whether he's really telling the truth or not."

Uncertainty about honesty was not a desirable trait in a county sheriff, but I knew what Margot said was true.

"I can't wait until she leaves, so I can put all of this behind me. That's what I need to do. I need to refocus on the village and my family—I mean my husband and children. Zara was not much of a mother to me in the first place. I shouldn't have expected her to change this late in life."

"She does care about you," I said. "She asked me to help look into the investigation to protect you. She could tell that the sheriff's department wants to blame you for the murder, but she knew you wouldn't do such a thing."

She frowned. "Or she wanted to protect herself. Even if we are estranged, who wants a murderer for a daughter? If she really cared about me, she wouldn't have brought my husband's name up yesterday with the police and put him through all that."

I frowned and left it alone. I wasn't going to be the one

to convince Margot that her mother cared about her. Mother-daughter relationships are some of the most complicated. I knew that my own relationship with my mother could be tense, and it wasn't nearly as bad as the relationship between Margot and her mom.

"You'd better go home and get that powdered sugar off. You looked like you got into an argument with a chalk board and lost."

I shook more sugar from my sleeve. "I feel like it too. Before you go, can you tell me exactly what you had Leon doing at Thanksgiving?"

"Leon?" she asked.

"Leon Hersh, the young Amish teen who has been helping you on the square."

Her face cleared. "Yes, I know who you mean. Since Uriah Schrock moved back to Indiana last summer, I've been testing out caretakers. Leon is the latest candidate."

"Why haven't you replaced Uriah yet? He's been gone for months."

"He's not easy to replace. He was a stellar caretaker. He always knew what needed to be done long before I was aware there was a problem. I just haven't found a person who can step into his shoes."

I kicked sugar from the toe of my boot. "Leon isn't the right person?"

"Leon is young and has a lot to learn. He's a good craftsman and handy like most Amish young men are, but he doesn't have much life experience. He doesn't always know how to carry himself in social situations."

"Aren't many Amish seen as shy even when they aren't?"

"It's more than shyness. I've been told he was raised alone by his father in the woods. His father still lives out there, but Leon has struck out on his own. I think he's renting a room somewhere, maybe in a boardinghouse."

"A boardinghouse? Like the eighteen hundreds?" I asked.

She shrugged.

That was why he was desperate enough to work so many jobs to earn money. He was on his own.

"Did you ask Leon to keep an eye on your mother on Thanksgiving?" I asked.

She nodded. "I did. I needed to get her out of my hair that day. It was such an important event for the whole community. So I assigned Leon to fetch her everything that she and Blaze might need. It was a lot better if they pestered Leon rather than me. He was to be her servant for the day."

I didn't like the sound of the word *servant*. "What did she ask him to do that afternoon?"

"How would I know? The whole reason he had the job was to keep her away from me. I took care not to pay attention to her. I wanted it to be a happy and peaceful day. At least that was my intention before the meal started."

"Would he have had any reason to be upset with her or Blaze?"

"I don't know what you're getting at. Leon doesn't know my mother. He wasn't even born when she moved to Florida. Besides, he wanted the caretaker job on the square so badly. He would never do anything to put that in danger."

I thought about telling her what Ansel had revealed to me about the church spread, but I thought better of it. It seemed to me that it would be better to wait and see what Aiden could confirm about those details. I snuck a peek at my phone. So far, he had been completely silent.

"Your mother gave me a list of people who might be holding a grudge against her because she sentenced them to prison years ago."

"She has a list of names—"

"I passed them on to Aiden."

"Who are they?" she asked.

I rattled off the names, but she stopped me when I came to Allen Shirk.

"I know it wasn't Allen." She folded her arms.

"How do you know that?"

"Because he wasn't at Thanksgiving. He wasn't at Thanksgiving—because he's been dead for over a year."

"Dead?" I asked.

She nodded. "He died in some sort of accident at work."

"Where did he work?"

"His family owns a cabinetmaking business. I don't know the particulars. He left behind a widow and seven children."

"That's awful," I murmured.

"As for Levi Wittmer, I can't see him doing it. I've worked with him for years on Harvest events. He has supplied a lot of the poultry for meals, although nothing on the scale of this Thanksgiving. He's never once mentioned my mother or seemed to be reluctant to work with me because I was her daughter."

"Maybe he doesn't know you're Zara's daughter."

"I suppose that's possible. It's certainly not something I advertise when I meet people."

I shook sugar out of my hair. I would need to leave soon and take a shower; I could feel the powdered sugar beginning to cake. "And what about Clyde Klem, who works in the market?"

She shrugged. "I have never spoken to Clyde, and he's never spoken to me. But I guess he could still be holding a grudge. It's impossible to know all the slights and grievances a person holds close to their heart."

It was the truest thing that I had ever heard Margot say.

After leaving her on the square, I stopped by Swiss-men Sweets to drop off the sugar and to tell the ladies that I needed to go to my house for a little while to clean up.

Charlotte gawked at me. "What happened to you?"

"Jethro," I said. And really, it didn't need more explanation than that.

She slapped a hand over her mouth to hold back a laugh.

I walked out of the shop with my head held high.

As I reached my driveway a little while later, I spotted Penny in her yard raking leaves. She saw me and gasped. She held up the rake as if it would afford her some sort of protection.

I forced back a groan and plastered a smile on my face. "Hi Penny. Cold today, isn't it?"

"What happened to you?" she asked.

"A little mishap with powdered sugar. Nothing to worry about."

She had a look on her face as if she believed that it *was* something to worry about and worry about very earnestly. I sighed. Penny and I had never been close neighbors, but our exchanges had never been this uncomfortable before. It was as if her whole attitude about me had changed when she learned Aiden was staying at my place for a few days. Apparently with her, that was more than enough to damage my reputation in her eyes. Part of me wanted to remind her that this was not the Regency era, and my reputation wasn't the be-all and end-all of my life. I didn't though. Any discussion would just make things that much more uncomfortable.

I gave a little wave and started toward my door.

"I heard that you are investigating that man's death on the square," she called after me.

I slowly turned around. "How did you hear about that?"

"There wasn't much to hear. It seems that every time something odd happens in Harvest, you have your hand in it somehow." Her words didn't sound like a compliment, and I certainly didn't take them that way.

"I'm just helping Margot out, that's all."

She chewed on her lip. "If you want to help Margot, you might want to ask her why she hired the man's nephew to work on the square."

"The man's nephew? What man?"

"The Englisher who died." She leaned on her rake.

I stared at her. "What?"

"Leon Hersh is that Englisher's nephew. The Englisher who died."

"*What*?" I asked again, knowing that I sounded like a broken record, but it couldn't be helped. What she said made no sense at all. Blaze had been the most English English person I had ever met. It was impossible to think that he might have once been Amish, wasn't it? Just to be sure, I said, "You're saying Blaze is Amish?"

"Did you really think his mother named him Blaze?"

"I'm certain that there are people in this world whose mothers gave them that first name, yes."

"Well, not people in Holmes County. I can tell you that."

"Why do you think he's Leon's uncle?" I couldn't

even believe that I was asking the question. It seemed too crazy even to voice.

"I never forget a face. Never. It doesn't matter if I don't see the person for thirty years. I can tell that this man who called himself Blaze made a lot of changes to his appearance, maybe even a few to his face, but he's Marvin Hersh. If you saw him side by side with his brother Melvin, you wouldn't question me on that."

"The brothers were named Marvin and Melvin." Poor guys. It was no wonder he chose the name Blaze even if Ansel said it sounded like a name better suited for a dog.

"Yes. I never forget a name or a face or a detail. I have a perfect memory."

I could vouch for that. She still reminded me to bring my trashcan out to the curb every week for trash day because one time I had forgotten. That was well over a year ago now, but when Thursday morning came, she would be out looking for my trashcan to double-check that I hadn't forgotten.

Taking her perfect memory into account, I gave more weight to Penny's story. I mean, it was possible that Blaze was an Amish man named Marvin Hersh, right? Maybe?

"How did you know Marvin?" I asked.

She sniffed. "He used to work with my late husband at a cabinet factory in Charm."

Charm was another small village in Holmes County a few miles away from Harvest. However, if what she said was true, then the detail that most caught my attention was the mention of the cabinet factory. Hadn't Margot just told me that Allen Shirk, a cabinetmaker, died a year ago? Cabinetmaking was a major business in Holmes

County, and it was very possible that they were two completely different cabinet businesses, but I had to ask. "Did a man named Allen Shirk work there too?"

She stared at me. "How did you know that?"

"Someone mentioned it," I said.

She frowned as if she didn't believe that the answer was as simple as that. Penny always noticed when things were off. She not only had a good memory, but great attention to detail too. In fact, I thought if she put her mind to it, she might be better at solving crimes than I was. She was certainly already better than the sheriff.

"Yes, Allen Shirk's family owned the factory. He was my husband's boss, but my poor husband hated working for him. He wasn't a kind man. I doubt that anyone was upset when he died."

"Who runs the factory now?"

"That's the interesting bit, and unusual too. There were no men in the family to leave the business to, so his wife, Marilla, is now in charge." She began raking again. "But to be honest, I think she's been running the business ever since her husband went to prison. He was sickly when he got back."

I bit my lip and tasted powdered sugar. I needed a shower desperately. "How is it possible that of all the people at the Thanksgiving meal, you were the only one to recognize Blaze?"

She stopped raking and looked at me. "Why do you think I was the only one who recognized him? I was the only one brave enough to say it."

She was right, and my guess was that at least one other person had recognized Blaze. That person was the killer.

CHAPTER TWENTY

After I got cleaned up and fed Puff a snack of cabbage and broccoli, I called Swissmen Sweets on my cell phone. Charlotte answered.

"How's everything going there?"

"Good!" she said with her typical cheerfulness. "We finished all the Cyber Monday orders, and we're restocking and cleaning up for tomorrow. I know it's a bit early to be starting to put things away. It's only three, but the place is dead."

"That's great. Listen, since the shop is slow, I'm going to run a few errands."

There was silence on the other end of the line.

"What?"

"Errands?" she asked, her voice dripping doubt. "You're going to poke your nose into the case again."

"Fine. That's what I'm doing."

"You should just come right out and say it. It's not like it's a secret that's what you're up to anyway."

She had a point.

I said goodbye to Charlotte and headed out the door again. Twenty-five minutes later when I parked in the lot adjacent to the cabinet factory, I wasn't completely surprised to see Aiden's BCI SUV already there. It seemed that we had come to the same conclusion about Blaze. The only reason I could think of for him to be there was because he had also learned that Blaze Smith had been born as one Marvin Hersh.

I debated as to whether I should go inside. I didn't think Aiden would be thrilled to see me. He had asked me to stay out of the case. At the same time, he must have known that there was zero chance of that happening.

Before I could make up my mind, the front door opened, and Aiden and an Amish woman came out. The woman wore men's work boots under her plain Amish dress and a pair of leather work gloves peeked out of the front pocket of her apron. There was a smudge of soot on her cheek and sawdust in her hair. If this was Marilla Shirk, she was much more hands-on with the family business than I would have first guessed.

I slid down in the front seat, but I knew that was pointless. Aiden would recognize my car. There was nowhere to hide.

As if to prove my point, a few minutes later there was a tap, tap, tap on the roof of my car.

I looked up from my slouched position to find Aiden peering through the driver's side window with an expression on his face that was a mix of amusement and frustration. I'd seen that look directed at me many times before.

I sat up and rolled down the window. "Oh hey, Aiden."

"What are you doing hiding in your car like that?" Aiden asked.

"Hiding? I wasn't hiding." I struggled to sit up in my seat.

Aiden snorted.

"Agent Brody! Agent Brody!" a woman's voice called.

Through the windshield, I saw the woman with the work boots stomp in the direction of my car. Aiden stepped away from it to meet her, and I got out.

"Can I help you with something, Marilla?"

So I had been right, and the woman was Marilla Shirk.

"*Ya*, you can help me," she snapped. "You find either one of those Hersh brothers and make them pay for what they did to my Allen. Because of them, he was a broken man." She shook with anger. "If you're right and Marvin is dead, he got what he justly deserved. Now, my hope is the same for Melvin."

I shivered. She spoke with so much hate. At the same time, she confirmed what Penny had already told me, that Blaze Smith was Marvin Hersh.

Her dark eyes zeroed in on me. "Who are you?"

"I'm Bailey."

She folded her arms. "You're that *Englischer* who pokes her nose into Amish business. I should not be surprised you're here. I heard about you from Ruth Yoder."

So nothing good. Great.

"Are you here to find out what happened to my husband? Because I will tell you. The Hersh brothers are the reason he is dead today."

"You blame them for Allen's death?" I asked.

She glared at me. "Aren't you listening to me? It was all because of the Hersh brothers. If it weren't for them, he never would have been in any trouble, and he would still be alive today. Being in prison made him ill. He was never the same when he got out."

There were so many questions running through my head. How did the Hersh brothers get Allen in trouble? How did he die? He'd died last year—how was that related to his being in prison years ago?

"I'm not sorry that Marvin is dead," she said again defiantly. "If that makes me a bad Amish woman, so be it. I have suffered too much."

"What happened to cause your husband to go to prison?"

She scowled at me. "There was a fire and a schoolhouse burned down. Allen, Melvin, and Marvin were all there at the start of the fire. Marvin ran and Allen and Melvin stayed to try to put out the flames. The deputies arrested them as they were trying to put out the fire."

"How did the fire start?" I asked.

"They had been hired to burn the adjacent field for planting. Fire is the quickest way to clear a field. None of them had done it before. And they were sentenced to six years in prison because of an accident."

I gasped.

Her eyes narrowed. "*Ya*, that is because the judge hated the Amish. She wanted to make an example of them. Both Allen and Melvin were sentenced to *six years*. I was pregnant with our first child and was left to raise our son and manage the cabinet business alone. I was able to do it because I knew Allen would come home. What I didn't know was he would die young because of his ordeal."

"You said Allen and Melvin were sentenced. What about Marvin?"

"He ran away. No one saw him after that. It was assumed that he left to live *Englisch*. He not only ran away from the fire, but he abandoned his friend and his brother. I don't have an ounce of sympathy for him."

I glanced at Aiden. "Did the authorities search for him?"

Marilla took her gloves from her pocket and squeezed them tight. "They didn't know about him. Melvin wanted to protect his brother. Why, I don't know. Why would you protect someone who fled and left you to take the blame? Allen agreed not to tell the deputies about Marvin also being there. I didn't know about the role Marvin played until Allen was released from prison. By then, he was already sick. Had I known, I would have told the police myself."

"When was the last time you saw Melvin? Didn't he work here?"

"He did before the fire. He had the nerve to come back after both he and my husband got out of prison, but Allen turned him away. He didn't want anything to do with the Hersh brothers ever again. He wanted to start over." She twisted the gloves in her hands. "Those brothers ruined my husband's life. He spent six miserable years in prison because of him. He told me some of the horrors that he dealt with every day. He refused to tell me everything. Sadly, I have a *gut* imagination so I can easily picture how bad it really was for him."

I could only imagine. "Did you know in advance that Marvin Hersh was coming back to Harvest over the weekend?" I asked.

"*Nee.* That is a *gut* thing. If I'd seen Marvin Hersh walking down the street, he would have been dead a lot sooner." She spun on her heel and stomped back toward the building.

There were few times in my life when I was rendered

speechless. This was one of them. Such hate, such an open admission that she'd commit violence. It contradicted everything I knew about the Amish—or thought I knew. Then again, upon reflection, I admitted that the Amish were just as human as the rest of us. They loved, hated, forgave, mourned, struggled just like everyone else. Could I really fault this woman for harboring such horrible feelings? Her life had been terribly impacted and so had her husband's, all resulting from an accident. Six years in prison for an accident. I could scarcely wrap my head around it. It was little wonder that Zara would include Allen Hersh's name on her list as one of the Amish men harboring a grudge against her.

Aiden removed his BCI ball cap and rubbed the top of his head. It was a habit that he indulged when he was feeling particularly frustrated. "How did you know about Marilla Shirk?"

"Penny," I said.

"Your nosy neighbor Penny?"

"One and the same. She recognized Blaze as Marvin at the Thanksgiving meal." I shoved my cold hands into my pockets. It was time to get out the winter gloves, hats, and scarves. I had put it off long enough.

"How did she recognize him, when no one else did?"

"She thinks the killer did."

He frowned. "That's a good point."

"Was Marilla at the Thanksgiving feast?"

Aiden shook his head. "She doesn't live in Harvest, nor does she belong to any of the Amish districts that were there."

"So she's off the hook? She had a lot of rage against Blaze. . . ."

"That's one way to put it." He put his hat back on his head. "I don't know if I can say that she's off the hook, but she's not a prime suspect because she didn't have opportunity."

"But she had plenty of motive."

He nodded.

A light snow began to fall, and I wrapped my arms around myself for warmth. "What did her husband die of?" I asked.

"Cancer."

"Can you get cancer in prison?"

Aiden shrugged. "There is no way to prove now that his time in prison caused his disease, but that's what Marilla believes. I don't think anything is going to change her mind on that."

Neither did I.

"Where do we go from here?"

Aiden didn't meet my gaze but kicked the gravel at his feet.

I touched his arm. "What's going on?"

"I have to go back to Columbus tonight."

My heart constricted.

"I got a call from my boss. Sheriff Marshall has made a big stink about BCI overstepping its jurisdiction in this case." He looked at me. "I don't usually agree with the sheriff, but in this case, he's right. This should be his case. I guess I got blinded by the chance to be in Holmes County again. I've missed being here." He paused. "I've missed you."

If he missed me, why had I hardly seen him over the last few days? But I said, "I've missed you too."

He smiled.

"But do you really think it's wise to leave this case to Sheriff Marshall? When was the last time he solved a case correctly?"

"I don't know the answer to that, but Deputy Little is the point person. He'll do a good job. I taught him everything he knows. There's no one better in my book."

"Do you have to leave right away?" I asked.

He shook his head. "I have until the end of today, and I plan to make the most of it."

"Good. The next person we need to talk to is Melvin."

Aiden held up his hand. "Not so fast. The next person *I* need to talk to is Melvin, not you."

I folded my arms. "I'm the one who found out Blaze was Marvin."

"First of all, we have to verify with DNA that he really was Marvin, and second of all, you didn't figure it out. You suspected it because Penny told you."

"Do you have a sample of Marvin's DNA to compare Blaze's to?" I asked.

Aiden shook his head. "No, but Melvin is his twin brother. The genetic markers will be there for the match."

I raised my brow. "Identical twin?"

He shook his head. "Fraternal."

"You really think he'll just hand over his DNA?" I asked.

"No, which is even more reason you're not coming with me when I speak to Melvin."

"Why not?"

"From what we know, he's a recluse living in the woods. He's had very little contact with the outside world since he was released from prison."

It was no wonder that Leon wanted to move away from his father and make it on his own.

"I'll stop by and see you before I head back to Columbus." He kissed me on the cheek.

My heart fell.

He looked at me. "I should have told you this before, but I could be in Columbus for a long while. The bureau had to make some changes due to budget cuts, so they thought it was best to transfer me to where there was the most need. Even though I was hired to work in rural areas near the Amish, the crime rate here is a lot lower than it is in the cities. Right now, the cities are where BCI needs me most."

"I understand."

"It won't be forever."

I bit the inside of my lip to stop myself from asking him, if not forever, how long?

"I'm glad you have this opportunity," I said, and hoped that I sounded as if I meant it. Aiden deserved this job. He'd worked so hard for so long in the sheriff's department without the support of the sheriff. It had to be nice to be in a place where he was so valued. Columbus was the biggest city in the state and the state capital. BCI would not have sent him there if they didn't believe that he was a good fit for the responsibilities the appointment would entail.

He looked down at me. "Your support has meant everything to me, Bailey. You've been there for me every step of the way. I can't thank you enough for that. I know the wedding timeline we talked about last year has been turned upside down. Just know I will make it up to you." He kissed me. "Now, please go back to the candy shop and leave the murder investigation to Little and me."

He so easily dismissed me.

CHAPTER TWENTY-ONE

I thought maybe I should follow Aiden's advice and not go traipsing through the woods looking for a reclusive Amish man. There were a couple reasons for this. The first was that it was dangerous, and the second was that I had no idea where Melvin Hersh lived.

That didn't mean I couldn't track down his son though. The best place to start looking for Leon Hersh was the village square because he was vying for the care-taker job there.

I drove straight to the square. It was close to closing time at Swissmen Sweets, so I parked in front of the shop. I wasn't worried about taking any customer spots for my business or any of the other businesses on the street.

Esther stood outside the pretzel shop, sweeping the walk in front of her store. She glanced up, saw my car, picked up her broom, and was about to head back into her shop when I called out to her. "Esther."

Her shoulders tensed and she turned around, albeit reluctantly. It was just more proof to me that Esther and I were never to be the best of friends. But I hoped that we could be good neighbors for Emily's sake.

"What is it?" she asked, making it clear that she was busy and didn't want to be bothered by whatever I had to say.

"I saw Abel the other day. Is he living at your farm?"

She narrowed her eyes at me. "I don't know why that is any of your business."

I shrugged. "I guess it's not. I'm just worried about you. You were doing so well when Abel was away."

I thought "away" was a nicer way to put it than just saying "in prison."

"What would you have me do? Instead of taking my *bruder* in, I should turn out my own flesh and blood? It does not surprise me that you would think that a *gut* course of action. It is how the *Englisch* are."

I bit my tongue to keep from saying that's what she and Abel had done to Emily when she decided to marry. They practically disowned her and didn't speak to her for a year. I wanted to say it, but I didn't. Again, I planned to keep the peace for Emily's sake.

My shoulders sagged. "I just want you to take care of yourself too. Abel is a grown man. He can't be your problem for the rest of your life. It's not fair."

"Whoever said life was fair? *Gott* doesn't even say that life will be fair. It's not something that I expect." She picked up the broom and held it in her hand. "Now, I think you should spend some time working on your own problems, such as why Aiden Brody can't seem to stick around the village for more than a few days."

With that, she took her broom and disappeared inside her shop.

The door slammed closed after her, and I heard the dead bolt slide home.

I sighed and went into Swissmen Sweets.

Inside, Charlotte was in the front of the shop turning the chairs over on top of the tables so that she could start the evening sweeping and mopping.

"You were gone a long time," Charlotte said.

"I ran into Aiden."

She smiled. "I'm glad. Isn't it weird that he's in the county, and we have barely seen him at all? When he lived here, he came into the shop almost every day to say hello. He would even drop by when you weren't here."

I tried to keep my face neutral. "He's busy. His new job is a lot more responsibility. He's juggling several cases."

Charlotte wrinkled her nose as if she wasn't so sure about that, but I was grateful she didn't ask any more questions about Aiden.

"Did Emily go home?" I asked.

Charlotte nodded. "About an hour ago, and Cousin Clara went upstairs to lie down at the same time."

My eyes widened. "Is *Maami* all right?"

"Oh, I think so. She's just tired. We have all been pushing so hard this holiday season. It's a lot of work for such a small staff, and the business doesn't look like it will slow down any time soon. We got in thirty more Internet orders—"

"Thirty more!" I yelped. "I don't know how we're going to keep up with this pace."

Charlotte said, "What choice do we have? Business is picking up because of your show. You're so popular. It's something to be proud of, Bailey."

I shook my head. "Not if it's at the cost of my grandmother's health, it's not."

"She's not ill. She's tired. Cousin Clara would have told us if she was sick."

I wasn't as sure as Charlotte about that. For many of the older Amish, it was common to be stoic about illness. My grandfather had been a prime example. It wasn't until he was quite ill and needed serious medical attention that anyone knew he wasn't feeling well; he had been suffering in private for several years. I made a mental note to ask *Maami* about it at the next opportunity and to remind her of what *Daadi* had done, if need be.

Also, this talk about all the additional orders made me think of my idea for a candy factory again. Not only would it be good for my grandmother's health to have her less actively involved, but it would take away some of the stress on Charlotte and Emily. The factory could be the answer to all of our problems at the shop. It could be the start of some new ones too.

Charlotte stopped sweeping. "What are you thinking about, Bailey? You have a grimace on your face."

I shook my head. "This case with Blaze." I quickly told her what I'd learned about Blaze's past.

She stared at me open-mouthed. "He was once Amish? I never would have guessed that in a million years. He was just so, so . . ."

"Un-Amish," I offered.

"Exactly." She began sweeping again. "It just doesn't make sense. If he ran away all those years ago to escape what he'd done, why would he come back to Holmes

County? I'm sure he could have made an excuse to Zara as to why he couldn't come."

I wasn't so sure about that. Zara wasn't one to take no for an answer.

"Anyway, I'm going to see if I can track down Leon and ask him about his father. . . ." I trailed off.

"Please let me go with you, Bailey. I've been trapped in this shop all day, and I'm worried about Luke. He's been so stressed about this case. He's under a lot of pressure from the sheriff." She shook her head. "When he's stressed, I'm stressed. I need something to take my mind off my worry that he's chasing a killer."

I wished I could tell her that being in love with someone in law enforcement would get easier, but that was something I certainly had not observed and could not promise.

"Please," she begged. "I will mop the front and the back of the shop when I get back. The floors will be so clean when you come in to work tomorrow, you will want to eat off them."

"You don't have to do any extra work, but yes, you can come with me," I relented.

"Great!" She propped up her broom in the corner of the room. "Where do we start?"

"That's the question. I came back to town because I had hoped to see Leon on the square, but there's no one there. I don't know where else he might work or where he lives."

"Oh, I know where Leon lives."

I blinked. "You do?"

"Sure! He's renting a room in an Amish bunkhouse in Berlin."

"An Amish bunkhouse? What's that? Is it like a boardinghouse? Margot mentioned he lived in a boarding-house."

"I don't know if it's the same thing," she said. "You've lived in Holmes County for a while now, Bailey, and I'm still surprised by how much you don't know. An Amish bunkhouse is exactly what it sounds like, a place for Amish young men to live when they are traveling for work or moving to a new community. It's community living. Sometimes they have their own room and other times it's more of a dorm setting."

"It's sounds very nineteenth century and very much like the boardinghouse Margot mentioned."

She smiled. "Well, wouldn't *Englischers* say that about most of Amish life?"

That was a good point. "Anyway, I know he lives in the bunkhouse because I heard him talk about it at church. This was before I left the district. He had just finished school and was striking off on his own. He was proud of his independence and would tell anyone who listened."

I had to remind myself that when Amish talk about finishing school, they didn't mean they were eighteen and done with high school. When Leon struck out on his own as Charlotte described, he would have been only fourteen. I couldn't imagine it at all. When I was fourteen, I couldn't have taken care of myself. I didn't know many English who could.

"Isn't that young to be out on your own, even for the Amish?"

Charlotte nodded. "I thought it was very young, but he seemed happy about it."

Was he happy because he was getting away from his reclusive father? There was only one way to find out, and that was to ask Leon himself. "Let's go. This might be a good time to drop in on him because Leon will be headed home for dinner."

Charlotte ran upstairs to grab her coat and tell *Maami* that she was going to "run errands" with me. Even though I wasn't there when she spoke to *Maami*, I didn't for a second believe my grandmother thought that was what we were doing. She knew I was trying to find out who'd killed Blaze, and she knew that Charlotte liked to be my sidekick whenever she could.

A few minutes later, Charlotte and I climbed into my car just as snow began to fall in earnest. Charlotte shivered and snuggled into the passenger seat. "I don't know that I'm ready for winter."

I glanced at her as I drove away from the square and passed Harvest Market. "I thought you loved Christmas."

"I do love Christmas. I do." She blushed. "It was last Christmas when I learned that Luke cared about me."

I smiled at the memory. "It was very sweet how he told you."

She laughed. "*Ya*, but I'm not looking forward to the new year because I promised Luke we could get married next year. I'm not sure I'm ready."

I raised my brow. "Are you having second thoughts?"

"*Nee*. Not about Luke. He's the best person I have ever met." She sighed as if she couldn't believe her luck that such a man would care for her.

"Then what's the problem?" I turned up the car's heater.

"I'm just realizing that there is so much I don't know about *Englisch* life and need to learn. I don't know how to drive a car or use the computer properly or how to dress." She waved at her long skirt. "I mean, you would never be caught dead in this."

"I've worn a long skirt before."

"When? I've seen you in a skirt maybe four times, and they were never long."

"It's more comfortable to make candy in jeans. Do you want me to take you to Canton so we can go clothes shopping? It's something we could do on a Sunday when the shop is closed."

"I'd like that, but it's going to feel weird to wear jeans." She lowered her voice. "But I really want to."

I chuckled. "You'll get used to it, and you'll be able to learn all those things. Personally, I think driving a horse and buggy is a lot harder than a car. You don't know what the horse will do if it gets spooked."

She looked down at her puffy black winter coat and denim skirt. "But . . ."

I shook my head. "When Luke fell in love with you, it wasn't because you could drive or what you were wearing. It was because of who you are. But if you want to go on a shopping trip some Sunday, I would be more than happy to help you out. Honestly, I think Cass would fly in from New York for that. She would love to style you."

Her eyes went wide. "Cass is so cool looking. I could never dress like her."

"Not many people can, and I'm not saying you should dress like her. But she would have fun helping you find your own style. Besides, even she would know that her look wouldn't work for you. All she wears is black and you're not a black clothes person. You need brighter colors."

"I do like bright colors," she admitted. "That was one of the hardest things about living in my home district— we always had to wear black or gray dresses. It was so depressing. I was glad that Cousin Clara's district allowed more colors, but now that I'm *Englisch,* I'm overwhelmed by the fact that I can wear whatever I want." She sighed. "I just want to be a *gut* wife to Luke, and there are so many things I feel I should know before we marry. I don't want him to have to teach me everything. That could be frustrating for him and embarrassing for me."

"I'm sure Deputy Little just wants you to be happy. . . ." I trailed off as I drove out of town and saw a mostly empty lot to my left. The only structure on the lot was a ramshackle shed that appeared ready to cave in. There was a large "For Sale" sign on the edge of the unkempt, weed-ridden lot. I slowed the car. I had never noticed that sign before; it appeared to be new. At least it was in much better condition than the rest of the lot.

Bright white snow in large flakes floated to the ground around the sign. Despite the disrepair, I could see potential here. My heart began to race.

Charlotte looked around. "What are you doing? We aren't even out of the village yet."

I pulled over to the side of the road and took a photograph of the sign, which included the Realtor's name and phone number. I didn't know if I would do anything with it, but it was a start. For the first time in weeks, I felt excited.

"Why did you take a picture of that sign? Do you want to buy that place?"

I pulled the car back onto the road. "No reason," I said, keeping my eyes straight ahead.

I felt Charlotte watching me. She didn't believe me for a second.

CHAPTER TWENTY-TWO

An Amish bunkhouse was a house. The home where Charlotte believed Leon was living looked to me like a very large farmhouse on a side street in Berlin. From the driveway, I could see U.S. Highway 62, the main road through the bustling tourist area of Berlin.

Berlin was everything that Margot wanted Harvest to be. It had dozens of specialty shops and restaurants. Tourists walked up and down the sidewalks, loaded down with shopping bags as they looked for Amish Country souvenirs to take back home to friends and family. Despite today's cold temperatures and falling snow, there were still a good number of stalwart shoppers moving up and down the street with their heads down and a determined set to their jaws.

The bunkhouse was a large, two-story brick home. There was no sign outside announcing what it was. If I had been driving by it, I would have thought it was just any other single-family dwelling in Holmes County.

"This is the place?" I asked Charlotte.

She unfastened her seatbelt. "Yep." She got out of the car.

I did the same and followed her up the brick walk to the front door. Charlotte knocked, and a moment later, an elderly Amish man in overalls came to the door. He had a mug of hot chocolate in his hand.

The hot chocolate was the perfect drink for the snowy weather. It wouldn't be long before the green grass outside completely disappeared under a blanket of white.

"What do you want?" He pointed toward businesses up the street. "All the shopping is up there. There's nothing to buy here." He started to close the door.

I put my hand against the door to stop him. "Please, just one second. We didn't come here to shop. We wanted to talk to one of the young men living in this bunkhouse."

"You can't be talking to any of the Amish men living in this bunkhouse without talking to me first. I'm Jett. This is my place. I'm in charge here and I make the rules."

"Then can we speak to one of the young men with your permission?"

He eyed us as he sipped his hot chocolate. "I've told the young men who live here that I won't abide lady visitors. This is a place to sleep so that they can find work. There is no time for courting or any shenanigans here. I won't hear of it."

"We aren't lady visitors, or at least we aren't lady visitors in the sense you imply. We're here to talk to Leon Hersh. He has helped out with events on the Harvest Village square and we wanted to talk to him about his work there."

"Oh, why didn't you say that you were here for Leon?" Jett's demeanor completely changed. "He's a *gut* one. I know that he wouldn't be participating in any unseemly behavior." He shook his head. "I can't say the same for all the young men living here. At least once a month, I kick out a young guy for bad behavior. Just because a person is Amish doesn't mean he will always do the right thing. These kids find their own kind of trouble, I can assure you of that."

I had found that to be true myself since I'd discovered a number of Amish killers. I didn't say that to Jett though. He'd just passed his approval of us. I guessed that he would revoke it if I said that some Amish were killers.

"Let me get him. I know it's cold out, but I can't let you inside. No women in the place. I have to stick to that rule for the young guys. Sometimes to keep youngsters in line, you have to keep the world black and white, so the *gut* and the bad are clear to them."

"We can wait here," I said.

Charlotte shivered next to me. "I hope we can find a warm spot to talk to Leon. I don't want to stand out here. I'm freezing."

"I agree. We'll go to the coffee shop if Leon agrees. It's just around the corner."

"Oh!" Her eyes sparkled. "I love that place. It's where Luke took me on our first official date. It will always have a special place in my heart."

I smiled.

The front door opened again, and Leon stepped out. He wore a thick winter coat and a pronounced frown.

Jett patted him on the shoulder. "Now, don't be too long, Leon. You know curfew for the house has been moved up to nine because of how dark it is getting at night." He looked at Charlotte and me. "Nothing *gut* ever happens after sunset. That's when all the trouble comes out. People, and when I say people here, I mean *Englischers*, would do well to remember that." With that he closed the door.

"Why are you here?" Leon asked, speaking for the first time.

"We're here because we want to talk to you about Blaze."

"Maybe I don't want to talk to you or anyone else about that. I'm tired of talking about it." He wouldn't meet my eyes. "I don't know anything."

"All right, but did you know Blaze is also your uncle Marvin?"

He stared at me. "What?" All of the color drained from his face.

Charlotte flipped her braid over her shoulder and peered at Leon as if he was a challenging candy recipe. "Are you going to be sick?"

He breathed in and out through his mouth. "*Nee*. I don't think so. I need to sit down, and we can't go into the bunkhouse. No women allowed."

"We know," I said. "Jett was very clear on the rules. Let's just walk up the block here. There's a little coffeehouse on the corner. We will get you something hot for dinner and you can collect yourself."

He nodded silently, and not for the first time I was reminded of how young he was. Leon Hersh was only fifteen. In the Amish world that meant he was a grown adult who should be making a living and trying new things in *rumspringa*—the Amish "running around time" when young Amish men and women decided if they wanted to join the church or leave forever.

Charlotte didn't make that decision about leaving the church until she was twenty-two. That was an extremely long time for an Amish young person to take to make such an important decision, but it could take several years.

However, instead of sowing wild oats, as it were, Leon was working multiple jobs and doing his best to get a full-time gig as the caretaker of Harvest's village square. What had happened in his young life to make him so serious? Was that just the way he was or was it his upbringing? These were important questions but not ones that I was going to bring up with Leon, who likely would have no use for the nature-versus-nurture debate.

Leon shoved his gloveless hands into the deep pockets of his coat, pulled the wide brim of his black felt hat down over his eyes, and followed Charlotte up the sidewalk.

I brought up the rear.

When we reached the coffeehouse, Leon scurried ahead of Charlotte to open and hold the door for us. Inside, the room smelled like cinnamon, coffee, and herbs. There were people eating and chatting at the small café tables and on the wide leather couches. Everyone in the room was *Englisch* except for the three baristas working at the counter, who were young Amish women, probably not much older than Leon.

"There's hardly anywhere to sit. I'll hold us a table," Charlotte said. "Bailey, can you get me a red velvet mocha?" She hurried over to the open table by the window.

I glanced at Leon. "What would you like? Get whatever you want."

He stared at the menu and bit his lip.

"Get anything you like," I encouraged him. "Just tell the barista."

Leon moved up to the counter. "Hello."

The girl behind the counter smiled encouragingly at him.

"Can I have a large caramel mocha, and a grilled cheese sandwich with chips?" He glanced back at me as if to ask whether it was okay.

I smiled and nodded. Then I put in the order for Charlotte's red velvet mocha and ordered a latte with cream and sugar for myself.

After I paid, the barista said she would bring the drinks to our table just as soon as they were ready. Leon and I joined Charlotte at the table.

Charlotte sighed. "This is the table where Luke and I sat for our first date."

I smiled at her daydreaming face and prayed she would never lose her sense of wonder over being in love. I wasn't sure that I'd ever had that. It wasn't my personality to look through rose-colored glasses, much as I wished it could be at times. Being skeptical could be exhausting.

Leon removed his hat and held it in his lap. "I'm not sure why the two of you want to talk to me about Blaze— I mean my uncle." He licked his lips. "And I didn't know he was my uncle when he died, I promise you that."

I sat across from Leon, and Charlotte sat between us.

"The thing is, Leon," I began, "Margot is in trouble, and I think you want to help Margot because you want her to give you the caretaker job on the square. If you help her out, I bet it will go a long way toward your getting that job."

"Margot is scary, but *ya,* I want that job. I like working outside and taking care of plants. I've always liked the events that she plans for the square—except this last one because of the dead man."

"Great," I said. "Then tell us what you know about what happened on Thanksgiving Day."

Again, he looked as if he might be ill. I was becoming increasingly concerned for Leon's health. It seemed that he could go from pale to dead white in a matter of seconds.

Just when I thought he was going to finally open up, the barista arrived with our drinks and Leon's food.

"Oh," Charlotte said. "There is a little Christmas tree design in the foam on all our drinks. That's so clever."

Leon looked from Charlotte to me and back again. "How did you find me?" His voice was on the edge of panic.

"I overheard at church one day where you were living," Charlotte said in a matter-of-fact way. "It was a while ago, but I thought you might still be here and it was the best place to start looking."

He slumped in his chair without touching his drink. "I'm not going to get away with this, am I?"

I leaned forward. "Get away with what?"

He met my gaze and there were tears in his dark eyes. "With killing a man."

CHAPTER TWENTY-THREE

Charlotte's hand hit her mug and some of the mocha sloshed out. Thankfully, she caught it before the hot liquid covered the table. "Are you saying you're a murderer!"

"Charlotte," I hissed. "We're in public."

She clapped a hand over her mouth, and then looked around the room as if to see whether anyone had overheard her outburst.

I turned my attention to Leon. "What do you mean when you say that, Leon? You shouldn't make a statement like that lightly."

"I don't make it lightly. Trust me. I don't. But it's the truth, and something that I will have to live with the rest of my life." His face fell. "I'll go to prison like my father did and turn out just like him. I left home because I wanted to make something of myself. I didn't want to follow in his footsteps, but that's what I'm doing."

"Do you know how Blaze died?" I asked, calling the dead man Blaze because I thought if I reminded Leon again that the dead man was his uncle, he would go into a complete tailspin.

He swallowed. "He ate the church spread I put in his marshmallow fluff."

I stared at him. "*You* did that?"

He nodded and stared down at his hat. "I'm a criminal just like my father."

"You wanted to kill him?" Charlotte asked.

"*Nee! Nee,* I never would want to hurt anyone, but I followed the directions given to me. . . ."

"Whose directions?" I asked.

He looked me in the eye. "Margot's."

I blinked. "What? You're telling me that Margot asked you to kill Blaze?"

He shook his head. "Not directly."

"It seems to me that asking someone to kill a person is a pretty direct request," Charlotte said, gripping her mug.

He shook his head. "I told you that Margot asked me to take care of her mother and her mother's boyfriend on Thanksgiving Day. It was my job to make sure they were happy and to keep them away from Margot as much as possible. I was supposed to do whatever they requested. When they arrived at the Thanksgiving Day meal, Blaze gave me a two-page document of all their requests for the day. It included where they wanted to sit, that Zara would have a pillow, that there had to be another chair and pillow for her nasty little dog. Those were just some of the items on the list. There were many more things on the list. Buried in that very long list was an item that read, 'Put one teaspoon of church spread in Blaze's marshmallow fluff and stir thoroughly.' Blaze gave me the fluff and asked me to place it by his seat. He said he didn't want anyone else touching it except me."

"And you didn't find that odd?" Charlotte asked.

"It wasn't any odder than all the other items on that list. Some of them were really bizarre." He touched his mug for the first time, but he didn't take a sip from it. Instead, he wrapped his hands around the smooth porcelain as if to warm them. His hands were very pale. Just like his face, it looked as if all the blood had drained out.

"Who gave you the list?" I asked.

"Blaze did. He handed it to me just as they arrived, at the same time that he gave me the jar of marshmallow fluff. When he put the list in my hand, he looked me in the eye and told me to follow it to the letter. He said if I messed up one item on that list, I would never get the caretaker job at the square."

"How did he know you wanted that job?" Charlotte asked, and then sipped from her mug.

Leon shook his head. "I don't know."

"Blaze was deathly allergic to peanuts. He never would have given you that note if he knew what was on the list. Can I see it? Do you still have it?"

He looked down at his hands. "*Nee*. I misplaced it. I thought it was in my pocket, but when I got home after the Thanksgiving feast, it was gone."

I suppressed a sigh. That list might just be the clue we needed to find the killer. An idea struck me. "Could you have dropped it on the green?"

He shrugged. "Maybe. I assumed that's what happened, but when I went back Thanksgiving night to look for it, I couldn't find it."

"Someone must have picked it up," Charlotte said.

That's what I thought too. I asked Leon, "Did it look like everything was written in the same hand?"

"The same hand?" His smooth brow furrowed in confusion.

"Written in the same handwriting, I mean."

He nodded his head. "I think so. It was printed in block letters. My handwriting in school was terrible, so it all looked fine to me."

"Was there anything distinguishing about the paper it was printed on?" I asked.

"It was on the stationery from the hotel they were staying in. It was signed with Blaze's name. I just wanted to impress Margot and show her what a great job I could do fulfilling tasks. I never for a moment thought when I was adding church spread to his marshmallow fluff that the list would include murder."

Charlotte shook her head. "No one does."

I shot her a look. "We have to figure out who wrote that note, and then we will find the person responsible for the murder. I really don't believe it was written by Blaze even though his signature was on the list. He wouldn't sign his own death sentence."

Leon gripped his mug a little tighter. "You don't believe I killed him?"

I shook my head. "I don't. Someone used you, Leon. I'm sorry to say that. Someone used you, and we have to find out who that someone is. You were the killer's unwitting accomplice."

He stared at me. "Does that mean I won't be arrested and go to jail?"

I stopped myself from saying anything because the truth was I didn't know the answer to that question. I supposed the sheriff's department could arrest him, and it would be up to the DA to decide if charges would be filed. I wanted to think the system wouldn't charge a minor who had unknowingly facilitated the incident. But the reality was that a man was dead. What's more, rather than come forward, Leon had lost what little evidence existed in the case. With Sheriff Marshall in charge of the department, anything could happen.

He sipped his mocha for the first time as if the possibility of not going to prison restored his interest in the drink. When he looked up at me again, he asked, "You think that man was my uncle?"

"I nodded. The police hope to get DNA from your father, who is his twin, to prove it."

Leon's eyes went wide. "They will never get that from my father. I hope they aren't planning to go into the woods to talk to him. They will be sorry if they did. It's full of booby traps."

"Booby traps!" I cried. "What do you mean?"

"My *daed* was very paranoid when he got out of prison. When my *maam* died five or so years ago, he moved us out of our farm to this old hunting cabin in the Harvest Woods. My father spent all his time fortifying the cabin to keep us safe. It was a terrible place to live, and he had awful dreams. He would wake up screaming at night." He closed his eyes for a moment as if he could still hear the screams.

"How bad are these booby traps?" Charlotte asked.

"Bad enough to kill," Leon said in all seriousness.

"Kill?" Charlotte and I both cried.

I stood up. "I have to call Aiden. He needs to know

about this. He could be hurt. He might already be there."
I pulled my phone out of my pocket and called. There
was no answer. I sent him a feverish text message, but I
didn't have any reason to think he would get it in Harvest
Woods. I knew from experience that reception was terrible there.

I tapped my foot and called Deputy Little next.

He picked up.

"Little, thank God. It's Bailey. Where's Aiden?"

"Aiden?"

"Yes, Aiden. Where is he? He said that he was going to
track down Melvin Hersh to get a DNA sample for com-
parison."

"He didn't tell me that," Deputy Little said, sounding
mildly upset. "Aiden is my friend, but he's not supposed
to be on this case anymore. The sheriff called BCI, and
they pulled him off. He could get into a lot of trouble if
he's still working the case. A lot of trouble."

My heart sank. Aiden had told me that he thought he
would be pulled off the case, not that he had already been.
However, I couldn't worry about that now. I just had to
make sure he was okay. "Little, listen to me. You have to
meet me at Melvin Hersh's cabin to make sure Aiden is
okay. He's not answering my calls or texts."

"Okay? What do you think could happen? Melvin is
not a suspect as far as I know. He wasn't at the Thanksgiving dinner."

"That's beside the point. There are booby traps there,
and Aiden could be hurt."

"Like Indiana Jones style?" Deputy Little asked.

"I don't know. I'm in Berlin with Melvin's son, Leon,
and he says that his father has fortified the area around
the cabin. Charlotte and I—"

"You got Charlotte involved in this?" he yelped.

I ground my teeth. "Little, if you don't meet us there, we will just go without you."

"Don't do that. I'm on my way. What's the address?"

I sat in my chair. "Leon, what's the address of your father's cabin in the woods?"

"There isn't an address."

"But you know how to get there from here?" I asked.

He nodded but didn't look the least bit happy about the situation. However, I could not worry about Leon's feelings at the moment; I had to make sure Aiden was safe. That was the most important thing of all.

"If there's no address, how am I going to find this place?" Deputy Little asked.

I repeated the question to Leon.

"Tell him we'll meet at Oaktree School, and I will be able to lead the way. He needs to bring a flashlight," Leon said.

I raised my eyebrows and glanced outside. Sure enough, it was dark. What else had I expected this late in the year? Would Aiden go and talk to Melvin in the woods after dark?

I relayed the message back to Deputy Little.

"All right," he said. "I'm forty minutes away from there so I'll head out now. It will just be me. I can't call backup because if we do find Aiden there, it will get back to Sheriff Marshall that he's still on the case when he shouldn't be. It could hurt his career with BCI." He paused. "Let's just both keep trying to get Aiden on the phone through call or text. Maybe if one of us can get hold of him, we can avoid going out there altogether."

I ended the call. I looked at Charlotte and Leon. "Ready to go?"

Leon shook his head. "I can't go back there. I *won't* go back there. I promised myself when I left that I would never return. My father is not a kind man, and I knew if I stayed there, I would turn out just like him. Maybe I already have because of what I did to Blaze. What makes it even worse is the possibility that he was my uncle. I don't know if I can live with myself after what I have done."

"Leon, if you save Aiden's life, you can make up for what happened to Blaze. The police will look kindly on you for saving one of their own."

"I just can't go back there."

I bit the inside of my lip. "Leon, please. When we get to the school, you can just point us in the right direction, and you can stay in the car."

"I—I guess I could do that."

"Then let's go."

I herded Charlotte and Leon out of the shop and in the direction of my car, which was still parked outside the bunkhouse.

"I have to be back by curfew," Leon said when he climbed into the back seat. "I can't give Jett a reason to kick me out on the street."

"When's curfew?" I asked as I started the car.

"Nine."

"It's six thirty now. If we aren't back by then, we have even bigger problems than we thought," I said.

The schoolhouse was twenty minutes from downtown Berlin on a dirt and gravel road that looked better suited for the turn of the nineteenth century than the twenty-first. It was pitch black out, but the headlights of my car caught the simple whitewashed building and the small playground next to it, which had a swing set and a teeter-totter. Both pieces of playground equipment looked as if they dated back to the 1970s. I guessed that they wouldn't pass the safety standards of a modern playground.

A lone swing gently rocked back and forth on its chain. Had someone been here and just gotten up from the swing? It was impossible to know. The only light came from the headlights of my car, and it didn't even reach all corners of the playground.

"I went to a one-room schoolhouse growing up," Charlotte said. "And I always thought that the place was creepy at night. Schools are supposed to be filled with laughing children. When they're not, they lose all their life."

The lone swing rocked back and forth, and I shivered. "The school is closed for the day. There's nothing creepy about that." I said this both for Charlotte's benefit and my own.

I decided I didn't want to be looking at the rocking swing while we waited for Deputy Little, so I moved the car a little bit to the right. The playground was now in darkness, and my headlights fell on a hand-painted sign. The date on the sign was over twenty-five years ago. "The first Oaktree School was lost, but the Good Lord allowed us to rebuild. Bless the children who walk through these doors today and every day."

I stared at the sign. This couldn't possibly be *the* school, the school that burned down while Allen Shirk and the Hersh brothers were clearing a field using flames. Could it? It was too dark to see beyond my headlights whether there was a field behind the school.

"Leon, is this the school that your father went to prison for burning down?" I unbuckled my seatbelt and turned around in my seat to face him.

Most of his face was in shadow, but his glasses caught

the ambient light that fought its way through the windows. "It is."

I gripped the seat between us. "Why would he want to be so close to a place that caused him so much pain?"

Leon sat back in his seat, and now his entire face was in shadow. "He said that he wanted to stay close to it as a reminder."

"A reminder of what?"

"I don't know. I never thought to ask. My father was a very private person even with me, and I was his only child. I learned to stop asking questions. He would grow very angry if I asked too many questions."

Not for the first time, I wondered if Melvin had hurt his son, perhaps even hit him. I knew that talking about child abuse was taboo in the Amish community. I was relieved that Leon had been strong enough to escape that toxic environment on his own. He probably could use some therapy to unpack the trauma he might have suffered, but Amish and therapy didn't mix. I doubted that he would even consider such an idea. Maybe twisting Leon's arm to get him to show me the location of his father's cabin was putting Leon through too much. I didn't want to traumatize the Amish teen any more than necessary.

I turned back around and felt Charlotte watching me.

"Bailey, are you okay?" my cousin asked.

"Maybe we shouldn't be here. It's cold and dark, and I don't see Aiden's car." To Leon, I said, "Where else would someone park if they wanted to get close to the cabin?"

"There's a small buggy path that leads into the woods just a bit down the road. In the daytime, you're able to see the end of it from here."

"Should we drive over there and check it out?" Charlotte asked.

I was wondering the same thing, but before I decided, a pair of headlights turned into the tiny school lot. I don't think it could hold more than four cars or maybe five horses and buggies. I knew that most Amish children walked to school. Some were bused to public schools.

At times, Englishers were surprised that many Amish went to public English primary schools. Fewer went to the English middle school, and if they did, they had special permission to sit out particular classes that were contrary to their religious beliefs, such as science and health.

Deputy Little climbed out of his SUV and walked over to us.

I rolled down the window and he leaned inside.

"You really did bring Charlotte with you," he said with a bit of awe at my boldness.

Charlotte leaned forward and gripped her seatbelt. "Bailey didn't ask me to come, I just did because I wanted to."

Deputy Little pressed his lips together as if he wanted to argue with his fiancée. Maybe he was learning early on what it took to be a husband. The first rule of any marriage according to my mother was to pick your battles. This was a lesson I needed to work on with Aiden.

Deputy Little looked in the back seat and must have seen Leon cowering there. "Leon, can you show us the way to your father's cabin?"

I looked behind me, and it seemed that he somehow managed to make himself even smaller.

"If you're going in, we need to go now. The temperature will be dropping as the night goes on. I don't think any of us want to be out late in the cold."

"I'm not going." Leon spoke for the first time. "Bailey said that I don't have to."

Deputy Little looked as if he wanted to protest.

"I did tell him that," I said before Deputy Little could try to negotiate. It was already hard on Leon to be so close to his father's cabin. I couldn't imagine how he would react if his father came out of the woods.

"If there really are booby traps we have to worry about," Deputy Little said, "how are we going to avoid them if we don't have a guide?"

I hadn't thought about that. I had been so laser-focused on finding Melvin's cabin that I hadn't thought much more ahead.

"I'm not going to know where all of them are," Leon said. "He may have moved some since I left."

"But you may know where some are," Deputy Little said.

Leon didn't speak. I assumed that meant yes. "Before we drag Leon into the woods, let's look for Aiden's car. If his car is not here, he's probably not here either. If it's here, we'll decide what to do."

"Fair enough," Deputy Little said. "Aiden might not be answering our calls or texts because he's on a completely different case."

"Right," I said, but in my heart, I doubted that was the reason.

"Leon said there's an access road there, just beyond the end of the playground. Since Aiden's car isn't here, that's the place where he would most likely park."

"How far is it?" Deputy Little asked.

"Four hundred feet that way. You can't miss it."

Deputy Little stepped back from my car. "Let's go."

Charlotte and I climbed out of the car, but Leon didn't move.

"Charlotte," Deputy Little said. "I want you to wait here with Leon until we see if Aiden's car is there."

"Why?" Charlotte said.

"Because Leon needs someone with him." The deputy's voice left no room for debate.

Charlotte pressed her lips together as if she didn't believe him, and I suspected too that he just wanted to keep his fiancée out of harm's way. I had no idea what he planned to do if we did find Aiden's car on that access road.

As Deputy Little and I walked in the direction of the access road, the deputy asked, "What's wrong with Leon?"

"I don't know exactly. He has a hard relationship with his father. He left about a year ago when he was of age. My best guess is there is some abuse there, but he hasn't come right out and said it."

Deputy Little nodded. "Talking about abuse of any kind in the Amish community is taboo. I think you will be hard-pressed to get any such admission out of Leon. However, I'm glad the kid got out and seems to be doing well on his own. That's not always what happens."

I nodded and my heart ached for Leon as I realized everything he must have been through in his young life. Despite all that, he'd escaped and made a life of his own. I promised myself that when this was all over, I would talk to Margot about giving Leon a chance at the square's caretaker job even if it began with a trial run. I suspected that she was leery of hiring someone so young, but Leon was more mature than a lot of adult men I knew. We could make sure that he had a good support system around him, and could help him get access to resources.

There had to be services to help someone so young—counseling, child services, and the like—even if it wasn't exactly the Amish way to take advantage of them.

Deputy Little's flashlight moved back and forth around the patchy grass in front of us. "Watch your step," he said. "There are a lot of ruts in the ground. Looks like they're left over from old plowings. I would guess the spot where the schoolhouse stands used to be a farm field at one time. Be careful. The ruts are hard to see in the snow."

"This field must have been plowed a long time ago," I said. "That schoolhouse is rebuilt on the same place as the one that Melvin and Allen were arrested for burning down."

"Why would Melvin want to live close to this site?"

"I don't know. I asked Leon, and he doesn't know either."

"There's the road," Deputy Little said.

The beam of his flashlight reflected off something red. My heart sank as we came closer. It was clear the flashlight reflected off the back taillight of a car, Aiden's BCI vehicle to be exact.

CHAPTER TWENTY-FOUR

Deputy Little shone the flashlight down the narrow lane in front of Aiden's car. It was about the width of two adults. I corrected myself. It wasn't a lane; it was little more than a path.

I shivered. "Do you think Aiden went down that way?"

Deputy Little didn't answer. Instead, he walked up to the car and tried all the doors. They were all locked. Then he shone his flashlight in through the windows.

I tried to peek around his shoulder, but from my angle I couldn't see anything but the glare from the windows. "Do you see anything?"

"Not anything that will tell us if Aiden went down that path."

I looked at my phone. It showed that I had called Aiden five times that evening and sent him ten text messages. Surely, if he got that many messages from me, he would have responded. He had to know I would only pester him so often if something was really wrong.

I put my hand on the hood of Aiden's car. It was cold. That could've been a result of the temperature continuing to drop dramatically, or, more likely, it spoke to the fact that Aiden had arrived here some time ago. Neither thought comforted me.

"Do you need to call backup?" I asked. "Maybe some other deputies should be here to help look for him?"

Deputy Little shook his head. "Not yet. I told you what would happen if anyone in the department finds out that Aiden is still working on Blaze Smith's murder."

"But . . ."

"I will call them if it gets bad. Before I do that, I'll just see what I can find out. I'll walk down the path a little and scope out the area." He walked to the front of the car.

"What about the booby traps?"

He stopped midstride. "I forgot about those. Wasn't Leon going to tell us where they are?"

"I don't know where they all are, but I can tell you some."

I pivoted quickly to see Leon standing at the top of the path just behind Aiden's car.

"You didn't think I was really going to sit in the car all this time?" Charlotte said. "Did you?" She shook her head. "I had a nice talk with Leon, and we both think it's best if he helps the two of you so that we can all go home."

"Are you willing to help, Leon?" I asked. The Amish might think of him as an adult because he'd graduated from eighth grade, but in the English world that I lived in, a fifteen-year-old was still a minor and needed extra protection.

"I'll help," he said. Leon's Adam's apple bobbed up

and down in the glare of Deputy Little's flashlight. "I want to help."

"All right," Deputy Little said. Some of the sternness had gone out of his voice.

If Aiden's life wasn't potentially in danger, I would've been shooing Leon back to the car, but as we had no idea what to expect, I said, "So what kind of things does your father have in store for us?"

The glow of Deputy Little's flashlight glimmered off Leon's eyeglasses. "He didn't want any cars coming back by the cabin so he put nails and screws about a third of the way down this narrow road. That was to keep cars away. Sometimes people would see them in time and turn around; sometimes their tires would get blown out. It didn't happen often. There are not many people in this world who want to come talk to my father."

"What else?" Deputy Little asked.

"There are a lot of bear traps and rabbit snares in the woods. I don't know where they all are. Stay on the path. If you go off, there's no telling what you could step on."

"Aren't traps illegal?" I asked.

"Yes," Deputy Little said. "Because they're inhumane. Ohio outlawed them decades ago."

"Well, let's go," Charlotte said. "The only way to know if Aiden is down this path is to look." She stepped in front of the car.

Deputy Little caught her arm. "No, the three of you stay here by Aiden's car while I search."

Charlotte looked up at him. "Luke, I'm not letting you go in there by yourself."

"You don't have a choice. I'm the officer here. I'm trained to deal with things like this."

Charlotte folded her arms. "I'm not budging."

The deputy's jaw twitched. "Charlotte," I said. "How about if you stay here with Leon and I will go with Deputy Little?"

She looked as if she was going to argue with me too. I pulled her aside. "Please. I won't let anything happen to Luke, I promise, but I'm worried about Leon. He needs someone here with him."

She looked over her shoulder at the Amish teen, who had his arms wrapped around his waist and his chin bent down to his chest. He seemed to be trying to make himself as small as possible. "All right, but I'm only doing it for Leon because he's a *gut* kid. I don't think many people have cared for him in his life."

I didn't think so either.

We walked back to Deputy Little.

"Charlotte will stay here with Leon," I said. "I'm going with you. If we don't see anything in fifteen minutes of searching, you will call in reinforcements. I don't care what repercussions this might have on Aiden's career. His safety is more important."

Deputy Little nodded. "Agreed."

Charlotte and I stood in front of the deputy with our arms folded. We were a united front.

Deputy Little's shoulders sagged. "Fine. Bailey, come along. But you stay close to me all the time. Don't wander off."

"Got it."

I took one glance back at Leon before Deputy Little and I walked down the path. He was looking up now and his face was a mask of fear.

The ground along the path was a mix of rocks and clay and rapidly being covered with snow. The earth was just beginning to freeze, but a week ago there had been a hard rain in the county so the ground was still soft enough to give under our feet. Ice cold muddy water seeped into the sides of my shoes. I had a feeling the tennis shoes I was wearing would have to be retired after this nighttime hike.

Deputy Little wore boots that were more appropriate to the seasonal changes. I supposed as an officer of the law he had to be ready to walk through any terrain. As a candy maker, I usually wasn't called upon to do the same.

His flashlight's beam was powerful, almost as bright as the headlight of a car. It reflected over something in the middle of the road in front of us. We inched forward, and sure enough, there was a foot-wide line of nails, screws, and razor blades in the path. It had a thin layer of snow over it, but the swath of sharp objects was so thick, the snow hadn't completely covered them yet.

"Leon wasn't lying about the booby traps," I said.

"Apparently not," Deputy Little replied, and he didn't sound happy about it. He shone his light on either side of the road. Frowning, he picked up a large, long stick and threw it into the woods.

It landed and a millisecond later there was a great cracking sound as the stick was snapped in two.

I stared open-mouthed.

"Bear trap," Deputy Little said.

"Geez," I murmured.

"Let's stay on the path like Leon said."

"Definitely," I agreed.

We stepped over the line of nails and screws. I took care to make sure I didn't step on any of them. Not only were they sharp but they were rusted from being exposed to the elements for who knew how long.

We walked in silence for a few minutes. Both of us were frantically looking for any hint that Aiden was nearby or had been there. It was nearly impossible to know in the dark. All we could see were objects in the direct beam of Deputy Little's flashlight or those illuminated by the moon, which peeked out from the clouds every now and again. It was a cloudy night, so that didn't happen often, but at one point I saw smoke catch in the moonlight at the end of the path and the simple silhouette of a cabin.

"That must be Melvin's cabin," I whispered. "It's up ahead."

Deputy Little nodded and he turned off his flashlight. At the same time the moon dipped behind a cloud and we were in the dark.

It took several second for my eyes to adjust to the blackness. Even when they did, I couldn't see much in front of me at all. However, I could see the smoke coming out of the chimney of the cabin and smell the scent of it. The faintest glow of a lamp shone through one of the windows in the front.

"What do we do now?" I whispered.

"I'm not sure knocking on the door is a good idea."

"I wouldn't advise it," another voice said.

I yelped, and a hand was slapped over my mouth to keep me from screaming.

When Aiden removed his hand, I punched him in the shoulder. "What are you doing here?"

"I could be asking the two of you the same exact thing." Aiden looked from Deputy Little to me and back again. He rubbed his shoulder. "Good thing I have a winter coat on or that might have hurt."

"We were worried about you. I knew you planned to speak to Melvin, and Leon told me that the area around his cabin is booby-trapped. We thought something happened to you when you didn't answer the phone or either of our text messages."

Aiden's eyes went wide. "I have my phone on silent. I don't want the ringer to go off and scare Melvin. The guy is jumpy. I have been here observing him for the last hour trying to plan an approach."

"And you haven't looked at your phone at all in the last two hours?" I hissed.

Aiden sighed. "I'm sorry. I suppose I was too absorbed in what I was doing. There are booby traps everywhere. I almost got caught in a rabbit snare."

"We could take him in for the traps and snares," Deputy Little said absently. "I didn't want to call for backup if you were here. . . ." He trailed off.

Aiden shoved his hands into his pockets. "Because I'm not supposed to be on the case any longer? I'm guessing that you know this too, Bailey."

I nodded.

"Right. I plan to drop it. I just wanted to do this last thing."

Deputy Little's jaw twitched as if he wanted to say something but held it back.

There was a cocking sound like a gun. The three of us spun around.

An Amish man with a long, grizzled beard stood in front of us with a shotgun pointed in our direction. "Those traps were supposed to keep people like you out."

Both Deputy Little and Aiden pulled out their guns and aimed at the man. Aiden pushed me behind them.

"Mr. Hersh," Aiden said in a calm but authoritative voice. "Put the gun down. You are pointing it at officers from BCI and Holmes County Sheriff's department. Just doing that could send you back to prison."

The man dropped the shotgun on the ground. "I don't want to go back to prison."

Deputy Little scooped up the gun and opened the chamber. "It's empty."

The moon came out from behind the clouds, and I could see Melvin's features clearly now. Even in the moonlight, I noticed that his skin was crusted with dirt. I wondered when he had last taken a bath. He had the traditional Amish beard with no mustache, but his hair was much longer than that of any Amish man I had ever seen. It came all the way down to his shoulders in unkempt curls. I couldn't even guess what Ruth Yoder would say if she met an Amish man who was so terribly groomed.

"Of course it's empty," Melvin said. "I haven't bought bullets for years. I'm Amish, aren't I? That makes me a pacifist, doesn't it?"

"Do you think setting traps and putting nails in the road that could hurt people makes you a pacifist?" Aiden asked.

"That has nothing to do with shooting at a person. Those are there to protect what is rightfully mine." He narrowed his eyes. "Why are you here? This is private land. Does it have something to do with my son? I don't know anything about him. He ran off just as soon as he finished school and I never saw him again. He's a perfect example of an ungrateful child. He should have stayed here with me so that we could take turns caring for things around here. Instead, he ran away like a coward."

I bit my lip to stop myself from coming to Leon's defense. The less Melvin knew about his son's life now, the better.

"We would like to talk to you about your brother, Marvin," Aiden said.

"Marvin? I don't have a brother named Marvin. He's been dead to me for years."

"We think he actually died this Thanksgiving. He's been living under the English name Blaze Smith. He was at the Harvest community Thanksgiving meal. He had an allergic reaction to peanuts we believe."

"He was here?" Melvin asked. "He was here in Holmes County? As far as I know, this was the first time he ever came back, although I was in prison for six years because of him, so he might have come and gone from the county many times while I was locked away."

"You don't seem surprised that he used the name Blaze," Deputy Little observed.

"He wrote me some letters when I was in prison. He used that name. I thought he used it just to avoid the prison knowing about him. It was the dumbest name I had ever heard, so I wasn't surprised it was the one he picked. My brother was never the practical sort."

"Why do you say it's his fault you were locked away?" I asked.

Melvin looked at me as if seeing me for the first time. "Who are you?"

"She's with us," Aiden said as if that was answer enough.

I expected Melvin to protest that statement, but he just shrugged as if he didn't have enough energy to argue with Aiden over my presence. Instead, he answered my question. "He was the one who started the fire. He didn't know how to use the torch to control the burn. He got too close to the school, and it went up like a tinderbox. It just took off. The fire was in August, when it's the driest. There was no stopping it once it was headed toward the school. My brother knew that too, and he just took off like the coward that he is."

"You don't seem upset at the idea that your brother is dead," Deputy Little observed.

"I'm not. Like I told you before, he was dead to me the moment he ran away from that burning school. I decided when he ran that I never had a *bruder,* and I believe that to this very day."

"But you never told the police about him?" I asked.

Melvin balled the hands at his sides into fists. "What *gut* would it have done? As soon as Allen and I were arrested, the sheriff and the courts decided to make an example of us."

"Listen, Melvin, there are some violations on your property," Aiden said. "You could get in a lot of trouble with those traps."

Melvin scowled at him. "What I do on my land shouldn't be anyone's concern but my own."

"It's a concern if someone is walking through the woods or if an animal is caught in one of those traps. That would be considered poaching, which is a serious offense. It will definitely send you back to prison."

"I'm not on parole any longer."

Aiden put his hand on the hilt of his gun. "Do you think that matters? You have a record. A judge won't be lenient on you when he or she sees that. You need to take them out. If you agree to do that in seven days, Deputy Little and I will look the other way. I don't think you want to go back to prison."

Melvin ran his gloved hand over his sweaty upper lip.

It was clear that the idea of going back to prison got to him. "I'll take them down."

"You have seven days."

Melvin nodded.

"We have another request too. Marvin was your twin."

"My fraternal twin. I'm not identical to that fool."

"All right. Your fraternal twin. In any case, he was your brother. We're fairly certain, but we need to prove that the man who died on Thanksgiving was your brother."

"I don't want anything to do with it," Melvin snapped.

"All we need from you is proof that you are his brother in order to prove his identity."

"I don't leave my woods, so if you're asking me to go somewhere and look at a dead person, you are out of luck."

"That's not what we're looking for. I need to swab the inside of your mouth for a saliva test. That will tell us if he is your brother."

Melvin frowned. "And if I do this, you will go away."

"Yes, but a sheriff's deputy will be back in seven days to make sure that you have removed those traps."

Melvin's scowl deepened, but to my amazement, he let Aiden swipe the inside of his mouth. It took all of five seconds. Aiden put the sample in a plastic tube and secured it in an evidence bag. The test was over in no time at all.

"There. Now, you can leave me in peace, and if you see my son, tell him that I don't want him to come back. He's no better than his traitor uncle." He turned around and shuffled back to the cabin.

"He didn't ask for the shotgun back," Deputy Little said.

"Leave it here. He'll find it in the morning."

Deputy Little nodded and set the empty shotgun on the edge of the path. "Either I'll come out next week or I'll let whoever does know that Melvin might brandish an unloaded weapon."

Aiden nodded. "Let's leave."

I looked at my phone. It was twenty minutes before eight. "We have to be quick about it. I have to get Leon back to his bunkhouse. If he's not there before nine, he'll get in trouble." I hurried down the path and could hear Aiden and Deputy Little behind me.

When we reached the spot where Aiden's car was parked, Charlotte went limp against the passenger door. "Oh, thank the Lord you are all okay! Leon and I were just deciding whether we should go in there and look for you."

Leon stood a few feet away. His arms were still wrapped tightly around his narrow waist. It was almost as if he was wearing a straitjacket.

Aiden handed the DNA bag to Deputy Little. "This is your case. You take it to the lab. I'm done with it now."

Deputy Little appeared to be unsure when he took the bag from Aiden. I knew that he looked up to Aiden. It might be difficult to be the one taking over from his mentor.

"Leon," I said. "Let's go so we can make it back to the bunkhouse before your curfew."

He nodded, and Leon, Charlotte, and I hurried to my car by the schoolhouse. Now that the clouds had cleared, it was light enough to find our way with just the moonlight to guide us.

We jumped in the car and drove to the bunkhouse in silence. I pulled up in front of the bunkhouse.

"Thank you for your help, Leon," I said. "We never would have been able to find your father without you."

He opened his door and paused. "Did my father say anything about me when you spoke to him?"

I gripped the steering wheel. I didn't want to lie to Leon, but at the same time I didn't want to repeat the words that his father had said.

"I can tell from your face that he did and it was un-kind." He closed the door and ran into the bunkhouse just as the clock struck nine.

CHAPTER TWENTY-FIVE

I dropped Charlotte off at Swissmen Sweets, and we agreed that our adventure in the woods was not a story to share with my grandmother. *Maami* worried about us enough as it was.

When I got home, I was happy to see that my neighbor Penny wasn't lying in wait for me as usual. Honestly, it seemed that it didn't matter what time of night I came home from the candy shop; she knew when I was going to stroll up the sidewalk or, in tonight's case, pull into the driveway.

Just to be on the safe side, I parked my car in the one-car detached garage and bolted for the house. After the night I'd had, I didn't feel like being quizzed by Penny about what I had been up to and with whom. In fact, I never felt up to being quizzed by Penny on those things.

A very irritated Puff met me at the back kitchen door.

She shuffled over to her empty food bowl and lay on her side as if to illustrate that she was at death's door.

For Puff, having her dinner delayed was akin to death.

Just as I fed the rabbit, there was knock on the front door of the house.

"If that's Penny, I'm going to play dead too," I told the rabbit.

I walked over to the front door and looked through the peep hole. Aiden stood on my doorstep.

I opened the door. "I hadn't expected you to come back here tonight. I thought you were headed to Columbus."

"I am. My boss wants me back at work on my cases there bright and early tomorrow morning. I just wanted to say goodbye to you first."

My heart ached at the idea of saying goodbye to him again. It always seemed that our time together was too short, and this visit had been interrupted by murder. I wished I could say that this was the first time murder had played a role in keeping us apart, but it wasn't.

"Come on in." I stepped back from the door. "I know Puff missed you."

As if she knew we were talking about her, the fluffy rabbit hopped into the living room from the kitchen and made a bunny beeline for Aiden's shoes. She loved to sit on his shoes.

He carefully removed his feet from under the rabbit. "Puff, you can sit on my shoes, but I want to have a seat first." He walked over to the loveseat and sat down. Puff hopped after him and settled on his shoes.

Aiden looked at me. "Has anyone ever mentioned that you have a very peculiar rabbit?"

"Ruth Yoder has said it more than once when she's

seen Puff curled up with Nutmeg at Swissmen Sweets. However, when I see the two of them together, my thought is that Nutmeg is the peculiar animal for not wanting to eat the rabbit."

Puff's long white ears twitched as if she had heard what I'd said and didn't approve.

I tucked myself in the corner of the sofa, sitting cross-legged so I could face Aiden.

He leaned forward and wiped something from my cheek. "I think you had a speck of dirt on your cheek from our adventure in the woods."

I touched my cheek. "That was quite an adventure."

"And one you and the others wouldn't have undertaken if I had looked at my phone. I'm sorry about that. I was just so laser-focused on this case that I ignored everything else."

I tucked my knees up under my chin. "What's going on, Aiden? You've been focused on cases before, but never anything like this."

He rubbed the back of his neck. "I know I've been distant. I just realized being back in Harvest that *this* is where I want to be. I love this county and the people here. I don't want to be in the city; I wasn't made for it. I dread the drive to Columbus tonight."

I stared at him. It was the last thing I'd expected he would say. "I thought you like working for BCI."

"I do, and I don't want to sound ungrateful for this opportunity. But now I'm at the will of the bureau. They can move me to any part of the state and give me any assignment they choose. I have very little say in it. Right now I'm two hours away from you, but it could be farther. It depends on the needs of the department."

"I can't leave Harvest, Aiden. There's *Maami*, the

shop, Charlotte, Jethro . . ." I trailed off, and confusion flooded through me. If I really loved this man, shouldn't I be willing to move with him wherever he went? What if we did get married and he was assigned to a post that was five hours away? Could a marriage sustain that kind of distance over the long term? I didn't know.

Aiden put a hand on my knee. "I'm not asking you to leave Harvest, and my mother would be heartened to know that Jethro was on your list of reasons to stay in the village."

"The little oinker has grown on me." I covered his hand with my own.

He laughed. "He has a way of doing that. I'd never ask you to leave Harvest. Your life is here, and your business. I know how many plans you have for the candy business. What you've done with it so far is amazing."

He didn't know all that I wanted to do. I hadn't told him about the factory idea. My mind wandered back to the property for sale that Charlotte and I had seen when we left Harvest to find Leon.

"Then what?" I asked. It was a vague question, but at the same time it was all I could manage.

"I need to think of a way to get back here." He removed his hand from my knee and let it fall on his lap. My heart caught in my throat, and I felt my body tense. I wanted Aiden to come home. I wanted him to come home more than anything, but what would it cost him to do that? His career?

"And leave BCI?" I whispered.

"If I have to, yes. I hope it doesn't come to that. I was hired on the understanding that I would work in this area with the Amish and other plain communities because of my connection to them." He shook his head. "But if they don't let me come back to Holmes County, I may have to leave."

"And work for the sheriff's department again?" I couldn't hide the doubt in my voice.

He grimaced. "The sheriff will never rehire me. I basically ran that department in spite of him for years, and now that I'm gone and they have fumbled their way to get the department on track again, he won't take me back. Nor do I want to work in an environment where I'm not wanted. Furthermore, Luke Little is my friend. I wouldn't want to go back and force him to a lower rank. He's worked too hard and grown so much as an officer of the law. I'm proud of how he's conducted himself and how far he's come."

"What are you going to do?" I asked.

He shook his head. "I don't know. I just know now, leaving here, leaving *you*, was a huge mistake. Being here with you is more important than any job. I'm not happy. I haven't been happy since the day I left, and maybe that's why I've been distant." He met my gaze with those deep chocolate-brown eyes.

I grabbed his hands. "I haven't been happy since you left either. It's been so hard to be separated from you. Even when we talked on the phone, I could tell you were distracted by other things. I was so afraid of losing you."

"You won't lose me. I swear you will never lose me." He looked into my eyes. "I had my guard up. I didn't want you to know that I couldn't handle being away from Holmes County. You're so strong and successful, and I felt embarrassed to come back to Harvest with my tail between my legs. You juggle the candy shop, your show, and a hundred other things while I can't manage one career."

"In my career, I'm not putting my life on the line the way you do. Yours is more difficult. Anyone would agree with me on that. And if you're not happy where you're working, that's a problem. It doesn't matter what you're doing if you're not in the place that feels like home."

"It didn't feel like home, that's for sure. And all that may be true, but the bottom line is I was embarrassed to tell you. I didn't want you to think I was flighty or unstable just when we are thinking about the next step in our life together."

Next step in our life together? Aiden and I hadn't seriously talked about marriage since he'd joined BCI. I wanted to ask him exactly what he meant by that, but I held off. We needed to close some of the distance that had been opened between us first before we could talk about being engaged again.

"There's nothing wrong with trying something new, and then deciding that it's not for you," I said. "I think it's brave to be able to say that, and on a selfish level, I'm elated. I want you back here. Harvest needs you. Your mother needs you. Jethro needs you." I looked into those chocolate-brown eyes. "I need you the most of all. I love you, Aiden. I always want you to be nearby me."

Tears gathered in his eyes. "I love you too. I always want to be close to you too." He touched my leg. "I should have known that you would be understanding about all of it. It's a male pride thing, I suppose. I'm proud I got tapped by the bureau, but in reality, I'd rather be here with you. This whole thing has taught me what's really important to me and what I really want in life."

"So if you have to leave BCI and can't work for the sheriff, what will you do?" I grabbed his hand. "I don't ask that in criticism. You could be anything—a brain surgeon, a trash collector; I don't care as long as you're with me." Tears pricked the corners of my eyes.

He laughed. "Well, neither brain surgeon nor trash collector was on my shortlist, but thank you for reminding me of all my options."

He shifted in his seat. "I have thought about it a lot, especially over this last week, and I'm going to finish out my full year with BCI. It's over in June. I think for the opportunity they gave me, I owe them that, and I'm learning so much more about investigations that I didn't know before. The resources they have access to are amazing, light-years ahead of what I had at the sheriff's department. In some ways, it will be hard to go back to a more primitive way of investigation, but really most of investigating is asking the right questions, listening, and observing. That doesn't require a fancy lab full of gadgets. It's just attention to detail."

"Will you leave law enforcement? It's been so much a part of who you are."

Aiden shook his head. "I love investigating, and more than that, I love helping people. I think I'll always stay in investigations. I had another idea."

I frowned when he didn't say what that idea was. I felt like I was pulling information out of him. "What's your idea?"

His face flushed red. "I could hang up my shingle as a private investigator."

I stared at him. "Like Sherlock Holmes in Amish Country?"

He laughed. "I don't think it would be completely like that, but it would give me more freedom to investigate outside the confines of law enforcement."

I had a million questions. Were there enough cases for

a private investigator in Holmes County or even in Canton, which was the biggest nearby city? Would he be able to make enough money to pay his bills? Would the police be willing to work with him? Would the sheriff? I already knew the answer to my last question was a no. All of that was "practical" Bailey talking.

However, instead of asking any of those questions, I said, "I just want you to be happy. In whatever you do, I want you to be fulfilled and happy."

He grabbed my hands and pulled me toward him in a hug. "I love you more every day. I'm so grateful for your support."

I didn't know if he would feel quite so grateful if he could see all the questions swirling around inside my head. I'd be lying if I didn't say that I had doubts his idea could work or that I didn't think it was going to be harder than he thought it would be. I knew from running a business that it wasn't easy, and candy was a natural in a tourist village like Harvest. I didn't know if PI services would be quite as simple.

But I also knew Aiden, and he could do anything he put his mind to. Knowing that, my fears fell away. I hugged him and then pulled back. "If you hang up your private investigator shingle, can I be your Girl Friday?"

"Always," he said.

"But my Girl Friday would not be an assistant. She's an equal."

"I wouldn't have asked for anything else," he murmured.

CHAPTER TWENTY-SIX

T he next morning, it was back to business as usual at Swissmen Sweets. Aiden had left for Columbus the night before.

Maami and I were in the kitchen making up more Jethro bars for online orders. The pig was a popular Christmas stocking stuffer this year, I would give him that. Charlotte was up front, and Emily was at home. She had worked some extra hours for us over the last several days, but now that she had two young children to care for she typically only worked two days a week.

Charlotte came into the kitchen with the typical bounce in her step. By looking at her, you would never know that she had been in the woods the night before asking about booby trap danger.

"Bailey, did you make an offer on that piece of land?"

I froze. Milk chocolate dripped from the piping bag that I was using to add Jethro's polka dots to his design.

Maami looked up from the white chocolate she was tempering. "What's that? Bailey, you are buying land?"

Charlotte clamped her hand over her mouth. Behind her there was the telltale jingle of the door opening. A customer had arrived, and Charlotte dashed through the swinging door. She had literally been saved by the bell.

"What did Charlotte mean when she asked that, Bailey?" *Maami* asked.

I set my piping bag on a piece of parchment paper and wiped my hands on a paper towel. "There is a large plot for sale at the end of the downtown part of the village. It's just beyond Harvest Market."

She nodded. "*Ya*, I saw that when I went to church at Ruth Yoder's home on Sunday. It is quite a big piece of land. Why would you need it?"

I took a deep breath. I had wanted to propose my idea to my grandmother after the Christmas rush, but it seemed that I was backed into a corner. If I said I didn't want to buy it, I would be lying, and if I didn't tell her the specific reason I wanted to buy it, that would be lying too.

"I thought it would be a good way to expand Swissmen Sweets." I winced as I waited for her reaction.

My grandmother's mouth fell open, and I knew that expansion of the candy shop had never once entered her mind. Why would it? She and my grandfather ran this shop just as they always had for nearly sixty years before I came along. They made a good living at it and had everything they needed. They were Amish through and through. They didn't have the English desire for more, better, faster, bigger, but I did. I was an equal partner in

Swissmen Sweets with my grandmother, but I had made most of the big decisions about the business in the last two years. *Maami* loved making candy. She hadn't enjoyed the business side of things. She always let *Daadi* deal with that. After he died and I took his place, she had done the same with me. She left all the business to me. I'd made an online store and made improvements to the shop, like the awning over the windows and replacing some of the equipment.

However, starting an online store and building a brand-new factory were two totally different things.

"Expand it how?" she asked carefully.

I turned to face her on my stool. "You know we have been having trouble filling orders and finding enough space for all of us to work in the shop. We were barely able to keep up this holiday weekend with all four of us working around the clock. We can't fit any more people in the kitchen to help. We need more space. If we had a factory with more employees, we could fill more orders and serve more people. We could expand our reach exponentially."

"What would happen to this place?" Tears gathered in the corners of her crinkled eyes, and my heart clenched.

"It is my home," she said in a hurt voice. "It's the home I shared with your grandfather for over sixty years. I don't want to leave the place I shared with Jebidiah. It would break my heart."

"Nothing about the original shop will change. I'd never ask you to leave here. I don't want this place to change at all. You will still work and live here, and it's where I will be most of the time. It's the brand and the flagship shop. The factory will be used for mass production so that we can expand in the online space. It gives us the opportunity to distribute to other stores. I'm not talking about the few specialty shops in Holmes County that hand-sell our candy, but in state and national grocery stores." I let out a breath.

"Why?" *Maami* asked with less emotion this time. I was glad I was able to reassure her that she wouldn't have to leave the store and home she'd shared with my *daadi* for so many years. But her final question didn't have a simple answer or any answer that my grandmother would understand.

"To keep up with demand and to grow the business."

"Why?" she asked again. "If we are not able to fill all orders, we tell people items are limited. We do not need to grow. What would we be growing for?"

I bit the inside of my lip. "*Maami*, I see so much potential for this business. It could be bigger than any of us ever dreamed."

"But it is not the Amish way to be bigger. It is the Amish way to be closer to *Gott*. My fear is this will distract you, Charlotte, and me from *Gott*. If we are too focused on the here and now, we lose sight of heaven."

I wasn't particularly religious, but my grandmother was devout. There was nothing I could say to her to change her mind on this point.

"I don't want to do this without your support. We're partners in this business, and we both have to be on board with the decisions. It's what *Daadi* would have wanted. My only request is will you think about it?"

"I will think and pray about it." She looked at her wrinkled hands on her lap. "I wish I could ask your *daadi* about this. Since he has been gone, I have struggled. There is so much that I miss about him: his sparkling eyes, his smile, his love of making up new candies, but the thing I miss the very most is talking to him. I miss asking his advice and giving him mine. A marriage, a *gut* marriage, is built on conversations over a lifetime. How those conversations are begun, delivered, and received make all the difference in the happiness and contentment of a husband and wife." She looked up from her hands. "Your *daadi* and I had *gut* conversations. Even when we didn't see eye to eye, we could still speak to each other. That is what kept our marriage strong for so long. We'd reached the point that we already knew what the other person would say; we knew each other that well."

"What would *Daadi* say about my idea?" I asked softly.

"He would tell me to trust you. He would say that you would never do anything that would compromise my beliefs or my standing in the district. He would be happy that you don't plan to change this place. Even though he was Amish, he would recognize that sometimes one must try something new."

Tears sprang to my eyes. "Thank you."

She leaned forward and squeezed my hand. "It won't be easy to build a factory from the ground up, but I have never known you to take the easy way. You didn't as a child, and you certainly don't as an adult."

"I'm ready for the challenge, and I really do think this is the best idea."

She smiled. "I will trust that and trust in *Gott*. With both, we will be fine."

After I finished my conversation with *Maami*, I excused myself, saying that I was going to take a little break by walking around the square.

The shop was quiet, so Charlotte and *Maami* would have no problem helping any customers who wandered in.

As I went out the back door of the shop into the alley, my mind was full. Now that I had my grandmother's blessing to go forward with the candy factory idea, it felt overwhelming. My brain whirled over how much it might cost, how many people I would have to hire, how to do training, where to get the extra supplies we would need, and the list went on and on and on.

I supposed I never really thought *Maami* would agree. Since I had expected all this time that the answer would be no, I hadn't allowed my brain to go to the next step, to consider logistics and money.

"You look a bit confused," a deep voice said as I was about to walk up the alley between the pretzel shop and Swissmen Sweets.

I felt my shoulders sag. It was Abel Esh again. Really, when would I be rid of this guy lurking around Swissmen Sweets? Those few short months he had been in prison sure had been nice, if all too fleeting. "I don't have time for your games today, Abel." I started to walk up the alley.

"If you don't have time for my games, then you certainly won't want to know anything about how the death of the *Englischer* happened on Thanksgiving Day."

I spun around. "What do you know?"

He grinned his creepy grin. "Oh, that caught your attention, did it? I'm not surprised since you love to poke your nose in other people's business when it's your own business that you should be most concerned about."

"Tell me what you know or leave," I snapped.

"I saw the person who put the peanut butter church spread in the *Englischer's* marshmallow topping."

"I know," I said. "It was Leon Hersh. I already knew that."

His eyes went wide, but then they cleared. Perhaps I'd taken away some of his bluster.

"So what are you going to do about it? Are you going to tell your cop boyfriend?"

Now that he'd said that, I realized that I hadn't told Aiden the night before what Leon had done. I hadn't said anything.

"Oh, I see. You are just going to let that boy get away with murder. Perhaps you only tattle on people that you don't like, people such as me? If you like a person, it doesn't matter what he's done. That's an interesting moral compass you go by. *Englisch* justice is clearly not your guide."

"He didn't know that Blaze was allergic to peanut butter," I said defensively.

He touched his smooth cheek. "He told you that, did he? I would think by this point you would be used to people lying to you. However, it seems that a *gut* liar can trick you much more easily than I would have thought. Duly noted."

I turned back around and marched down the alley without another word. Behind me, I could hear Abel laughing because he knew he'd successfully put a seed of doubt into my mind.

Across Main Street from the candy shop, I saw Margot Rawlings and Ruth Yoder having an animated conversation on the square. Usually when I saw such a scene, I turned the other way, but standing a few feet from them with his arms wrapped around his waist again was Leon Hersh. He seemed to be frozen like a deer on the side of the road that didn't know whether to run or play dead.

I sighed and crossed the road, knowing that I would likely come to regret my decision.

"The position of square caretaker is a lot of responsibility," Margot said. "I don't know that a fifteen-year-old boy is up to the task."

"Maybe in the *Englisch* world fifteen is a boy, but in the Amish world, the world *Gott* intended—"

Margot snorted. "You think God intended that everyone live like the Amish? How would the world accomplish anything? Where would you go to get medical help? I bet you go to an English doctor."

Ruth glowered back at her. "Leon is a responsible young Amish man who will do well caring for the village square. I believe he should be given the job. You have put him on trial for too long. Did you make Uriah Schrock go through a trial when he held this position? How is it fair that you make this young man wait so long?"

My eyes went wide because I thought for the first time ever I was in total agreement with Ruth. I glanced at Leon, who said nothing and kept his head down. Maybe Margot was right. He looked very much like a child. Standing there like that he appeared no more than twelve years old, but I also knew that he was a strong young man, who was a hard worker and who had removed himself from a rough childhood all on his own.

I doubted that Margot and Ruth would want me to butt into their conversation, but that's what I was about to do.

"It is my job to ensure that everything on the square goes well—"

Ruth interrupted her. "Like Thanksgiving went well? Your mother's fiancé was murdered."

Margot balled her fists at her sides. It was time to break this up.

"Hi!" I said in my most cheerful I'm-just-out-for-a-walk voice.

Margot and Ruth turned to me so quickly I was surprised that neither of them twisted a hip.

"Bailey King," Margot said. "You're the perfect person to ask since you have been involved in so many events on the square. Don't you think Leon is too inexperienced to have the job of caretaker?"

"I don't," I said.

Ruth fluffed her cape and smiled. Margot opened and closed her mouth as if she couldn't believe what she was hearing. Since I wasn't Amish, I was sure that she thought I would automatically agree with her. However, Margot should know me better than that by now. I don't automatically go along with anyone.

"Leon is a responsible young man, and I think he will do a great job caring for the square. You will be hard-pressed to find someone who would care more about doing a good job."

Margot shot a glance in Leon's direction. "But he's so young."

"He's young, but he grew up fast after a very difficult childhood. I would think that's something you could relate to."

Margot scowled and looked from Ruth to me and then back again. She threw up her hands. "Fine. Fine. I'm tired of debating this any longer." She turned. "Leon, come here."

The Amish teen shuffled over to us.

Margot pointed at him. "The job is yours. Just remember that I will be watching you."

For the first time since I had met him, I saw Leon's face break into a beautiful smile. "*Danki. Danki.* I promise I will do a *gut* job. You won't have to worry about anything on the square."

"That's good to hear because you start right now." She

rubbed the back of her neck. "Now that that's over, I have to get my mother to the airport."

"She's leaving?" I asked.

Margot nodded. "The sheriff's deputies visited her this morning and told her the truth about Blaze. She's no longer interested in waiting to take his body back to Florida. Since they weren't married yet, I guess she doesn't have to."

"What's the truth about him?"

Margot sighed. "It's hard to believe, but he was former Amish. It seems he lied to my mother about his past for years."

I glanced at Leon. "Do you know his Amish name?"

She shook her head. "My mother was too upset to tell me. I'm sure that I will learn it soon enough. However, between you and me, I'm happy to put her on a plane and say goodbye. It's been difficult with her here. My mother is very exacting."

"That's why you asked Leon to help her and Blaze as much as possible," I said.

She glanced at Leon. "Yes. My mother said Leon did a perfect job and carried out everything she requested." She sighed. "She's very particular and doesn't care for the Amish in general. From her, that's high praise. I suppose I should have hired Leon for the caretaker job on that very recommendation." She looked at Leon. "I'm sorry if I've been harsh. You're just so young."

"I will do my very best."

"Well," Ruth said. "If we are done with all that, I have a quilting circle meeting to get to." She pointed at Leon. "Don't make me regret intervening on your behalf."

Leon's Adam's apple bobbed up and down. "I will get to work right now." He walked over to a rake that leaned against the gazebo and started to pull fallen leaves out from under the bushes.

"You made the right choice about Leon," I told Margot.

"I hope you're right. I'm ready for a fresh start. I want to put the last week behind us." She shoved her hands into her coat pockets.

"We can't put it behind us completely," I said. "We still don't know who killed Blaze, and I think you're technically still a suspect."

"They can't prove that I killed him, and I'm trusting in that. I just need to have all of this behind me so I can refocus on the square. We are starting the Christmas season now, but I'm already thinking about the new year. We'll come back bigger and better."

I shook my head. Despite everything that had happened, it was the activities on the square that still were most important to Margot. If murder couldn't change that, I doubted anything else would.

"My mother is waiting now in the Sunbeam Café for me to take her to the airport." She started to walk across the square. Over her shoulder, she said, "I have some great plans for the square next year and a new role for you and Swissmen Sweets. You won't be disappointed."

That sounded ominous.

CHAPTER TWENTY-SEVEN

I knew I should go back to Swissmen Sweets. I promised myself that I would in a few minutes. My mind was just so jumbled over the murder, the possible candy factory, and the idea of Aiden leaving the benefits and job security of law enforcement to be a private investigator on his own.

I climbed up the four steps to the gazebo and sat on edge of the bench that encircled the perimeter.

Remembering that I had the suspect list that Zara had given me in my pocket, I removed it and looked it over. The three names on it had not offered a great deal of help finding the killer. Clyde Clem worked at Harvest Market and had an alibi. Allen Shirk was dead. Levi Wittmer had been so occupied with the turkeys on Thanksgiving Day, I didn't know how he could be involved. And in truth, I couldn't see any of these men having access to the list that Leon had been given by Blaze when they arrived.

What it came down to was knowing who had written, "Add church spread" to Blaze's marshmallow fluff on that note.

Someone cleared their throat and I jumped. The paper fell out of my hands and drifted across the gazebo floor.

Leon scooped it up, but not before he looked at it.

I took the list from his hand.

"I'm sorry if I scared you, Bailey," Leon said.

"Can I help with something?" My tone was a little harsher than I intended it to be, but I was flustered that he'd so obviously read my note.

He apologized again. "I just wanted to thank you for speaking to Margot on my behalf. I know that she puts a lot of store in what you think, so it really made a difference."

I felt my body relax. "You're welcome, but you're giving me too much credit. Margot doesn't put a lot of store in what I think."

"She does," he insisted. "Many times when we set up on the square she will ask us how we think Bailey would do it. You're the only Bailey anyone around here knows, so it has to be you."

I blinked. "Wow. That comes as a bit of a shock."

He nodded. "I just wanted to say thank you again." He turned to go and then stopped.

"Is there something else?" I stood up. "I need to get back to the shop. There's always candy to be made."

"Can I see that piece of paper again, please? It's important." His eyes were wide behind his glasses, and his expression was so earnest that I turned over the piece of paper to him.

He unfolded it and stared at the piece of paper. "This is it."

"What? What is it?"

"Before you asked me if the item about putting church spread in Blaze's marshmallow fluff was in the same hand as everything else on that list. It was. This one. This is the handwriting of the person who wrote the list for me on Thanksgiving Day."

"It's on hotel stationery," I whispered and I almost slapped myself on the forehead. How could I be so stupid? Of course, Zara wrote this list as well as the list of duties for Leon. She must have been the one who wanted him dead. She hated the Amish and somehow, she must have learned of his ties to the community. Would that have been enough reason to want him dead?

I looked at the Sunbeam Café and saw Margot and Zara coming out the door. Lois was in the doorway, trying to put a bakery box in Zara's hand.

Once Zara boarded that plane, it would be hard to get her to come back to Harvest. It took a lot of proof to extract a person from another state. It would be Sheriff Marshall's call, and I didn't know that he would be willing to do that. Even though he didn't like Zara personally, he would sympathize with her distaste for the Amish.

I grabbed the list from Leon's hand, ran out of the gazebo, and across the street to the sidewalk in front of the Sunbeam Café.

"Whoa! Bailey," Lois said. "Where's the fire?"

I held up the list. "Zara, we need to talk about this before you leave."

She glowered at me. "I don't have to talk to you about anything. It's clear to me that I was a fool to put my trust in you to solve the murder of Blaze. Not that I think any of it matters now. I just found out he's been lying to me for the last two years."

Lois held the bakery box out, but still neither Margot or Zara took it.

"You wrote this list," I said.

"Yes, and I gave it to you," she snapped.

"It's not the only list that you wrote while in Harvest. I want to talk to you about the other one."

"What list?" Margot asked.

"It's a list of duties for Leon to take care of on Thanksgiving. One of the items buried in that list was to put church spread in Blaze's marshmallow fluff."

Zara narrowed her eyes.

"Do you deny it?" I asked.

She lifted her chin. "No, I don't."

"Mother!" Margot gasped.

"Don't you gasp at me. If I could have relied on you to take care of me when I was old, I wouldn't have had to find a young husband to take care of me."

"Who said that I wouldn't take care of you?" Margot asked.

"Please," Zara spat. "You have made no secret of the fact that you hate visiting me in Florida and can't wait to get home. If it was up to you, I would go straight into a nursing home."

Margot bit her lower lip. When she didn't say anything, I guessed Zara had been right in thinking what her daughter planned to do with her elderly mother.

"How long have you known Blaze wasn't who he said he was?" I asked.

"For several months. I found a letter that he had been writing to his brother. In it, he promised to make it up to Melvin by marrying me and taking all my money. He promised to give most of the money to his brother for abandoning him at that fire all those years ago. I was furious."

"Why didn't you just break up with him?" I asked. "Why did you have to have him killed?"

"He was Amish, and he'd betrayed and humiliated me. I wasn't just going to walk away from that. I knew forcing him to come back here would be the perfect punishment. He deserved to die for what he did. It was more fitting that he died here in Harvest."

I licked my lips. "Zara, you can't go home to Florida today. The police will want to talk to you."

"I have no intention of talking to them. My daughter is going to take me to the airport and I'm going to fly home. There will be other young men who will want to marry me and be willing to take care of me for my money. I will find another."

"I'm not taking you to the airport, Mother. You have to talk to the police." Margot took a step back from Zara.

Zara glared at Margot. "You are my child and you will do what I say."

"You were willing to let me be framed for murder! You didn't care that my husband was dragged to the police station and questioned in the middle of the night."

"Rupert was never good enough for you. You never should have married that truck driver in the first place. I told you not to marry him. You're my daughter and could have done much better," Zara snapped. "If that's the case, I will drive myself." She ripped the bakery box from Lois's hands and hit Margot in the face with it.

Margot cried out and dropped her car keys. Zara picked them up.

"Oh!" Lois said. "That was a butterscotch pumpkin pie!"

I jumped between Zara and the driver's side of the car. "Zara, stop. Think about what you're doing. They will never let you on that plane once the authorities are notified."

Lois disappeared into the shop. I knew she was calling the police. They couldn't get here fast enough in my opinion.

"Then I will drive to Florida."

"They will catch you on the highway. You're a judge. Take a breath and look at this logically. You might get away today, but you will be caught eventually," I said.

She reached into her handbag. Gator growled as she removed a small gun from it. "I think of everything logically, and this is my best choice."

"If that's true, why did you call me in the first place?" I asked. I felt beads of sweat form on my forehead as I looked at the gun. "You could have gotten away with this without involving me at all. You wanted the truth to come out about Blaze."

The gun wavered in her hand. "What are you talking about?"

"You wanted the truth to come out. Why else would you have written Allen Shirk's name on that list you gave me? You had to know it would lead me to Melvin Hersh, Blaze's twin brother. Why else would you have asked me to help find the killer?"

"Yes, I wanted the truth to come out," she snapped. "I wanted the world to know what a double-crosser he was. I wanted everyone to know he was a coward who left his brother and friend to take the blame for a fire he caused."

I heard sirens. I had been right in thinking Lois had called the police.

She leveled the gun at me.

"Zara." I held up my empty hands. "You are already in enough trouble. Don't make it worse for yourself. If you shoot me, you will."

"It doesn't matter what happens now." Zara's voice was choked with tears.

"Zara, you don't want to spend what's left of your life in prison. You spent so much time building the life you wanted, but you threw it away over a guy."

She glared at me. "No one betrays me like that and lives to tell about it. I would never allow it."

The sirens grew louder as three sheriff department SUVs careened around the square and pulled up in front of the Sunbeam Café.

"What I've just realized is there is one solution to avoid all of this unpleasantness and to avoid dying sick and alone." She moved the gun so that it no longer pointed at me but pointed at the side of her own head.

"Mother, no!" Margot screamed.

Deputy Little and the others jumped out of their vehicles with their guns drawn.

Just as Zara was about to fire, Gator leaped out of her purse and bit her hand. She squealed.

The mean little dog saved her life.

Epilogue

Margot stood outside of her car just feet from the live nativity. The nativity parade only happened at night, but all the animals were there during the day. Tourists and locals liked to visit and give the animals carrots and other treats.

A little girl giggled as Melchior the camel took a carrot from her outstretched hand. Jethro waited patiently for his carrot. A big red and white polka-dotted bow was tied around his neck. Margot had tried to tell Juliet that the animals would not have been wearing satin bows at the first Christmas, but Juliet would not hear of it. She said her famous pig needed to stand out. As if his black and white polka-dots weren't enough.

"While I'm gone, you will take care of the square?" Margot asked me for the tenth time. "You know how important the Christmas parade is for this village."

"Yes, Leon and I can handle it. In fact, Leon is doing such a good job as caretaker that there's not much I will have to do."

She nodded. "I'm glad I hired him. He was the right choice." She spoke as if hiring Leon had been her idea all the time.

I held back a smart comment on that.

"All right." She got into the car and spoke to me through the open window. "I hate to leave this close to Christmas, but I want to get my mother settled. I want to show her I will care for her."

"You're a good daughter."

After she was arrested, Zara had had a stroke while she was in custody. She became paralyzed on one side and confined to a wheelchair. Her attorney entered an insanity plea and asked for a deal due to Zara's condition. I didn't think anyone in the county wanted to put an ill woman in her late eighties through a long trial. Instead, they sentenced her to a long-term mental facility. In the end, Zara got what she most feared, being disabled and sent to an institution for the remainder of her life. What she'd done was horrible and inexcusable, but I would be lying if I didn't admit that I had some compassion for her. It would be wrong of me to wish a person's worst nightmare on them.

Zara was in the process of being transferred to a facility in Florida. Margot thought she would be happiest there. As everyone knew, Zara didn't like Ohio. Just a week before Christmas, Margot was headed to Florida to get her mother settled and take care of her affairs there.

Gator sat on the passenger seat and growled at me. Margot had decided to take him in after her mother was arrested. I knew that it was the right thing to do. It wasn't the dog's fault he had belonged to a killer. At the same time, the little dog scared me, and I was always waiting for him to bite. I had a feeling that Gator would become a fixture on the village square, and he wasn't an addition that I was happy to see.

"We have everything under control," I reassured her. I had learned over the last couple years that Margot would check and recheck that everything was perfect on the square.

She nodded, and I stepped away from the car as she drove away.

Across the square, Leon adjusted the lights on the pine trees to make sure that every holiday light on the branches was perfectly positioned. I smiled at how seriously he was taking the job. I hoped that this was a new beginning for him and he could leave his difficult past behind.

The front door of Swissmen Sweets flew open. "Bailey! Bailey!" Charlotte ran out and across the street without looking for traffic. An Amish buggy driver had to pull back hard on his reins to keep from hitting her.

"Charlotte! Be careful. You were almost hit!" I cried.

"I was?" She looked around, confused.

I shook my head. "Are you okay? Is *Maami* okay?"

"*Ya*! The Realtor is on the shop phone."

I frowned. "Oh, why didn't he call my cell?"

"He said he tried."

I sighed. "All right. I'll come talk to him."

"Bailey!" She grabbed both of my arms. "You got it!"

"I got what?"

"The open lot. Your bid won. You just bought a spot to build your candy factory." She jumped up and down.

My mouth fell open. I had never for a moment thought

my low bid would win. At the same time, the reality of winning the bid hit me like a wall of chocolate bark.

"Come on!" Charlotte tugged on my hand. "The Realtor is waiting on the line for you."

My future was waiting for me across the road in Swissmen Sweets. I walked toward it.

Maami's Buckeyes

Ingredients

1 stick softened butter
1½ cups peanut butter
1 pound powdered sugar
1 teaspoon vanilla
12-ounce package chocolate chips

Directions

1. Blend butter, peanut butter, powdered sugar, and vanilla well.
2. Roll into balls and chill overnight.
3. Melt chocolate chips in a double boiler.
4. Dip the balls into the melted chocolate using a toothpick in the center of the peanut butter balls.
5. Let cool and enjoy!

Please read on for a sneak peek at Amanda Flower's next Amish Matchmaker Mystery, **Honeymoons Can Be Hazardous!**

Widowed matchmaker Millie Fisher is anything but lonely between her mischievous goats, her quilting circle—and her habit of solving the odd murder or two. . . .

Millie's decidedly *not* Amish best friend, Lois Henry, is outspoken, colorful, and so hopelessly romantic, she's had four husbands. Millie doesn't judge, and she also doesn't expect to run into Lois's most recent ex, gambler Gerome Moorhead, in small-town Harvest, Ohio. With him is the very young, new Mrs. Moorhead, aka "Honey Bee." Lois is outraged, but Millie is completely shocked to learn the next day that Gerome is already a widower.

When a large wood carving at the cozy Munich Chalet falls on Honey Bee, all eyes turn toward Lois. Who else would want a tourist—a complete stranger—dead? And half of Harvest witnessed Lois's enmity toward the young woman. Suddenly Millie must put aside her sewing needle and flex her sleuthing skills. She's no stranger to a murder investigation, after all, and if she doesn't learn who killed Honey Bee, Lois could go from Millie's boisterous best friend to her horrified prison pen pal. . . .

CHAPTER ONE

"Can you smell the love in the air, Millie?" my dearest friend, Lois Henry, asked as she walked across the Harvest village square and inhaled deeply. "It's positively magical."

I didn't know anything about the air being magical. It wasn't something Amish women thought or spoke about. Then again, I was Amish, but Lois most certainly was not. She wore a bright red beret over her short purple-red hair. Pink plastic hearts hung from her earlobes and she had completed the outfit with a neon pink winter ski coat over light blue jeans.

I glanced down at my black boots, long navy skirt, and black wool coat, and then touched the wide brim of the black bonnet that covered most of my head. We could not have been more different.

"I just smell snow," I said. The ice crust covering the

snow blanketing the square crackled with every step we took across the lawn.

Lois held her arms in the air and took in a long breath. Her arms fell at her sides. "Oh, Millie, your literal Amishness can get old at times." However, she said all this with a smile to prove she was teasing me. "On a side note, what does snow smell like? It's just water, right? How can it smell like anything at all?"

"I think it has a scent, or maybe not the snow exactly. The air does. Clean and crisp, I suppose."

Lois cocked her head as she considered this, and the bright red beret slid to one side. She caught it before it fell off completely. "This silly thing. It won't stay in place." She stopped in the middle of the frozen square, opened the giant purse that was always at her side, stuck her hand in, and came out with a fistful of bobby pins.

It was amazing to watch. There was no limit to the items Lois could pull out of that bag, and she always seemed to know the exact location to each and every thing she sought. It was like pulling a rabbit out of a hat. Which proves I knew a little bit about magic, or at least the traveling kind that comes to the Holmes County fair every year.

She adjusted her beret on her head and jabbed half a dozen bobby pins into it. "There. This sucker isn't going anywhere now!"

"Isn't it the purpose of a winter hat to sit down over your ears to protect them from the cold?" I asked.

"If I did that no one would see my earrings." She tapped the back of her left ear and the chain of pink and red hearts swung back and forth from her ear lobe. "What would be the point of my outfit without the earrings?"

It wasn't a question I could answer. I had essentially

been wearing one form or other of the same dress since I was a toddler. Even with my own plain background, I could recognize that her ensemble was something noteworthy. She stood head to toe in red, white, and pink. No one could get into the holiday spirit quite like Lois, and it didn't even have to be a major holiday like Christmas or Thanksgiving. Lois dressed up for all holidays. It didn't matter how small. She donned a top hat on Lincoln's birthday, for example.

A flyer posted on the gazebo flapped in the winter breeze.

"Oh," Lois said. "That's going to fly off, and then won't Margot pitch a fit?"

Margot Rawlings was the village's community organizer. I honestly didn't know what her real title was, but I knew she was responsible for spearheading all the events that occurred on the square, and thanks to Margot, there were a lot. Her goal was to make Harvest as much a tourist destination as the more well-known villages in Ohio's Amish Country, such as Sugarcreek and Berlin.

The flyer was for the Valentine's Day spaghetti dinner, and it was happening that evening at the church on the square. The event was to be hosted by the village of Harvest, the church, and several Amish communities to raise money for a drug counseling center in the village. The church would donate the space for the counseling center, and the fundraiser was to hire trained drug counselors for those seeking help. Over the last decade, drug use in rural Ohio had skyrocketed, and the Amish weren't immune to it either, although it was only whispered about in the community. Lois and I both had tickets to the dinner.

Lois reached into her purse, came out with a staple gun, and stapled the flyer back to the gazebo post. I didn't even blink at the staple gun. It was par for the course with her.

She tucked the staple gun back into her purse and patted her hat one final time. "We had better pick up the pace. I promised Darcy I would be back by now. She usually doesn't mind my running a little late, but tonight she has a date. She wants to go home and get ready," Lois said in a loud whisper. "On Valentine's Day weekend. Isn't that wonderful? Who wants to be alone on Valentine's Day?"

"Is the date with Bryan?" I asked.

Bryan Shell was a writer, working on his first novel, or so he had told us. He wrote at the café every day. However, he spent more time watching Darcy than typing into his computer. Finally, he got up the courage to ask Darcy on a date after months of pining for her.

"Bryan Shell?" She shook he head. "Oh no. Darcy said that she wasn't interested in him, and I haven't seen him in the café for over a month. He fled. We haven't seen him since."

Now that she mentioned it, I hadn't seen Bryan in the last several weeks when I popped into the café to see Lois and have some of Darcy's blueberry pie. That came as a relief to me. I was a matchmaker and had a sense when two people should and shouldn't be together. It was a gift from *Gott*, but one I only used when asked.

I didn't charge money for my matchmaking services. I didn't see that it was right to make money off of someone else's happiness. It was just something I did because I cared about my community and wanted to see as many people happy in life and as happy in love as my late husband Kip and I were for our full twenty years of marriage.

Darcy never asked me if she thought Bryan was right for her, so I never shared my opinion on the topic with her. I was glad to hear that she came to the correct con-clusion on her own. However, I was just as curious as her grandmother about this mystery man.

"You won't be alone. We are going to the spaghetti dinner tonight. Half the village will be there. It seems to be how many villagers are spending their Valentine's Day." We left the gazebo and walked side by side across the snow-covered square. I was grateful for my sturdy boots, which kept me from slipping in the snow.

"Half the village, but not my better half because I don't have one." She sighed. "I'm starting to get the itch, Millie."

A gust of wind blew a chilly draft into my bonnet, and I tied its ribbons more tightly under my chin. "The itch?"

"Yes, to get married again. I know, I know what you're thinking. That's how I ended up married to Rocksino-Guy, which by any accounting was a disaster. He was a weasel through and through."

"You pushed him into a swimming pool," I said. A small part of me wished I had been there to see it. Lois did everything with a flourish. That was sure to have made a big splash, both literally and figuratively.

"He deserved it," she said with an uncharacteristic scowl on her face. Just as quickly, the scowl changed into her more common beaming smile. "And I have to say it was memorable. It's the best way I could have imagined to tell a man I wanted a divorce. I would know too, since it wasn't my first time around the block."

It certainly wasn't. Lois had had a string of marriages since her twenties. Four to be exact. She'd divorced three of those husbands, while her second husband had died. By her account, her second husband was the only man she'd ever truly loved. She'd married the other two after him just searching for that spark again. So far, she hadn't found it.

"Are you sure that you want to marry again?" I asked. "It hasn't been easy." I thought, as her closest friend, it was my place to talk some sense into her.

"Nothing worthwhile is easy, Millie. You know that better than most people." She sighed. "I don't ever want to give up on love. When I do, well, that would be the end of me."